"Humor and heart blend together to make *Latte Daze* the perfect pick-me-up novel of this year! Maya Davis and her brew of family and friends are guaranteed to put a smile on your face and to freshen your own faith journey. Erynn Mangum has concocted yet another best seller !"

—DEENA PETERSON, independent book reviewer,
A Peek at My Bookshelf

"Only Erynn Mangum can make a reader crave coffee and romance in equal quantities, and this sweet story delivers generous helpings of both. Fresh, fun, and relevant, Erynn's storytelling skills are even better than your favorite caffeine fix."

—BETSY ST. AMANT, author of *A Valentine's Wish* and
Rodeo Sweetheart

"*Latte Daze* is absolutely ideal when you need a lift, a laugh, or just a good read. Maya Davis and her pals are hilarious, but there's sense in what they say and do. And only Erynn Mangum can consistently describe weather in ways that make me laugh out loud. But beware, this mocha maven will leave you wanting more."

—LORI FOX, reviewer, TitleTrakk.com

"Maya Davis—barista, beagle lover, and fledgling girlfriend—returns in *Latte Daze*, another hilarious adventure by the talented Erynn Mangum. Laughter, love, and life lessons abound as Maya negotiates her best friend's wedding preparations, the revelation she is to become an aunt, and her new relationship with Jack. Tender, sweet, and authentic, *Latte Daze* affirms that relationships of integrity and purity are not only possible but also well worth pursuing. I'm ordering a *Double Shot* to go!"

—REL MOLLET, Relz Reviewz

a maya davis novel

book two

LATTE DAZE

erynn mangum

NavPress is the publishing ministry of The Navigators, an international Christian organization and leader in personal spiritual development. NavPress is committed to helping people grow spiritually and enjoy lives of meaning and hope through personal and group resources that are biblically rooted, culturally relevant, and highly practical.

For a free catalog go to www.NavPress.com
or call 1.800.366.7788 in the United States or 1.800.839.4769 in Canada.

ISBN-13: 978-1-60006-712-9

Cover design by Studio Gearbox
Cover image by Dallas Event Inc, Shutterstock

Library of Congress Cataloging-in-Publication Data

Mangum, Erynn, 1985-
  Latte daze : a Maya Davis novel / Erynn Mangum.
    p. cm.
  ISBN 978-1-60006-712-9
  1. Coffee shops--Fiction. 2. Weddings--Fiction. I. Title.
  PS3613.A5373L38 2010
  813'.6--dc22

                          2010001728

Printed in the United States of America

1 2 3 4 5 6 7 8 / 14 13 12 11 10

For the ladies in my life: Susan Mangum, Cayce Mangum, Eloise Terry, Connie O'Brien, Vicky O'Brien, and Ashlee O'Brien. Thank you for all the sweet encouragement you've given me, the celebrating you've done with me, and the help you've given me. I love you all!

ACKNOWLEDGMENTS

My Savior, Jesus Christ — I want everything I write to be out of love for You. Continue to teach me to rely on You for everything. You know the end from the beginning! I love You, Lord.

My amazing husband — Jon, you are the best part of my day. I love you more than you will ever know! I'm so excited about this new chapter coming up for us.

My family — Mom, Dad, Bryant, Caleb, and Cayce, I couldn't ask for a more amazing family. Thank you for always being there for me. I love you all!

My grandmother — Nama, you are wonderful! Thank you for sharing your wisdom and for our long phone chats. I love you!

My in-law family — Greg, Connie, Allen, Vicky, Tommy, and Ashlee, thank you for being such a fabulous family to marry into. I couldn't ask for better! I love you all!

Our extended families — Thank you for everything you have done for Jon and me! We love you lots!

Barb and Walt Kelly, Jen and Greg Fulkerson, and our Mars Hill community group — Y'all make life fun! Thank you for the prayers, the support, and the friendship! Love ya!

My sweet friends — You are such a wonderful part of my

life! Thank you for the breaks from writing, the lunches, and the coffee dates. I love you all!

The incredible NavPress team — Thank you for everything you have done and the friendships we've made in the process! Special thanks to Rebekah Guzman, Kris Wallen, Amy Parker, Tia Stauffer, and Arvid Wallen.

My agent — Steve Laube, you are awesome! Thank you for your patience with me as I bombard you with questions and e-mails. You are great!

The Christian Writers Guild — I'm so grateful for your friendship and support! You all are wonderful!

And last but definitely not least, to YOU — Thank you for reading this book! I hope it makes you laugh, reach for a mocha, and remember how great our God is.

CHAPTER ONE

Reasons I Don't Like Water Ballet:
1. The weird arm motions
2. The weird leg motions
3. The thought of dancing in public under water
4. The thought of dancing in public . . . period
5. Olympic sport? Pshh!!

"Seriously, Maya, it's a *great* form of exercise." This is said by my best friend and roommate, Jen Mitchell. She's standing in the middle of our living room wearing a quite ugly, red one-piece swimsuit and one of those sarong things around her waist, and she's tying her super long, incredibly gorgeous blond hair into a bun on the top of her head.

"Sorry, Jen. I draw the line at aquatic dance forms."

"Don't think of it as dancing. Think of it as upright Pilates."

I exchange a look with my beagle, Calvin, and look back at Jen. "Um, no."

She shrugs. "Suit yourself."

"No, they're ugly. And red isn't my color."

Jen rolls her eyes.

I grin at my own joke. Calvin gives a little "Roo!"

Good to know someone thinks I'm funny.

"Okay. I'm off to the gym." She picks up her purse. "Travis and I are watching a movie tonight."

"Find another place to go, got it." I smile at her. Travis Clayton is Jen's boyfriend and actually an old high-school flame of mine. But that's a long story involving ice cream, tears, lies, ice cream, skipping Bible reading, guilt, ice cream, and, eventually, loads of prayer, lots of hugs, and again . . . ice cream.

I frown and look down at my waist. Maybe I should consider synchronized swimming.

Nah. All that was a good four months ago, and since then, we've been very good girls and switched to the half-the-calories ice cream. Never as tasty as the leaded stuff, but I will admit it keeps my thighs in nicer shape. And considering it's the middle of April and nearly time for shorts here in Hudson, California, in-shape thighs are a nice thing to have.

Jen lets out her breath at my earlier comment. "Maya, you know you're always welcome to watch movies with us."

So she's said before. But being the third leg of a two-leg ladder isn't my best idea of a good time. "I know," I say, wanting to pacify her but having no intention of joining them tonight.

"Besides, we're going to the theater, so you can stay here if you want."

Lovely. An evening alone with just my pajama pants, a good-looking man who doesn't care (Mr. Darcy), and a batch of chocolate-chip cookies.

I'm starting to get excited.

"Invite Jack over," Jen says, ruining my excitement over an evening spent in my PJs.

Real boys care if my hair is styled or not.

"Jen, I'm the girl," I say.

"So?"

"So, he's supposed to ask *me* out."

Jen sets her cute canvas tote she bought specifically for synchronized swimming on the couch. "Oh boy. Here we go again."

"Well, it's true."

"No, it's not."

"Uh-huh," I retort, using my best junior-high defense.

"Maya, you've been dating for four whole months. I think it's time you asked him out occasionally. Jack's been working his tail off romancing you. Give him a break!"

My mother would disagree with Jen's philosophy. "The man should always be the initiator," Mom always said.

Which, so far Jack has been, I guess. We've been "dating" four months, and I put the word in quotes because I'm not sure I'd call it that.

Jack is one of my best friends and currently my co-worker for another two weeks until he stops brewing espressos and starts mucking elephant dung. I shared the comparison with him and figured that would convince him to stay at Cool Beans forever, but he actually thinks the elephants sound exciting.

Dung and all.

All that to say, we talk every single day, and when we do go out on a "date," it's more like an extension of our current day than anything else.

When I dated Travis, it was actual dating. I didn't see him until at night, I dressed up in my best skirt, I was on my best behavior, and I got butterflies in my stomach every time I looked at him.

And Jack? I'm usually in jeans so I can wear comfy shoes after a long day standing behind the coffee counter, I'm never on my best behavior because he would totally call me on it, and usually my stomach hurts after we've gone out because I've been laughing so hard.

It's different.

And weird.

Jen's staring at me, and I shrug. "Maybe I'll ask him," I say, just to pacify her so she'll leave for her Drowning Nutcracker routine.

"Good." She shoulders her tote and slides on her sunglasses. "I'll be home later. Have a good afternoon!"

She leaves. I lock our apartment door behind her.

It's Saturday morning, and for once, my schedule has switched around enough that I'm actually home on the weekend. I'm working Monday through Friday, like your normal, average working girl. No nights, no weekends. I could seriously have been in that Dolly Parton movie about nine-to-fivers. It's like my boss, Alisha, has finally decided she likes me.

I watch Calvin circle around and lie down in front of the couch while I try to decide what to do today. Tonight has officially become my Mr. Darcy date night; tomorrow I've got dinner plans with the parental units and my brother and sister-in-law, Zach and Kate.

My family lives an hour away in San Diego, and I drive there every Sunday for dinner. I'm a good daughter.

And I'm working on being a good sister. Zach and I haven't always gotten along, but I'm trying to be better about the whole sibling-rivalry thing. So what if he's a doctor and I'm a barista. Does that really matter?

I frown.

Well, anyway, I'm working on it.

My cell phone rings, and I answer it, opening a box of Lucky Charms in the process. "Hello?"

"Good morning." It's Jack. His voice is so thick and groggy that I barely recognize it.

I smile. "Someone woke up on the wrong side of the bed."

"I just woke up."

I glance at the clock. "Jack, it's almost eleven."

"You're one to talk. I can hear you pouring your cereal, Nutkin."

Jack has always thought that my brain activity is similar to that of a squirrel — fast, pointless, and frenzied. Which is somewhat less than flattering, I might say. He doesn't seem to care about my feelings on that, since he persists in calling me all sorts of names that relate to it. Honestly, I've gotten used to them over the last few years, but seriously . . . Nutkin? It sounds like a brand of birdseed.

"Well, at least I've been up for a little bit," I say.

"What are you doing today?"

"I've got a date tonight."

"Well, great! I'd love to go out," Jack says.

I squint at an unidentifiable pink marshmallow in my bowl. "I don't believe you were invited, and I'm not going out." Play hard to get. That's my motto.

He's quiet for almost two seconds, which is saying a lot for Jack Dominguez. "You're seriously going to watch *Pride and Prejudice* again? Didn't you watch it two weeks ago?"

I sigh.

"You'd think for someone with such an exciting personality, you'd have a more diverse movie life, Pattertwig."

"Hey!" Fine if he guessed who my date was with, but he doesn't have to mock me for it.

"I'm coming over, and we're going to watch something you've never seen before. Preferably something with more action, too."

"What if I want to spend my evening with Mr. Darcy?"

"Please. You would seriously pick a prideful fictional man wearing weird pants over your perfectly normal boyfriend?"

"Now wait just a minute!" I object.

"It's true. You know it's true."

I close my eyes and shake my head. "Well, you're one to talk about prideful. Mr. Darcy was extremely fashionable in those days."

"The only reason you like him is the accent."

"Nuh-huh." Oh boy. Here we go again.

"That was mature. I'll see you tonight at six. I'll bring dinner and the movie. And I'll even wear weird pants if you want."

"What movie?" I ask cautiously. Last time Jack was in charge of picking out the movie, I had to sit through three hours of one bloody massacre after another. And while, all in all, I think *Braveheart* is a decent movie, I did not enjoy watching it while eating, especially when dinner was spaghetti and meatballs. Some scenes were a little too similar to what was in my bowl.

I make a face and shove my cereal away, remembering.

I hear Jack sigh. "Hmm. How about *Hancock*? Have you seen that?"

"No."

"Done. I'll be there at six. Have a good morning, Maya."

I hang up and look at the Lucky Charms. Will Smith. He's a good actor. Could be a good movie.

Here's my thought about new movies: Why mess with a good thing? If I like watching *Pride and Prejudice* and *While You Were Sleeping*, why would I stop?

Jack says I must get bored, but honestly I don't. I like knowing what's going to happen next.

I pull a marshmallow from the bowl and chew on it. It tastes stale, but that's probably because this box is getting old. Jen's been hiding the sugary cereals behind the granola, so I forget we have them.

It's not a very nice thing to do.

Jen likes the granola that feels like crackling leaves.

I like cereal with *taste* as opposed to feelings.

It's nearly eleven, and I'm still in my PJs. This is probably the best way to spend a Saturday.

I finish my bowl of Lucky Charms, hop in and out of the shower, and get dressed. I'm wearing jeans and a wrap-style cranberry-colored shirt because I heard on the Style Network that wrap shirts are very flattering on women with a small bust-line.

Somehow my parents gave me all the recessive genes. My brother, Zach, is well over six feet tall. He has straight blond hair, green eyes, that consistently tanned look going on, and he has no problem staying thin and in shape. Same with my parents. Dad's six one, with the same hair and eyes as Zach. Mom's five eight or so, with the most perfect body shape in the world: big boobs, tiny waist, no butt.

Then there's me. I'm five two, with chocolate-colored hair that curls in ringlets Shirley Temple would be proud of. Gray eyes. Definitely a butt, not-so-definite boobs. Pretty much, I look identical to what my grandma used to look like. When we were little, Zach convinced me I was adopted.

I am impressed by how the wrap shirt makes a little look like more and give points to the Style Network.

Mom calls right as I'm setting the curling iron down and giving up on taming the tangled mass of curls. I cut my hair above my shoulders about a year ago, and it looked cute but took too much time to style. Now, it's grown out to about three inches below my shoulders and just looks poofy and wild, as if

I should be living on a ranch somewhere like that girl in *The Man from Snowy River*. I'm trying for a romantic curly style like Minnie Driver in *Return to Me*. But it's not working.

"Hey, Mom."

"Hi, honey. What are you doing?"

"I'm going to shave my head."

"Be careful not to nick yourself. Head wounds bleed a lot."

This is my mother for you. No sympathy.

"I hate my hair," I say, trying again.

"I can see why. Thick. Curly. Natural highlights. No widow's peak or cowlicks. You lead a horrible life."

I give up. "Never mind. What are you doing today?"

"Mostly errands, which reminds me why I called. I was thinking about having steaks for dinner tomorrow night."

She waits for my response, so I say, "Yum. Sounds good."

"How many should I get for you?"

Wow. What does that mean? *How much are you eating these days, Maya?*

"What?" I ask.

"Well, I mean, are you planning on having one steak or two?"

I gape at the phone and rush to the mirror. My wrap shirt is nicely accentuating my waistline, which, despite the lack of genetic shortcuts, I still manage to keep in check by running with Calvin.

"Have I ever eaten two steaks, Mom?"

"Okay! All right," Mom says, sighing heavily into the phone. "Are you going to bring Jack or not?"

"That's what this is all about?"

"Well, honey, it's been four months, and he's never come with you to visit us. I'm just wondering if you're embarrassed of us."

"Mom." I rub my forehead.

"No, I mean, I understand. We're very embarrassing. Who wouldn't be embarrassed of your parents? They're both successful, live in a decent house, fairly young, attractive, if I say so myself—"

Squeezing my eyes shut, I interrupt. "Mom."

"Or maybe it's Zach? I mean, he is a doctor and your sister-in-law is a lawyer. They're definitely a pair to be ashamed of."

"Mom."

"Is it the house?"

"Mom, stop," I say, groaning. "It's not you; it's me."

She pauses. "Are we breaking up?"

"Mom!"

"All right, sheesh." I can hear her laughing. "What is you and not me?"

I clear my throat, thinking. "I don't know. That would just be kind of *serious*, you know?"

"It's not like we haven't met Jack, Maya."

"I know. But remember the first time Zach brought Kate home for dinner?"

"Maya, that was completely different. We'd never met Kate, and they were already engaged."

It's true. Zach had met Kate while he was off at medical school, and the most we knew about her was what she looked like because Zach posted a picture of them together on his Facebook page.

That first dinner was awkward. Actually, that first year of dinners was awkward. It hasn't been until these last few months when they've been living back in California that we've gotten to know the real Kate. It takes her a long time to warm up to people.

Jack, on the other hand, has yet to meet someone he couldn't talk to.

"Maya, please bring Jack. If not this week, then next week. I really want to get to know him better."

I sigh. "Okay."

It's not that I don't want my parents and Zach and Kate to get to know Jack; it's just that asking him to family dinner seems like such a huge step forward. I mean, yeah, we're dating, but it hasn't really felt like *dating* dating. It's like hanging out with my best friend all the time.

Dinner with the family? That's a serious relationship.

"All right," Mom says, obviously smiling. "Text me with his answer because I need to buy an extra steak if he comes."

"Okay." Mom's all into texting these days. Zach taught her how to do it, and now it's a rare day when I don't get some random text that goes something like this:

Hi. R U hving a gd day. <3 U.

I have only a few major pet peeves, but not spelling out a word just because you're texting is one of them.

"Love you, honey. Talk to you soon." Mom hangs up.

I close my phone and stare in the mirror. Maybe I should consider hats. Jen looks great in hats.

Of course, Jen looks great in everything, so I shouldn't take that as a sign that I would. Jen can wear that puke-green color and manage to make it look girly and adorable. I wear the puke-green color and look like some sick poster child who's about to be adopted by Angelina Jolie.

I try squirting hair spray on my hands and mashing my hair down, but it doesn't do anything. I'm not sure there's a worse curse in the world than curly hair. Especially ridiculously thick curly hair. Not only am I dealing with humidity-happy frizz, but

I'm also trying to stop the triangle effect.

I give up and finger comb it into a low ponytail. So much for the romantic curly style.

My phone buzzes, and it's a text.

Dd u ask hm yt?

Mom. Clearly, typing a vowel in between two letters is too much work.

I type back. *Not yet.*

Im @ th stor. Ask hm pls.

I guess I'm not going to be "accidentally" forgetting to ask him to dinner.

I text Jack. *Do you want to go to my parents' with me tomorrow night? Mom's making steaks.*

It's a dumb question, really. What twenty-five-year-old guy is going to turn down free steaks?

Definitely! Thanks! he writes back two seconds later.

I call Mom. "He said yes."

"Honey, the man is the one who is supposed to propose. And besides that, it's only been four months. That's awfully quick, Maya."

I just shake my head.

CHAPTER TWO

Jack shows up at exactly six o'clock. He's carrying a rental copy of *Hancock*, a large pizza box, and something in a plastic grocery bag, and he's wearing a pair of black starchy-looking pants with racing flames down the sides.

"What are you wearing?" I frown.

"Weird pants. I said I'd wear them and I did. You like weird pants, remember?"

I stare at him. "You're weird."

"No, the *pants* are weird. I'm just a pleasing kind of a guy."

"Oh boy." It's going to be one of those evenings with Jack. I open the door wider. "Come in before the neighbors see you."

He walks in, grinning, sets the pizza on the counter, and pets an ecstatic Calvin on the head. "So, I got us a Hawaiian pizza with extra cheese."

"Yum," I say. My mouth immediately starts watering.

"And if you're nice to me tonight, I might show you what's in the bag."

I smile sweetly at him. "I like your weird pants."

"You lie. And you have to earn this." He puts the bag in the freezer, and I clap excitedly.

"Ice cream!"

"Maybe. Maybe not." He smiles. "I'm going to change because as attractive as these pants are, they are not very soft. You want to get the movie ready?" He disappears into the bathroom and comes out a minute later wearing straight-cut denim jeans. He's wearing a black T-shirt that says *Hudson Zoo* in small letters on it.

See? This is exactly my point about dating. Before we started dating, we would both have been in sweatpants right now. I wouldn't have on any makeup, and he'd probably be wearing a baseball cap instead of actually taking the time to shower.

Jack isn't especially drop-dead gorgeous, but he's good-looking in a friendly kind of way. He has short, straight black hair (straight hair . . . kills me), dark, dark, dark brown eyes, and a really cute smile. And a dimple. On his right cheek. It's adorable.

He's very tall and fairly skinny. I know he's got muscles because he's pretty strong, but they aren't the obvious kind. He's lanky.

I stand up from where I was kneeling in front of the DVD player and join him in the kitchen, salivating over the pizza. "Yay!"

"Such a simple woman to please." Jack grins.

"And that's a good thing for you," I say. "Please pray so we can eat."

He holds out his hands, and I take them. "Why don't you pray tonight?" he says.

"Okay." I bow my head. "God, please bless this pizza and help it to be more nutritious than fattening. And please help me to be nice to Jack so I can get ice cream later. And, Lord, I pray that the movie has no resemblance to dinner. Amen."

Jack looks up at me, still holding my hands. "You have the

most interesting prayers of any person I know."

"Thanks. I think."

"No, it's a good thing. You're very real, and I appreciate that." He squeezes my hands. "Hungry?"

I hand him a plate, and we dig in, carrying the food to the couch. Calvin follows us excitedly, and I shoo him to his doggy bed.

"Poor Cal," Jack says.

"Not poor Cal. He's a food stealer."

"Oh. Not poor Calvin." Jack takes a huge bite.

I press Play, and we manage to keep quiet for the entirety of Will Smith's sad adventure.

The movie ends, and I stand to put the three remaining pieces of pizza in the fridge. Jack can put away food like no one's business. Incredible that he's so thin. Incredible and slightly disgusting.

"Well, that was sad," I say.

"What was sad?"

I frown. "The movie, Jack."

"Oh. It wasn't sad."

"Was too. They didn't end up together." I plop the now-cold pieces of pizza in a plastic baggie.

"So that makes it sad?" He stretches and joins me in the kitchen. "She's better off with the other guy."

"So, he gets to be alone forever." I toss the bag in the fridge. "That's horrible."

Jack sighs. "You know, every movie doesn't always have to end in a 'happily ever after' type of way," he says.

"Why not?"

"That's not real life, Nutkin."

"So? A movie isn't real life. It's fake life. And fake life

should be happy. If I wanted to watch real life, I'd just go stand outside the front door and watch tired, cranky people come home from work."

My logic makes sense and Jack knows it. "Never mind," he says, rubbing his forehead.

I'm not finished. "And you're comparing *Hancock* to real life? It's about a superhero! He should definitely be happy. That was wack."

He snorts and starts laughing. "Oh. My. Gosh. What did you just say?"

I bite my lip. "Can't pull it off?"

"You should never use slang again. Oh wow. That was hilarious!" He's grinning so wide that his dimple is showing.

"Okay. All right. Point made."

He snorts again. "Oh, Maya." He grins and pulls me into a hug. "You're awesome; did you know that?"

"Of course. Can I have the ice cream now?"

He just squeezes me tighter and laughs.

Jen doesn't get home until I'm washing the ice-cream bowls after Jack has left. She comes in the door humming.

"Hey," I say, waving a soapy spoon at her. "How was the movie?"

"Ah," she sighs, pressing her hands to her chest.

"That good, huh?"

"Oh my gosh, Maya, I will never get tired of *Sleepless in Seattle*."

I frown at her. "I thought you were going to the theater?"

"We went to that new one on Birch Street. It shows an older movie every Saturday night for a discounted price." She slings off her purse and sets it on the couch. "How was your night with Jack?"

"Fine. We had pizza and watched *Hancock*."

She makes a face. "I hate that movie."

"It's not my favorite either."

"He should at least end up with the girl."

I grin at her. There's a reason Jen is one of my best friends. "What else did you guys do?"

"We ate at Luigi's. Then we just did some window shopping."

Luigi's is an Italian restaurant in the newly renovated boardwalk area of Hudson. How we have a boardwalk is beyond me — we don't have a beach, and we're at least an hour away from one. But our mayor is very into all things outdoors- and fitness-related, so we're becoming proud citizens with tons of walking trails, parks, and evidently boardwalks.

"I haven't been down there since they finished it," I say, smashing the empty pizza box in the trash can.

"It's nice. It's also kind of weird because you're expecting to see an ocean on at least one side of you, but there's only the dirt path leading up to the back of Luigi's."

I grin. "Sounds scenic."

"My thoughts exactly." She sits at one of the kitchen chairs, pulling off her jacket. She's wearing a short black skirt with a flippy fringe and a hunter-green, short-sleeved satin shirt. Her hair is straight and shiny, and I'm again trying not to be jealous.

"So you're going to your parents' tomorrow," Jen says.

"Yeah." I wipe the pizza crumbs off the counter, avoiding her gaze. "I'm taking Jack with me."

"What?"

I hurry on. "Actually, he's taking me. He's doing the driving."

Jen's staring at me with her mouth open. "You're actually taking Jack with you?"

"Mom's making me."

"Wow. Family dinner. Serious."

"See? That's exactly what I told Mom." I bite my lip. "You don't think Jack is reading too much into this, do you?"

"What do you mean?"

"I mean, thinking I'm pushing him to the next step or something."

Jen rolls her eyes. "Oh, please, Maya. He's only going over for dinner. I mean, if he'd never met them before or if your mom were like mine, then maybe you could be concerned."

There are few people in this world I really can't stand to be around, and Jen's mom is at the top of the list. She's rude, stuck-up, and just plain mean. She's tried to control Jen her whole life, which is probably why Jen moved out the moment she turned eighteen.

Jen's dad, on the other hand, is a workaholic. I've never met him, but I hear his eyes are always glued to his computer screen and his ear is always glued to the phone. And that's on Christmas Eve. I'm not even sure he knows Jen's middle name. He sends her a hefty check several times a year and then a massive one sometime in April. I guess that's when he thinks her birthday is.

Jen's birthday is in October.

Jen calls the check "Guilt Change," which it probably is.

I join her at the table, pushing a package of Oreos over to her. She's too thin. "You're right."

"See? Travis still hasn't met my father and probably won't unless we get married or I get in a car accident and they cross paths at the hospital or something." Jen pulls three Oreos from the package, which shows how she's feeling. Jen's not one to snack.

"I'm sorry. You know my parents will adopt you anytime."

She smiles. "I might take them up on that."

"Do you want to come to dinner too?"

She shakes her head. "No thank you. I think I'll leave it a family affair."

"Funny."

She grins cheekily. "I thought so. No, Travis and I are going hiking tomorrow with one of his friends from work." She sighs and cracks an Oreo in half before eating it.

I frown. "Which friend?"

"The dorky one. Nick? Mick? Something like that. And his girlfriend. She's an IT specialist." Jen sighs again. "Should be a rousing afternoon."

I hide a smirk.

"It's not funny, Maya."

I guess I'm not hiding it well. I offer her another Oreo. "I'm sorry."

"Anytime Travis gets around his work friends, he morphs into this insurance-talking guy and becomes the biggest nerd ever." She sighs. "He's not like that when it's just the two of us."

"Well, that's good."

"Maya, we wouldn't be dating still if he were like that." She quirks her head at me. "Was he like that when you guys dated?"

"Dorky?"

"Just nerd-like."

I squinch my eyebrows together, thinking. It's still awkward to talk to Jen about when Travis and I dated. "Not that I remember," I say. "He wasn't working for the insurance company yet."

"I mean, I really don't care about the adjustable rates and whatever, but I don't know how to tell him that without sounding mean."

I frown. "You tell me when I'm talking too much about work."

"Yeah, but you're different, Maya."

"Well, thank you."

She rolls her eyes. "Not like that. I mean, it's different talking with you."

"Because I've seen you doing water ballet?" I crunch an Oreo.

She closes her eyes. "It's synchronized swimming, Maya. Synchronized swimming!"

"Whatever."

"And, no, it's not because of that. I feel totally comfortable with Travis, but I just don't know how to tell him I'd rather he didn't talk about work all the time."

I finish chewing. My mother would tell Jen not to worry about it — she'll be nagging him enough if they ever get married.

If they ever get married. Right. They are so getting married; you can tell every time Travis looks at Jen that he's already debating how many carats. And if the looks weren't enough, the amount of money he's spent on tulips for her is another good clue. Our apartment looks like we have some kind of weird pollen obsession.

Jen brushes some Oreo crumbs into her hand and carries them to the sink. "Anyway, I'm tired. We've got church in the morning."

"I'm tired, too."

She pauses in the doorway of her bedroom. "Hey, Maya?"

I flick the kitchen light, which sends the apartment into darkness. "Yeah?"

"Have you and Jack kissed yet?"

I'm suddenly very thankful for the inky blackness because it hides my immediate spastic reaction. My left eye is winking involuntarily, my hands are seizing into fists, and I'm having trouble getting my lungs to expand.

"What?" I manage to gasp out.

"Apparently not." Jen turns her bedroom lamp on and a warm glow floods her room. "Just curious. Night, Maya." She closes the door behind her.

I make it to my room and collapse on my bed, where Calvin was curled up in a little ball, asleep. He bounces a little bit when I fall down, and it makes me wonder if those memory-foam mattresses where the lady jumps up and down next to a glass of wine are really true.

That could be fun.

I shake my head slightly and focus on my seizure. What happened? My eye isn't blinking anymore, and my hands are more relaxed.

Kiss Jack?

I fight the half-laughter, half-horror in my chest. This is not a good sign. Don't get me wrong: I'm attracted to Jack, but *still*. Thinking about kissing Jack is a little like thinking about kissing Prince Edward in *Enchanted*. You just don't go there.

I look at Calvin, who's giving me the evil eye since I disrupted his precious sleep. "Sorry," I say.

He grunts and squinches his eyes shut again. Sheesh. For a dog that gets about eight hours of sleep every day, you'd think he'd be more supportive when I need him.

I push Calvin off the bed.

He makes a sad little sigh as he drags himself to his dog bed, but I'm not feeling sorry for him tonight. "Tough luck," I say. "Be more compassionate next time."

I change into my PJs and climb into bed, pulling the covers up under my chin.

Maybe it's because Jack and I have been friends for so long that it seems weird.

That must be it.

I pull my Bible onto my chest and prop it up, flipping to Proverbs. Right before Jack and I started dating, I was really struggling with trusting God—especially when Jen began dating Travis, who I thought I'd marry someday.

Before all that happened, I thought I had a fairly strong relationship with God. I read my Bible every day, prayed every day, and even made little sticky notes about what I learned.

I love sticky notes.

But there's a difference between learning and applying, and as much as I had learned about trusting God, I had never applied it.

Which led to some major problems a few months ago—but that's another story.

So, I'm reading Proverbs. I figure wisdom is definitely something I need, and Proverbs has to be one of the best books on application.

"The fear of the LORD is the beginning of knowledge" (Proverbs 1:7).

I remember something my pastor, Andrew Townsend, said in one of his Wednesday-night twentysomethings Bible studies. He was teaching on Matthew. "The disciples asked Christ why He was speaking in parables. Why use a story when You can just tell them what You mean?" Andrew pointed to his Bible. "And this is what Christ said: 'The knowledge of the secrets of the kingdom of heaven has been given to you, but not to them' (Matthew 13:11, NIV). Then listen to what He said a few verses later: 'For I tell you the truth, many prophets and righteous men longed to see what you see but did not see it, and to hear what you hear but did not hear it' (verse 17, NIV). Guys, don't ever take for granted the knowledge you have."

I write *Matthew 13* in the margin of my Bible. If knowledge is knowing Christ, the fear of the Lord is definitely a requirement for knowledge.

As I reach for the light, something on the ceiling catches my eye. I look up. There's something taped up there.

I squint. It's a piece of paper with blue pen scribbled on it: *Sweet dreams, Nutkin! See you at church in the morning.* ☺

Jack. How did he get in here to hang that up?

I grin and flip off the lamp before snuggling under the covers.

CHAPTER THREE

I'm ten minutes late for Sunday school the next morning. Mostly because I thought my blow-dryer had broken, when really I just wasn't very awake and didn't realize for a few minutes that it wasn't plugged in.

I seriously wouldn't survive without coffee.

I try to sneak in the back door unnoticed, but Andrew Townsend is big into preventing tardiness by bringing tons of attention to those poor people who are.

"Well, look who's here!" he half-shouts.

The whole class turns to look at me.

I have two personas—one is the Cool Beans Maya, who is friendly and outgoing and chatty. And here's the thing about her: She's so fake! My real personality is way shier. Actually, only a few people in this world know the real Maya: my parents, my brother, Jen, and Jack.

I blush, give the class a little wave, and drop into the first seat I find, which is on the back row next to a guy I've met six times and still can't remember his name. Jack, sitting beside Jen in the third row back, grins sympathetically at me.

Sorry, he mouths.

I glare at Andrew, who returns a cheeky smile. Andrew

knows I hate attention. He's just doing this out of spite for all the girly mugs I give him at Bible study on Wednesday nights.

Our twentysomethings Bible study is held at Cool Beans. It's great because I get free coffee since I work there. It's not great because I usually have to stay late and clean up. But Jack is always working too, so it's almost like a working date. It's late, no one else is there, and Jack turns on Elvis.

We love Elvis. It makes cleaning the coffee filters more fun.

Lately, we've only been working nine to five, so we haven't had to clean up. This forces our co-workers, Lisa and Peter, to hear the Bible study while they clean . . . which is a good thing.

I think God's got His eye on them.

"Okay, back to the opening passage of 1 Corinthians," Andrew says, and I quietly turn the pages in my Bible. I actually dressed up today, which is probably another reason I'm late. I'm wearing a short brown skirt and an off-white lacy top. My hair actually curled nicely today, so I'm not constantly blinking away a wayward curl.

Andrew is balancing on his little rickety stool, holding his Bible in both hands. "All right, guys, let's start with the basics. Who is this book written to?"

Nick, an outspoken musician type, answers, "The Corinthian Christians."

"Brilliant." Andrew grins. "Anyone want to take a stab at a major sin the church in Corinth struggled with?"

"Sexual immorality." This is said by Kara Thompson. She's one of those girls who knows everything about the Bible. Maybe I'm just jealous, but sometimes it's annoying that she always knows the answer.

Andrew nods. "Right. And the infamous chapter is . . .?"

"First Corinthians 13," Liz Chapman says. Liz is a beautiful redhead who has a very obvious crush on Andrew. Which, truth be told, I've never exactly understood. Andrew is nice-looking in an ex-hockey-star-with-all-his-teeth kind of way, I guess, but he is sarcastic, annoying, and has a very strange sense of humor.

But to each her own, I guess. I'm dating a guy who shows up to my apartment in racing flame pants, so, I shouldn't pass judgment.

Andrew teaches for forty-five minutes on why Paul decided to write the book of 1 Corinthians. "What I want us to take away from this is our responsibility as believers to constantly encourage each other and, in some way, provoke each other to lead godly lives," he says at the end.

I write on a sticky note in my Bible: *Provoke Jack more.*

Andrew prays, and class is dismissed to partake in the goodies a few of the girls brought in. Each week a couple of people are supposed to bring in snacks. We used to have the boys help, too, but there were a few weeks in a row where we had random stuff like health-food cookies that expired two weeks before and a half-eaten box of Rice Krispies without milk or bowls.

Ever since then, the girls have split up the calendar and resigned themselves to taking care of the men.

This week, Liz and another girl brought in homemade blueberry muffins with those little sugar crystals on top.

"Sorry to point out your tardiness," Andrew says, coming up behind me.

"No oo awnt," I reply, mouth full of muffin. I swallow, sighing. "Those are so good!"

"Thanks," Liz says, gliding over like she's Michael Caine's character in *Miss Congeniality.* She glances shyly at Andrew and then picks up a muffin. "Kayla helped me bake them. It's definitely berry season." Another glance in Andrew's direction.

Andrew swallows a muffin whole. "Definitely." He wipes his mouth with a napkin. "These are definitely some of the best muffins I've ever had."

"Thanks. Like I said, it's definitely because of the berries."

"Yeah, definitely."

Too much *Rain Man* going on for me. One of them will start boasting about driving skills at any moment. I nod. "All-righty then." I take my muffin and find Jack and Jen, still sitting.

"And then he took me home," Jen is saying to Jack as I walk up. "Did you have a good evening?"

"Definitely."

Seriously, how many times can I hear that word in a two-minute segment?

"Hey, Maya." Jen smiles up at me. "How come you were so late? I thought you were right behind me."

We took two cars because she's got a lunch date afterward. With Travis. I swear, his dining-out bills have to be as high as his mortgage payment. "I thought my blow-dryer broke, but it didn't." I don't elaborate. I like to keep my humiliating moments to myself.

Jen nods. "Oh, you look cute. I love your skirt!"

"Thanks."

Jack nods toward my legs. "You need a tan."

"Thanks," I say again. "In case you haven't noticed, the creamy natural color is in, Jack. All the celebrities are doing it. Haven't you noticed Anne Hathaway lately?"

"Which one is she?"

"The one I pointed out on TV the other night."

He frowns. "The pale, sickly looking one?"

I just rub my forehead.

"She's not pale and sickly," Jen says. "She's being her natural self. You know, in the olden days a tan was considered a bad thing. Read *Pride and Prejudice*."

"I'll take your word for it," Jack says. He grins. "Didn't mean to offend."

"Plus, it's only April. Give me a month, and then you can complain," I say.

Jack gives me a look, because he knows I don't tan easily.

"This year will be different," I promise.

"Right."

Jen claps her hands together and stands. "Okay, well, I'll let you two argue." She straightens her skirt and fluffs her gorgeous shiny hair.

"Has there been a day when you haven't seen Travis?" Jack asks. I think it's a valid question.

Jen pauses to think about it, gathering her purse and Bible. "I don't know," she says. "I'm sure there has been. We've been dating for almost seven months."

"Has it been that long?" Jack whistles. "Time flies."

"Seems like longer to me." Jen has one of those squishy, doe-eyed smiles. "He's so wonderful!"

Jack's looking a little sick to his stomach. "Have you two had a fight yet?" he asks, obviously trying to turn the conversation from Travis's wondrous personality.

"Of course we've had our disagreements," Jen says. "That's a normal part of any relationship." Now she sounds like Dr. Phil.

"Well, good."

Jen smiles. "And I need to go. We're meeting for lunch." She waves and disappears.

I look at Jack. "Four weeks."

"What?"

"That's my bet. I bet they're engaged before June."

"June, huh?" Jack squinches his mouth for a minute. "Yeah, I think you're right. She's head over heels."

I nod. Jack's smiling up at me, and then he looks at his cell phone. "Okay. What time are we heading to your parents?"

"Maybe around four?"

"Sounds good."

Awkward pause. I'm not sure if I should ask him if he wants to hang out before then. I had planned on taking Calvin on a walk and going grocery shopping. I guess I don't have to do that, though.

I'm a horrible girlfriend.

Sheesh.

"What are you doing today?" I ask, caving to the awkwardness.

Jack shrugs nonchalantly. "I was hoping to work out at some point. You know that new gym by my apartment? They sent out a free one-day pass, and I figured today was probably the only day I'd get any decent amount of time to go. Other than that, just hanging out tonight with you and the parental units."

"Sounds fun."

"What are you doing?"

"Taking Calvin on a walk and buying Oreos. Jen ate the rest of mine last night."

"And thus the end of the world."

"You know, my mom says that's caused by all these baby boomers going through menopause."

"What?"

"The end of the world. Global warming. She says that scientists should just forget the air-pollution theory and find a cure for hot flashes."

Jack just squints at me. "I will never understand women," he says finally.

I shrug this time. Too bad for him. I think I speak for all womankind when I say that we probably have more fun.

"So, I'll see you at four then," Jack says, standing. "Have a good time at the grocery store."

"Hope you burn a lot of calories."

"Thanks."

Jack arrives at four on the dot, just as I'm putting the Lucky Charms and Cocoa Puffs I bought in the cabinet. I open the door for him and frown.

"Where are you going? The prom?" I ask.

"Am I too dressed up?" Jack's wearing freshly ironed khakis, a white collared shirt, and a navy blue suit coat. He looks like he could launch into a sales pitch about stock with Ralph Lauren at any point in time.

"A little overdressed." I nod. I, on the other hand, have on my ratty jeans with the soon-to-be hole in the left knee and a white slightly oversized T-shirt that I stole from Zach in high school. While my hair did look nice this morning, chasing after Calvin in the park changed it back to my normal, insane curls. I pulled it back in a ponytail.

Jack sighs. "Okay, well, I'm glad I brought changes." He grabs a duffel I didn't see by his feet. "You get to help me pick out something to wear."

I watch him pull four different types of pants, six shirts, and three different pairs of shoes from the bag before I smile.

Jack's nervous.

It's kind of cute.

He rakes both hands through his hair and then points to the clothes. "Which ones?"

I walk over and look at them. "Jeans are a must."

"Done."

"And I don't know. . . . Wear that black Air Force shirt your friend gave you."

"Okay." He grabs it and then pauses. "Wait. What are your parents' political views?"

"What?"

"Well, what if they're all antiwar and I come in wearing an Air Force shirt?"

All right, the nervousness was cute. Now it's getting weird.

"Jack, you've met my parents multiple times," I say.

"I know, but I never asked them about their political ideals."

Nervous and using words like *ideals*. Never a good combination. I sigh and pick his normal sneakers off the couch.

"I think you're safe with the Air Force shirt." I hand it, the jeans, and the shoes to him and send him toward the bathroom. "And change quick, because I told Mom we'd be there around five, and if we're even three minutes late, she panics that we've broken down on the side of the highway."

He runs for the bathroom.

What a dork.

Jack comes out a few minutes later as I'm clipping Calvin's leash to his collar. Calvin loves going over to Mom and Dad's. They spoil him rotten. He even has his own toys over there. And Dad always buys Cal those pretzel bones.

"Ready?" I ask. He at least *looks* normal again.

"I think so."

"I don't understand why you're so nervous," I say as we leave the apartment. I lock the door behind me and follow him down the metal staircase. "You've met them before. They were nice to you."

"Yeah, but I haven't seen them since you and I started dating," he says, opening the back passenger door of his crew cab truck for Calvin. I have to lift my beagle in. Beagles weren't built for anything bigger than a sedan.

Jack opens the passenger door for me, goes around, and hops in the driver's seat.

"Well, I think you're panicking for nothing," I say.

"Nothing? I'm meeting my girlfriend's parents."

"You've already met!"

"Before you were my girlfriend."

I grab my head with both hands. This conversation is making me dizzy. "Jack, why does that matter?"

"Because I was just Jack the Co-Worker and Jack the Friend the last few times I saw your parents. Now I'm Jack the Could-Be In-Law. That's totally different!"

I feel my lungs catch a little when he says the word *in-law*. Or is that two words? Whatever, I definitely had trouble drawing a breath.

Isn't it a bit soon to be using that word? Or those two words?

I try to ignore it. "Okay, well, I think you're overreacting. But that's not out of character, so I guess we're okay."

Jack shoots me a glance as he turns onto the frontage road leading to the interstate. "What does that mean?"

"Nothing. Just that occasionally you overreact." I look out the window. It's not until you're on the interstate that you realize how small of a town Hudson is. It's tiny. Especially compared to San Diego, where my parents live.

Jack is muttering now. "I don't overreact. I'm very level-headed and calm. Overreact. I do not."

I hide a smile and look out the window.

We get to my parents' house exactly one minute after five o'clock. Mom opens the front door before we get there, waving excitedly. Calvin goes ballistic.

"Hi, Calvin!" Mom squeals, trying to pet my ecstatic puppy.

Calvin dashes inside for the pretzel treat he knows is in there, and Mom turns her attention to the humans approaching.

"Hi, honey," she says, giving me a hug. She smiles at Jack. "I'm glad you could make it, Jack."

"Thanks for having me, Mrs. Davis."

Jack has nice posture when he's trying to make a good impression. I grin at him, and then we follow Mom inside.

I inhale, closing the door behind me. Then I start jumping up and down. "Double-chocolate brownies? Yay!"

Mom laughs, and Jack raises his eyebrows at me.

"Have you ever had double-chocolate brownies, Jack?"

"Only when I've eaten two brownies at once."

Mom politely smiles at his bad joke.

I'm not so kind. "That was terrible." I grab his shoulders and make him look at me. "Jack. Double-chocolate brownies are, like, the best food group on the whole planet. And my mom is the only one who makes them."

Mom waves her hand. "I am not the only one who makes them. There are plenty of people who do."

"None are as good as the ones you make."

"You flatter me, honey."

We all go into the kitchen, where the pan of infamous brownies is cooling. Mom's trick is she adds the tiniest trace of coconut and zested orange peel to the batter.

It's amazing.

Calvin is happily chewing his pretzel bone on the living-room floor in front of the fireplace. As pathetic as they are, winters are my favorite season in this house. Mom is a cold weather fan, so to make up for San Diego's excuse of a winter, she turns the thermostat down and there's almost always a fire crackling in the fireplace. It always smells like apple cider or spiced tea, and Mom's a big fan of chocolate doing the most to keep a person "warm."

It's April, so the fires are over, but Mom has candles burning all over, so it smells like a clan of vanilla beans bred with a family of cranberries. Plus the double-chocolate smell.

Mom's a scent addict. Anytime she comes over to my apartment, she always brings candles or reed diffusers or those Glade PlugIn things.

Dad waves through the sliding-glass door. He's out tending the steaks on the grill, Bobby Flay style. I get my love of the Food Network from my dad. When I was in high school we used to watch it together late at night.

"So, how was the drive?" Mom asks, her customary Sunday-night question.

"Fine," I say, my customary Sunday-night answer. I look around. "Where are Zach and Kate?"

"They called and said they were running a few minutes late."

"Typical of a doctor."

Mom sticks up for her eldest. "At least he has nice handwriting."

I concede. Zach has prettier handwriting than I do. When he was in the sixth grade, his teacher was convinced Mom was doing his homework for him because his papers were so neat.

Dad comes in and gives me a hug. "Hi, Maya," he says. He nods at Jack, sticking his hand out. "Jack, nice to have you here."

"Thanks for having me, sir."

This is the second time he's said this in three minutes. If he keeps this up, it's going to get very old, very soon.

"How do you like your steaks?" Dad asks, throwing a towel over his shoulder, all Emeril-wannabe.

"I like mine on a plate, maybe with a sprig of parsley," I say. Dad ignores me.

To use Stephanie's catchphrase on *Full House*, "How rude!"

"Uh, well done is great," Jack says.

"We like our steaks mooing," I tell him. "You'll have to wait for your dinner then, because I'm hungry."

"But any way you fix it is fine," Jack quickly adds.

Dad shakes his head at me. "We like ours medium well. Don't listen to her." He goes back outside, squeezing my arm on the way. *Be nice*, he mouths.

I smile, and he sighs and closes the door behind him.

Mom is talking to Jack. "I hear you're interested in zoo animals."

I snort. There's a sentence you don't hear too often. I fake an insulted sigh. "Well, thank you, Mother. Yes, I'm hungry, but you don't have to be so honest about it. Your tact is amazing."

Now Mom ignores me. Calvin gives a little "Roo!" from the living room, and once again, I'm grateful my dog has a good sense of humor.

"Yes, ma'am," Jack answers nicely, also not commenting on my hilarious joke. "I'm getting a job at the Hudson Zoo in two weeks."

"That'll be nice. What will you be doing there?"

"Specifically, I'll be interning with the man in charge of the African exhibit. So, I'll be helping oversee animals like the hippo, rhino, and giraffe." He grins, and I can see the excitement in his expression.

"Wait, tell her the best part," I say.

Jack sighs. "I have to wear a safari hat."

"Have to? No, you *get* to." I grin. "I think you should wear it this week at Cool Beans. Just to get used to it."

"No thanks."

"He also gets to wear a badge that says, 'Hi, I'm SAFARI JACK,'" I tell Mom.

"Maya, everyone has to wear those badges," Jack says.

"They all wear badges that say 'SAFARI JACK'? Then how do you tell who's who?"

Jack covers his eyes right as we hear the front door open. "Hey!" Zach yells into the house.

He and Kate walk in. They are a beautiful couple. Kate is tall and slender, and has shiny, straight chocolate-colored hair. Zach's also tall and on the thinner side, but he got Mom's honey-blond hair.

Both of them have an extra-dressy taste in clothes. Zach's wearing straight-cut dark-washed jeans with a gray polo shirt, and Kate's wearing an empire-waisted navy sundress and heels.

When they get to the kitchen, they exchange a weird look. Evidently, Mom forgot to tell them Jack was coming to dinner.

"You guys have met, right?" I say, trying to cover the weirdness.

"Jack," Jack says, holding out his hand to both of them.

"Right," Zach says, nodding. "Good to see you. Glad Maya finally brought you to dinner." He jabs his fist into my shoulder.

"Ow."

"Hi, Jack," Kate says nicely.

Dad comes in with the steaks right then, and Mom pulls a cheesy hash-brown potato casserole from the oven. "Hope everyone is hungry," she says, taking a mandarin-orange salad from the fridge. "We have enough to feed an army."

We all find seats at the table, Dad prays, and then we fill our plates.

"This is great, Dad," I say, digging into my steak.

Jack says, "Yes, it is. Thank you, sir."

Silence.

Jack's chewing, Mom's picking the oranges out of her salad, Zach and Kate are exchanging odd looks with each other, and Dad's grinning at me.

See? This is why I didn't want to invite Jack. Bringing in outsiders just makes the whole evening awkward, despite my ice-breaking jokes.

"So, next Sunday is Easter," Mom begins.

Zach nods. "Yeah, and since we're spending Easter with Kate's family this year, we thought we'd go ahead and bring you your present this week."

Kate gets up and disappears into the entryway, coming back a minute later with a package that looks like a DVD.

I swallow a piece of lettuce. I bet it's one of those corny Easter movies they show on the Hallmark Channel. Mom loves those. She calls me every time one of those movies is on. "Turn on the TV, Maya! That movie about the man who got in an accident and has amnesia after he married his first wife and now he's getting ready to marry someone else is on!"

Mom can't get enough of them. I, on the other hand, find them a little disturbing. I mean, I can accept that the man has amnesia, but what are the odds that his first wife would fall into a twenty-year coma, too?

Not likely.

Zach and I love to make fun of those movies in front of Mom.

Kate hands the present to Mom. "It's for you both," she says, taking her seat again.

Mom looks a little pained, and I'm sure it's because she didn't get them anything. I try to hide a smile.

"Honey, you shouldn't have," she says. She tears open the package; instead of a DVD, it's a picture frame.

"Oh, how nice. Thank you!" Mom says in her polite voice. This means she's not so sure she likes it. She shows it to everyone at the table, and I'll admit, it's a little weird.

The picture frame is that artsy, papier-mâché decorated style, and inside is a picture of Zach and Kate cooking. They're both bending over an open oven, reaching for a loaf of bread, smiling at the camera.

I look over at them, and they're holding hands, grinning ear to ear. Then I look at Jack, who is also grinning ear to ear. Dad's got the same confused look I imagine I have on, and Mom's still being polite.

"Do you like it?" Zach asks.

"Of course, honey. I like anything you two give me," Mom says.

"No, but do you like the picture?" Kate asks.

Dad pulls his bifocals out of his shirt pocket and balances them on his nose. He picks up the picture and stares at it. "What are you baking? Mini pizzas?"

"It's a hamburger bun," Zach says.

Mom nods, probably trying to end the conversation so she can stop pretending. "It's nice, sweetie."

Kate sighs. "Told you," she says to Zach.

"Give them a minute," Zach tells her in a low voice. Jack is staring at his well-done steak, still grinning.

I slowly cut a square of steak and put it in my mouth, chewing. Maybe Zach and Kate are trying to tell us they're going to quit doctoring and lawyering and start baking buns.

Bun. In the oven.

Then it hits me. "HOWY CWOW!" I shout, half-choking on my steak.

"She got it," Zach says.

"Got what?" Mom says.

"She knows." Kate's grin is wider than the Oklahoma panhandle.

Meanwhile, I'm now gagging on my steak. I swallow with difficulty, tears building in my eyes.

"You okay, Maya?" Dad asks.

"You need to take smaller bites. I've been telling you this for years," Mom says, while I gulp down some water.

"They're pregnant!" I shout. I look at Zach and Kate, who are beaming. "You're pregnant?!"

"WHAT?" Mom shouts.

"It's a bun in the oven." Kate giggles. "Get it? Bun in the oven?"

Jack starts laughing.

Mom bursts into tears. Dad just looks stunned, his fork frozen halfway above his plate, hash-brown casserole sliding off it.

I whack Jack's arm. "You guessed right away, didn't you?"

"Kind of," he says.

"How far along are you? Is it a boy or a girl? What are you going to name it? Are you feeling okay? Oh my gosh!" I shout.

Kate and Zach are both laughing, and Kate's brushing tears from the corners of her eyes. Mom gets up, still blubbering, and grabs Kate in a hug.

"Oh, sweetie!" she manages.

"So, what do you think, Gramps?" Zach asks, standing and

reaching for Dad's hand.

"Gramps," Dad repeats, standing, still in shock.

Kate looks at me. "I'm thirteen weeks along, we'll find out in a few weeks if it's a boy or girl, and I feel like I've got food poisoning." She turns toward Dad. "So no offense to your cooking, but I might stick with some crackers for tonight."

"Oh, honey," Mom says, pulling her back into a hug. "Oh, honey." Then she starts crying again.

Zach winks at me.

"Congrats, you guys," Jack says.

"Thanks," Zach answers.

"Gramps," Dad says again.

I'm in shock. "You kept it a secret for thirteen weeks?"

Zach nods, all proud of himself. "Well, actually we've only known for about six. But yep. We were going to try to wait until Easter, but Kate started showing."

She tugs self-consciously at her loose-fitting dress. Thus the empire waistline, I guess. "My mom had three miscarriages before she got pregnant with my sister. We figured it would be better to wait until the danger time was over before we told anyone."

"And the danger time is over?"

"I just started my second trimester. So, yes. They say the highest probability for miscarriages is during the first twelve weeks."

I nod like I know what she's talking about.

"Plus, I didn't really start feeling sick until these last few weeks, and we thought that would be harder to hide, too." Kate smiles sheepishly at Mom. "You're a little too observant."

"Obviously not *very* observant or I would have noticed you were putting on weight," Mom says, grinning.

"Well, I've been trying to dress in looser clothes. Lucky for me, the styles have kind of moved in that direction."

Zach is all smiles. "We've actually been trying for about five months."

"I didn't know that!" Mom exclaims.

"We didn't tell anyone. Figured it would be better to just surprise everyone," he says.

This is starting to verge on too much information about my brother and his married life. I change the direction of the conversation.

"What are some names you like?" I ask.

Mom finally lets go of Kate and settles back into her seat. Dad is back to staring at his forkful of casserole. Jack's devouring his steak.

Kate looks bright-eyed and is smiling at Zach, and he takes her hand. "Well," he says. "We are still working on that."

"I really love the idea of naming the baby a family name," Kate says.

"And I don't love the idea of a daughter named Olga," Zach pipes up.

I grin. Dad's great-grandmother will always live in infamy, even though neither Zach nor I ever met her. One of Dad's favorite stories to tell us is how he pushed for Mom to name me Olga. "Finally settled on Maya," Dad always finishes with a huge, sad sigh.

I love my mom.

Shocked as he is, Dad still cracks a smile at that comment.

Mom waves her hand. "Oh, please. You don't have to go that far back. Your Nana's name was Madeline Grace, and I've heard those names are very popular these days."

"Oh, I love the name Madeline." Kate sighs.

Zach nods. "For a boy, we like the name Jeffrey."

"Jeffrey," I repeat. "Jeff."

"Oh, no," Kate says quickly, shaking her head. "I cannot stand the name Jeff. It would be Jeffrey."

Jack looks at me, sharing my frowning expression. "You don't think people might shorten it?" I ask.

"They probably will," Jack says in a gentler tone than mine. "My full name is Jackson. The only person who calls me that is my mother."

"Oh," Kate says sadly. "No Jeffrey then. I hate the name Jeff."

Zach glares at me and Jack. "Thanks, guys. Six weeks of convincing her, and you've undone it in three minutes."

"Sorry, Zach."

"Sorry, Zach."

"It doesn't matter too much. My mom's maiden name was Hamilton, and I've always thought that was such a great name for a boy," says Kate.

"I don't. Jeffrey is a much better name than Hamilton."

"Hamilton was a president!"

"Jeffrey was a famous pine tree in Yosemite," Zach retorts.

We all just stare quizzically at him.

"Look it up," he says wearily to our unasked question.

Dad's still staring at his fork. He says it so quietly that it's almost imperceptive: "Gramps."

CHAPTER FOUR

I get to Cool Beans at 8:47 a.m. It's sunny outside but there's a chill in the air, so I'm wearing a fuzzy hooded jacket over my typical work outfit of a black Polo shirt and jeans. My hair is tied back in a curling-out-of-control ponytail. Sometimes I wish I was still living in the time of *Anne of Green Gables*, where I could braid my hair down. It would be so much easier. Just not very stylish.

And I love the Style Network too much to do that.

Jack's car is already in the parking lot, and he's busy grinding the Roast of the Day when I walk through the door. Elvis is crooning "Love Me Tender" softly on the speakers, and Jack's got a fire crackling in the fireplace.

I love my work.

If you mixed Johnny Rockets with Starbucks, you would end up with Cool Beans. Everything is decked out in fifties' colors, styles, and memorabilia. It's my boss's trademark. Alicia is the owner of Cool Beans and a similarly designed and decorated diner across town. She spends most of her time at the diner and just creates the schedule — at least two people for every shift — at Cool Beans.

There are silver and cherry bar stools, white- and cherry-cushioned chairs pushed under the silver tables, two awesomely squishy sofas in front of the fireplace, and two overstuffed easy chairs. Elvis, Sinatra, Dean Martin, and more have remembrance in the form of posters, clocks, and framed records on the wall.

"Morning, Nutkin," Jack yells over the coffee grinder's whirring.

"Hey." I go behind the counter and into the kitchen in the back, yanking my cherry red apron off its hook and hanging my purse there instead. I take off my jacket and pull the apron over my head and loop the strings around, tying them in front around my waist.

Jack's dumping the freshly ground beans in the coffeemaker. "What's our Roast of the Day?" I ask, pulling over the blackboard and some colored chalk.

"Hazelnut with a touch of Italian," he says. "I had a great time last night."

"Me too." And I really did. Once the awkward pauses that had to do with the impending pregnancy — and not Jack — were over, we all relaxed and talked until close to midnight. It was almost one before I got home and fell wearily into bed.

"Kate seems stuck on Hamilton," Jack says, measuring the beans for the dark roast into the grinder.

I write *Italian Hazelnut* on the blackboard in scrolling letters and nod. "Hamilton Davis," I say, testing it out. I frown. "It sounds like a designer label."

"That's bad, I take it?"

"Not bad, just weird."

"Well, maybe it will be a girl," Jack says cheerfully, always the optimist.

I must admit, sometimes that can be extremely irritating.

Especially when I want to sulk for a while. Jack doesn't believe in sulking. Unless it's his problem. Then he sulks. I guess he just doesn't believe in me sulking.

Not fair at all.

"Maybe," I say. "Then I guess we'll have a Madeline Davis. Maddie Davis." I try out that name.

"I don't know. Kate might not like Maddie either. For having a name that's a nickname, she sure is against shortening names."

"Then she should stay away from Hamilton. The kid will be called Hammie his whole childhood."

Jack grins.

I measure out our medium roast of the day. I decide on a nice blend of a dark French roast and a light Breakfast Blend. We'll call it Breakfast in Paris. Or better yet, we'll call it French Kiss and hope Meg Ryan comes in.

"Dark roast is Colombian," Jack says, hanging a little sign that says *Colombian* over the now-gurgling coffeepot.

"Medium is Touché de Paree," I say.

"What?"

"A Touch of Paris. Half French roast, half Breakfast Blend."

Jack frowns. "You do remember you work at Cool Beans? A fifties-style coffeehouse? Call it an Audrey Hepburn, and then maybe you've got something."

"Why Audrey Hepburn?"

"I don't know. Wasn't she in a movie about Paris?"

"She might have been in one about Rome, but I'm not sure."

Jack shrugs. "Close enough."

I acquiesce. "Fine." I write *Audrey Hepburn* under the medium blend section on the blackboard. I'm pretty impressed that Jack even knows who Audrey Hepburn is. "How do you know about Audrey?" I ask.

"My mom made me watch *Charade* when I was in middle school."

"With Cary Grant? Great movie."

He sighs. "Right. Sure."

I grin. Jack doesn't have any sisters, and I think sometimes his mom made him and his brother do things just to have company. Like watch chick flicks.

"What should we make for the light roast?" Jack asks, looking through the huge supply of coffee beans.

"What about that new Mexican Blend? Isn't that a light roast?"

He nods. "Sounds fine." He pours the beans in the grinder.

Neither Jack nor I are big on light roast. If you're going to have coffee, have *coffee*. Not this half-water stuff. By the time you add cream to the light roast, all you've got is something that smells like coffee but tastes like milk.

Others obviously agree with us because we always run out of the dark blends.

My favorite? Jack makes a perfect blend of dark French roast, dark Italian, and a smidge of cinnamon. It's amazing!

It's nine o'clock now, so I go flip over the open sign. Winter is by far our busiest season — probably because colder temperatures make everyone want a mocha. Come March, I sometimes feel like all we make are MixUps, our version of the Frappuccino.

A Bible study for retired men meets here every Monday at nine thirty, and they start showing up about nine fifteen, just as I'm pulling our famous cinnamon rolls from the oven.

"Smells great!" says Mr. O'Neill, one of the leaders of the Bible study. He has this amazing shock of sheet-white hair, and without fail, rain or shine, summer or winter, he's always wearing khakis and an army green sweater vest over his collared shirt.

"Hi, Mr. O'Neill." I grin.

"Hi, Maya. What's the decaf for today?"

Jack calls the answer from behind me, hastily spreading frosting over the cinnamon rolls before the rest of the men arrive. It's a Bible-study favorite. "It's Italian today, sir. Just finished brewing."

"Thanks, Jack." Mr. O'Neill smiles at me. "I'll take a medium decaf, Maya. And a cinnamon roll, as long as you swear under pain of death not to tell my wife. She's gotten into this whole natural-diet thing. All we eat is wheat germ and raw vegetables."

I fill a medium cup with the decaf, leaving plenty of room for cream, the way I know he likes it, grinning. "I swear."

"Good girl."

I ring up his total, and he pays me, dropping his customary dollar in the tip jar. "Thanks," I say, smiling. I hand him his coffee and cinnamon roll, still so warm that the cream-cheese frosting is melting off it.

My mouth starts watering.

Mr. O'Neill settles down at the three tables pushed together that Jack and I set up right before he got there.

All eight men make it today, so in all we sell eight cinnamon rolls, six cups of decaf, and two English Breakfast teas.

Jack dumps the used tea leaves into the trash and wipes the counter. I slide the rest of the cinnamon rolls under the warmer.

"Does it make you sad?" I ask him as he watches the men's group pray before digging into their cinnamon rolls.

"Does what make me sad?"

"That you're leaving in less than two weeks."

He smiles gently at me. "I'm going to miss you."

Feeling the blubber fest coming on, I change the subject. "But not the customers? Or the coffee?"

I notice the flicker of sympathy in his eyes at my quick questions, but he doesn't push it. "Some customers," he nods. "I'll miss those guys. I won't miss that group of middle-school girls who come here."

They all blush eleven shades of red whenever Jack talks to them. He's a regular celebrity to that group. There are about five girls who come almost every Wednesday after school, order caramel MixUps, and sit on the bar stools at the high counter, staring at Jack and slowly sipping.

Most weeks, he hides in the back.

"I'm sure," I say, rolling my eyes.

Jack grimaces. "You have to admit, it's a little creepy. And I won't miss the smell of coffee on my clothes, in my car, and stinking up my closet."

He has a point. In Cool Beans, coffee smells amazing. In my laundry basket, however, coffee smells stale, smoky, and pungent.

It's a little gross.

"Plus, it'll be nice to do something that actually makes me apply my major," he adds.

Jack majored in biology with an emphasis in animal behaviors. Ever since I've known him, he's wanted to be a zookeeper.

And I've known him a long time.

"Excuse me, Maya?" One of the men is standing at the register.

"What's up, Mr. Patterson?"

"Let me have one more cinnamon roll to go. Lindy isn't feeling so good today, and she'd probably like it," he says, referring to his wife.

I want to marry someone who brings me cinnamon rolls smothered in cream-cheese frosting when I'm sick.

I pack up the cinnamon roll and hand it to him, waving aside his money. "On the house, Mr. Patterson. I hope your wife feels better soon."

"Well, thank you, honey." He joins the men, setting the to-go box next to his Bible.

I make sure Jack is distracted as I put three dollars from my tips the day before into the cash register. The Bible says not to let your right hand know what your left hand is doing when you're trying to do a good deed. I figure, if my right hand isn't supposed to know, then Jack Dominguez definitely doesn't need to know.

My lunch break is from twelve thirty to one. This doesn't leave me tons of time to go get something to eat, so instead of driving in a panic to Panda Express's drive-thru, I've started packing my lunch.

"It's healthier," Jen told me.

That might be the case with *her* sack lunches. Every single day, she packs a Lean Cuisine frozen entrée, a Special K protein water, and an apple.

I unzip my Thermos lunch box and pull out leftover mac 'n' cheese, a breadstick, and a brownie. I find an orange in there too, and I did not pack an orange.

Jen.

Ever faithful in her quest to get me to eat better.

So my lunch isn't too healthy. At least it's cheaper than spending $7 at Panda Express every day.

I sit at one of the tables in the back room. This is Cool Beans' kitchen and storage, but the kitchen part is only used at night, when our chef comes in to whip up a batch of cinnamon rolls, scones, cookies, and brownies for the next day. There are two huge commercial fridges back here, floor-to-ceiling shelves of supplies like cups, napkins, stir sticks, and the nonrefrigerated food items, counters all along one side for food prep, and two big round tables with chairs.

I pop my macaroni in the microwave and dig into it a few minutes later. Kraft's mac 'n' cheese — for all its amazing cheesy goodness the moment it's made — does not, in my humble opinion, make good leftovers. There's no more creamy cheesiness, just sticky, cheese-globbed noodles.

A little gross, I'll admit.

It still tastes good though, so I finish it off. I'm halfway through the breadstick when I hear my phone buzzing in my purse.

I dig it out. It's Jen calling.

"Which dress do you like better?" she asks, not bothering with common phone etiquette like "hello."

"What?"

"Which dress do you like better? Did you not get my texts?" She groans. "Okay, listen, I'm hanging up. Check your text messages and call me back as soon as you look at them."

Click.

I guess if there's no "hello" there doesn't need to be a "good-bye."

I take another bite of the breadstick and click into my message box. I have four new picture messages, all from Jen. They're all taken in a dressing room, and I can see her from the neck down, holding her phone out, taking a picture of her reflection in a mirror.

The first picture is of a fire-engine red, sleeveless dress that is straight-cut down to her knees. Red is a great color on Jen, but this dress makes her look flat as a board. I'm not sure that's the look she's going for if she's going out with Travis, like I assume she is.

The second is a black V-neck dress with what looks like a sheer lace thing on top of the dress. The lace hangs a little bit lower than the black, which makes her knees look weird.

The third is a burgundy wrap-style dress with three-quarter sleeves; it ends around her knees as well. That one is cute.

The fourth is an empire-waisted dress, and even though that style looks absolutely adorable on my sister-in-law, Jen can't pull it off. Kate has curves up there, if you know what I mean, but Jen works out too much to have enough above the waistline for that dress.

I call her back, swallowing the rest of the breadstick.

"Well?" she says.

"Are you shopping right now? I thought you were supposed to be working," I say, looking at the clock. I've got ten minutes before my lunch break is over, and Jen is supposed to be a regular nine-to-fiver with an hour lunch break, but she always ends up working through lunch and later than five.

"I took my lunch break to go to the mall," she says. "Ate on the way. What do you think?"

"I like the wrap dress."

"Really? You don't think the color is too Christmasy?"

"Burgundy? That's not Christmasy."

"Yeah, it is. Everything is always burgundy and evergreen during December." She sighs. "Never mind. Anyway, you think that one looked the best?"

"What is this for?" I ask.

"Travis is taking me to this big office party he's having on Friday, and it's fancy."

"Oh." I think about it. "I'd go with the wrap dress. It's very flattering."

I can almost hear her nodding. "Okay. Okay, I'll do that," she says. "Thanks so much, Maya!"

"You're welcome."

"I know you're on lunch break, so I'll let you go. Thanks. Bye!"

I hang up, put my phone away, and act like a good girl and eat the orange. Jack comes in right as I'm swallowing the last of my brownie.

"Your turn," he announces, pulling off his apron. "I'm starving!"

"Going somewhere?"

"No, I brought a sandwich from home."

I smile, put my lunch container away, pull my apron back on, and give him a quick, apparently surprising, hug.

He doesn't let go right away, though. So, my quick hug turns into a long one.

"I like this start to my lunch break," he says quietly.

He holds me gently, and I let my head rest against him. I'm short to his tall, but there's this perfect little spot right beside his heart where my head fits perfectly.

I get this weird, squinching feeling in my stomach, and I swallow hard.

I pat his back and pull away. "I've got to go man the counter. Enjoy your lunch!"

"Shouldn't it be *woman* the counter?" Jack asks, and suddenly everything is back to normal.

I grin and leave.

CHAPTER FIVE

The week passes by quickly, and I wake up Friday morning curled into a little ball — not on my bed, but on the couch.

I squint into the sunshiny living room, confused. *How'd I get here?*

"Well, good morning, sleepyhead. I was about to wake you up," Jen says, standing in front of me. She's wearing a black A-line skirt, a gray blouse, and heels. Work attire for her.

I'm so thankful I work in a place that prizes podiatric support.

I frown up at her, stretching. "What time is it?"

"Seven forty-five. I've got an early staff meeting today, so I'm about to leave."

"How'd I get on the couch?"

"You fell asleep there last night during the movie." She sighs and rolls her eyes. "Though how you did is beyond me. *The Dark Knight*, Maya. Seriously! That's like one of the tensest movies I've seen in a long time."

I rub my eyes, remembering. Jack came over, and the three of us watched the movie. There is a reason it's called *The Dark Knight*; it seems like the whole movie takes place in dark scenes. This isn't the first movie I've fallen asleep during. Actually, in one out of every three movies we start after nine at night, I fall asleep.

It's a curse.

"You didn't even wake up when Jack left," Jen continues. She grins. "I had to walk the poor guy out."

"I'm an awful girlfriend." It's becoming public knowledge.

"Yeah," Jen says matter-of-factly. "But at least you're dating a nice guy who didn't wake you up."

I push myself off the couch and smile at her, rubbing my sleep-matted hair. "You look nice."

"Thanks. I'll be home around five. Travis is picking me up at six for his office party." She bites her lip. "You're sure the burgundy dress is the right one?" She bought it on Monday, but she's been bugging me about it being the right dress ever since.

"Yes, Jen."

"You're sure it looks nice?"

"Yes, Jen."

"And you really think it's flattering?"

"Yes, Jen." I squint at her and straighten up off the couch, catching my breath at the crick in my spine. Clearly, our couch does not have the proper pressure-relieving and support features that my mattress does. "Anyway . . ." I say, going into the kitchen to start the coffee. Jen's a tea drinker. "Why are you getting so stressed out about this work party? It's not like you haven't met his co-workers."

"I've met some of them," Jen says, following me into the kitchen. "But I've never been to a work party before. It seems really official. I have to make a good impression on everyone."

I scoop the coffee into the filter. "I think you're worrying for nothing."

Jen sighs. "Okay. Well, one of these days when Jack takes

you to his work party, you let me know if you get stressed out."

"If that happens, it'll be with people who work at a zoo, Jen. They'll probably be impressed that I have opposable thumbs."

She giggles. "True." Then she sighs again. "You're probably right."

"I know. Opposable thumbs are very impressive."

"Not about that. About me stressing out. I'll try not to think about the work party today." She fingers a tulip in the latest bouquet from Travis, frowning.

Yeah, she won't be able to do that. I finish with the coffeemaker, flip the switch, and it starts gurgling.

"Just focus on work while you're at work, and then come home and worry." I look over at her. "But remember that stress causes premature aging."

She smiles at my warning. "Will you be here?"

I nod. "I get off at five."

"Okay. I have to go. See you tonight!" She grabs her purse and leaves, half-tripping over Calvin, who is just coming out of my room, yawning.

"I'm going to assume you slept in the bed?" I ask him.

He stretches, which is a yes.

I take a shower, and by the time I get out, the coffee is done. I pour a cup to drink while I'm fixing my hair and putting on some makeup.

I peer in the mirror at my nose. It's only April, and already the curse of fair skin is showing up across my nose: freckles. I hate this part of summer. I spend the whole season looking like a well-developed twelve-year-old.

Mashing some concealer over my nose seems to do the trick for now, but after an hour of working around steaming cups of coffee, the concealer fades away.

I beat Jack to work. Cool Beans is cold and dark; I hate being the first one here in the mornings.

It's creepy.

I flip on the lights in the front and tiptoe to the back, turning on the lights in the kitchen. The kitchen is the worst place first thing in the morning and late at night — mostly because the fridges make this *ooohhmmmmm* sound, like miniature monks are meditating back behind the fridge.

I could never be our chef, Kendra Lee. She's in here all by herself, baking for the next day. She gets here at nine at night and doesn't leave until close to midnight. She says it is peaceful after being at home with her two toddlers and a baby all day. Her husband watches them at night. I used to see her more when Jack and I had the closing shift, but now I rarely do.

I hang up my purse, pull on my apron, and turn on the stereo, drowning out the monks with Dean Martin's classic "Return to Me."

It was a great movie, too.

I'm halfway through grinding a huge batch of French roast when Jack gets there. I was thinking about what I read in my Bible this morning. Since I fell asleep before I got the chance to read last night, I picked it up for a minute today before I left for work.

In Proverbs 3, it was talking about honoring God with my wealth. I work at a coffee shop, so I don't really have wealth. I make enough to pay the bills, buy an occasional lunch out, and put a few dollars a month into my savings account.

"Hey, Nutkin." Jack yawns and comes around the counter, smiling at me. He leans down and kisses my cheek, and I blink at him, the ligaments in my knees suddenly feeling spastic. "I still can't believe you fell asleep during *The Dark Knight*," he says, grinning.

"Sorry about that."

He shakes his head. "No apology necessary." He disappears into the back and returns, tying his apron around his waist.

"I'm just amazed you can sleep through such a nerve-racking movie," he continues, grabbing a bag of a light Breakfast Blend and dumping it in the grinder I just finished using.

"It was dark," I complain for the second time this morning. "And, sheesh, you of all people should know how often I fall asleep during movies!"

"Which is why I've never taken you on a date to the theater," he grins.

I sigh, thinking of movie-theater popcorn. Buttery, salty, delicious. "We could go in the afternoon, you know."

"Could. We'll see. It's dark in the theaters, though." He's still grinning unrepentantly, and I calmly ignore him.

By the time lunch comes around, I've made seven lattes and fifteen MixUps. Like I said, the moment it starts getting warm outside, our blenders start overheating.

I rinse out a blender and set it on the drying rack, looking over at Jack. "I'm taking my lunch break." The last of our lunch-break crowd just left, and the only people in Cool Beans are a group of three moms having adult-conversation time while their toddler-age girls play with Elmo on the carpet.

All the girls are dressed in the most adorable dresses ever, and I wish that clothes looked that cute on adults. Honestly, you can dress babies or little kids in anything, and they'll look like a million bucks.

I decide middle school is when that gift disappears. My middle-school years were awkward, to say the least.

"Go for it," Jack says, wiping some spilled milk off the

counter. "I think I can handle this crowd." He grins.

"I don't know, Jack. The little brunette in the pink dress seems to have a thing for you."

The baby, who has soft, wispy brown hair parted on the side and huge brown eyes, keeps looking up at Jack.

"I think she's looking at the lights over the bar, Pattertwig."

"You never know. Got to watch out for those adoring females." I go into the back and pull out my lunch. It's leftover pizza from our movie night. Bacon, bell peppers, and pineapple — probably the best combination ever.

I pop the pizza in the microwave and eat quickly. Fridays around two o'clock, we get a huge rush of high schoolers and people who, I guess, left work early. I jam through my lunch break so Jack can get his in before the rush arrives. He could just eat in peace and let me handle the crowd, but Jack feels bad about doing that. So he ends up skipping lunch, and then I feel bad.

So, we worked out a new system.

Jack is just coming back to the front after his lunch break, wiping his mouth with a napkin, when six high schoolers walk in, laughing and giggling loudly.

"Oh my gosh, he really said that?" one bleach-blond says loudly, obviously wanting some attention.

I sigh.

Some girls are genuinely outgoing, enthusiastic, and friendly. But I think you can tell the genuine girls from the just-wanting-male-attention girls by the way they dress and carry themselves.

This bleach-blond is wearing a top my mother would have sent me back to my room for wearing. Let's just say the secrets are out. She's slyly standing close enough to some guy to be brushing arms with him.

I'm not a guy, but I think that would be annoying not attractive.

"Can I help you?" I ask.

"How many calories are in the mocha MixUp?" the blond asks.

I dig out a nutrition card from under the counter and hand it to her. She proceeds to have a fit.

"HOLY COW!" she yells. "That's, like, half my daily calories!"

I frown. There are fewer than four hundred calories in a MixUp, and if this girl is only eating eight hundred calories, in a few years she's going to wish she'd eaten more while her metabolism was high.

I show great restraint and hold my tongue.

The girl keeps exclaiming, and another girl, a cute curly redhead about sixteen in jeans and a T-shirt, slides past the blond.

"Hi," she says, grinning. "I'd like a large caramel MixUp, please."

See? She's cute, she's friendly, and she's taking advantage of a good thing while it lasts. I like this girl.

"Whipped cream?" I ask, ringing her up. Jack starts blending her drink.

"Please."

She takes her cup of caramel goodness and sits at a big table. I hide a smile as I watch the boy who the blond was not-so-subtly flirting with keep looking over at the redhead.

The blond could take a few hints from the redhead. "You don't buy the coffee shop if the drinks are free" is what my mom always used to tell me.

My mom knows my language.

Every person in the group orders a MixUp except the blond, who orders a Splenda-laced iced tea.

Pitiful, really.

They all start talking loudly over Elvis crooning on the speakers.

A man in a suit, tiredly pulling his tie looser, comes in. "I need a large decaf mocha," he groans, the bags under his eyes telling me how his evenings are going.

"Sure you want decaf?" I ask. I don't usually question the customer, but seriously, the man needs caffeine or cucumber slices for those bags, and we don't have the latter.

He manages a weak smile. "It's for my wife. She's eight months' pregnant with our second child."

"Congratulations," I say. "How old is the first?"

"A year and a half and teething like you wouldn't believe." He sighs. "No one tells you how hard parenting is."

Thus the bags under his eyes, I guess.

The man pays me and slumps over on the countertop where we keep the milk, cream, and sugar. He's cradling his head in his hands, elbows resting on the counter. I tell Jack to make two mochas: one decaf, one regular. The poor man is nice enough to come by Cool Beans to get his wife a mocha when he's this tired. He needs all the help he can get.

"Wow, really?" he asks, a barely there spark showing up in his exhausted eyes. "Let me pay you for the regular."

"Spend it on teething rings, sir. Have a good day," I say, shooing him out the door. I want to marry someone who buys me mochas when I'm eight months' pregnant.

By five o'clock, I'm making a regular mocha for myself as well. Jack's tiredly wiping down the counter after our forty-second—yes, you read that right—MixUp.

"Wow," he says.

"Yeah. Wow."

"We haven't been that busy since . . ."

"Yeah." I look over at him. "Going to miss this?"

"The Friday rush? Not really, Nutkin."

I smile. I finish my mocha, pop a lid on it, and see Lisa and Peter, our replacements, coming through the door. "Let's go."

He nods and pulls off his apron, disappearing in the back. I wave at Lisa. "Hope you guys are ready for a crazy night."

"Busy day?"

"Insane."

She grins, all happy. I've never seen Lisa upset before. She's the queen of abnormal amounts of energy.

"Awesome!" she says, her eyes sparkling. "That means better tips, which means I'm that much closer to my Christmas in Vienna!"

"The place where those sausages come from?" Peter grins. "Why would you want those for Christmas?"

Lisa rolls her eyes. "Shhh, Peter. Hush."

I smile, grab my purse and coffee, and wave as I follow Jack out the door. He pauses beside his car. "What are you up to tonight?" he asks.

"I have to go help Jen get ready for her work party."

"Want to get dinner after that? Maybe around six or so? Gives me time to shower and get this awful coffee smell off me." He makes a gagging expression.

"It's better than a manure smell," I say. "See you at six!"

I drive home and hear the shower running in Jen's room.

Calvin's sitting on the sofa, watching the Food Network.

He looks over at me all casually, then immediately looks back at the TV, like if he doesn't acknowledge my presence, maybe he'll get to stay on the sofa.

"Calvin," I say, exasperated.

He sighs and hops off the couch, never taking his eyes off Rachael Ray.

I toss my purse on the bed, finish drinking my mocha, and throw the empty cup in the trash. I look through my closet, trying to find something to wear to dinner with Jack. I know I should be wearing something other than jeans for our date, but I really do not want to wear a skirt.

Mom always said that if the guy is paying, you should wear a skirt. If you're going to split the bill, then jeans are okay.

I sigh.

"Oh, good, you're home," Jen says from my doorway, her voice harried. I look at her, and she's got her hair up in a towel, her ratty snowboarding-penguins bathrobe on, and panty hose covering her toes.

"I need to know," she says. "Panty hose. In or out of style?"

It's a sad day when Jen Mitchell is coming to me for fashion advice. I stare at her, open-mouthed.

"What? You watch the Style Network, like, nonstop. I just don't remember right now."

I stutter for half a second before my inner Stacy London comes out. "What kind of shoes are you wearing?"

"My black heels."

"Panty hose is okay then."

She sighs. "Great! I don't have a good enough tan yet to go bare-legged." She manages a quick smile before she dashes off, yelling behind her, "Thanks, Maya!"

I consider my closet for a minute before I pull a white and blue sundress from the back. I bought it last winter, and it's just now warm enough to wear it. I could potentially wear it tonight.

Potentially.

"Maya!" Jen yells from her room.

"You are way too nervous," I observe, crossing the hallway and walking through her open doorway. She's wearing the dress, and it looks fabulous, but her hair is still wet and stringy from her shower.

"How should I fix my hair?" she asks me, pulling a comb through it. "Straight? Curly? Up? Which way goes best with this dress?"

"Way too nervous," I repeat for emphasis.

"I just want to look nice. His entire office is going to be there tonight. I need to make a good impression."

"Everyone would love you even if you showed up in jeans, Jen. You're too nice for people not to like you. A little too health-conscious sometimes, but nice nonetheless." I rub her shoulder. "Wear your hair down and curly. You know Travis loves it like that." Typical male.

I try to keep my voice all smooth and relaxing like the masseuse my mother goes to. I went once because I had a stiff neck, and Mom insisted this lady was worth her weight in gold. It was nice, but I have to admit, the massage didn't help my neck very much. Probably because I had to stifle my laughter every time she said, "Nowwww, cloooose your eyeeees and think deeeeep, meaningless thouuughtsss. . . ."

Admit it; that's weird.

Jen is nodding like a bobblehead doll. I pat her shoulder one last time. "Get busy. He'll be here in twenty minutes." As will my date, but obviously a work party takes precedence.

"Thanks, Maya."

I hop in and out of the shower, bypassing the shampoo due to a short timetable and deciding a couple squirts of perfume in my hair will cover the coffee smell just fine. It's not like I didn't wash it this morning. I think I'm okay.

Jen's banging on my bedroom door as I pull on the sundress. I open it and just sigh at her.

"Sorry, sorry," she says. "What do you think?"

"You look stunning." And she does. The burgundy dress hugs all her curves, which could be a bad thing, but as much of a stickler as Jen is about healthy food and exercise, she's got nothing but good curves. The neckline is low enough to be sexy but not so low as to be slutty, and the edge of the dress floats somewhere around her knees. The panty hose gives her legs a tan sheen, and the heels do something very nice for her calf muscles.

Her hair is in long, loose ringlets, and she's gone with classic smoky eyes. She's holding a little black clutch purse.

"You look amazing," I say again. "Travis is going to fall down the stairs when he sees you."

She giggles. "Well, maybe you can let him in then." She sighs nervously and looks at my bedside clock. It's two minutes until six, which means he's probably waiting in his car until *exactly* six o'clock. Travis is punctual.

Maybe it's just me, but I almost like it when a date is running late, because I'm always running late.

Travis and Jen, though, are a good match as far as punctuality goes.

"So, where is the work party?" I ask, trying to distract her from counting the seconds.

"At Philippe's," she says. It's a nice Italian place a few blocks away.

Remind you of the horse in *Beauty and the Beast*? Yup. Me too.

"Mmm. Breadsticks," I say, my mouth watering.

Jen's mouth tips in one of those distracted smiles, and I know she's not listening to me.

"I think we have assigned seating," she says nervously.

"I'm sure you'll be assigned a seat next to Travis."

Jen's getting worried again. I can tell by how she's twisting the clutch purse like she's trying to choke the truth out of it. "I'm a lefty!" she gasps. "What if I sit next to a right-handed person and we bump elbows, and I spill a whole plate of spaghetti in my lap?"

Jen has better table manners than the queen. She eats with her elbows tucked so closely to her sides that she could hold a few toothpicks there for after the meal. I don't think she needs to worry about this.

"Well, at least you're wearing burgundy," I say, trying to make her laugh.

She doesn't laugh. The doorbell rings, and she jumps.

"Look, calm down," I say. "You look gorgeous, you're going to have an amazing time, and I don't even remember the last time I saw you eat as many carbs as spaghetti has in one meal. My bet is you get a salad, which doesn't stain. So relax!"

She's back to imitating a bobblehead doll.

I go into the living room and open the door for Travis, who looks like an all-American guy in a snazzy black suit, white button-down shirt, and burgundy tie.

It appears that someone clued him in on the color of Jen's dress. I grin. Good old Jen.

"Hi, Maya," he says, smiling at me.

"Hey, Travis." Occasionally, it can still be a little weird

between the two of us, but tonight it doesn't seem strange at all. High school was a long, long time ago.

Travis's eyes about pop out of his head when he sees Jen. He whistles, she blushes, and I still my gag reflex.

"Wow, you look fantastic!" he says.

I watch her nerves melt away and smile to myself. They make a great couple.

"Thanks," she says, grabbing two lungfuls of air. "You look nice, too."

He holds out his hand. "Shall we?"

"Sure."

Travis holds her hand as she navigates the metal staircase, and I close the door after them, still smiling to myself.

There are times when I wonder why I had such a spaz attack when they started dating. Today is one of those days.

Someone knocks, and I open the door, expecting Jack. I know he said he was coming at six, but for Jack—who knows me well—that usually means six fifteen.

It's Travis. Without Jen.

I look around him, and she's nowhere in sight.

I bite my lip and look at him, deciding he must be a kidnapper and he's come back for the only witness.

"Jen will probably want a jacket," he announces.

"Okay."

"She said you knew where she kept her black blazer." He shrugs. "She's already in the car, and since it takes her five minutes to get in there in a dress, I didn't want to make her get back out." This makes sense. Travis drives a Nissan pickup. Jen needs help getting in there in a dress.

I nod and go into Jen's room, dig in her closet for a minute, and come out with her blazer, finding Travis waiting in the living room.

"Here you go," I say, handing it to him. "Have fun tonight! Try to get Jen on the edge of the table, okay? She's all worried about being a lefty and knocking a plate into someone's lap."

Travis grins suddenly.

I frown at him. "And if you're smiling at that, that's not very nice."

"We're not going to a work party, Maya."

I'm on the verge of violence. I glower at him. "You mean to tell me that this whole week," I say, very slowly, annunciating, "this whole week Jen has been agonizing over this stupid work party and irritating everyone around her, most of all *me*, and you're not even going to take her?" My voice ends on an octave not normally reached by humans. Maybe bats, but not humans.

Travis shushes me. "Not so screechy, if you don't mind," he whispers. "I'm taking her to Philippe's, but there's no work party." He gets all quiet and giggly like a little girl.

And suddenly I know. "You're going to propose."

He grins.

Now *my* eyes are going to pop out of my head. "OH MY GOS—"

He slaps his hand over my mouth, shushing me again. "She might hear you!"

"Mhgh mooghb meeegh!!" I screech, his hand still over my mouth. I start jumping up and down, which makes it harder for him to hold on. He finally lets go, putting his finger over his mouth like I'm back in my two-year-old Sunday school class.

"I'm quiet; I'm being quiet," I reassure him at a normal volume. I can't help the grin. "Wow. You guys are going to be engaged!"

He bites a grin. "I have to get back to the car. She's going to start wondering, but I had to tell someone. Don't tell anyone else, okay? I want Jen to be able to tell everyone." He grins wider. "See you later, Maya."

I close the door after him and stare in shock at Calvin.

"Engaged," I tell him quietly.

Travis and Jen.

Engaged.

CHAPTER SIX

"You look a little distracted," Jack says to me later at Olive Garden.

I frown at him, gnawing on a freshly baked breadstick. Jack was sweet enough to bring me here since I had a sudden craving for breadsticks after Jen mentioned they were going to Philippe's. We couldn't go to Philippe's, too, with the whole proposal and all, but we could go to Olive Garden.

So here we are.

I'm not sure how I could be acting distracted. We've been talking about his upcoming zookeeping job, and I made sure I nodded and *mm-hmm*ed at the right times.

"I'm not distracted," I protest, trying to keep Travis's secret. *Engaged.*

"Oh yeah?" Jack says, crossing his arms on the table and leaning forward. "What did I just say?"

"You said I was acting distracted."

"Before that, Pattertwig."

"You said you couldn't wait to skip while you're golfing."

He closes his eyes. "I said I couldn't wait to *swim* with the *dolphins.*"

"Oh."

He looks across the table at me and smiles while the server sets our meals in front of us. I ordered minestrone soup so I could also eat breadsticks and salad and still be hungry for dessert. Olive Garden has one of the best tiramisus out there.

I raise my eyebrows. "You get to swim with the dolphins?" I ask, all excited.

He sighs, tells the server thank you, and reaches for my hands. "I think we'll need prayer tonight," he says. He bows his head. "Lord, thank You for the food and the ability to take this gorgeous woman out on a date. Help us to focus, and be with us through these next few weeks of transitions. Amen."

I squeeze his hands. "Sorry. I guess I am distracted."

He picks up his fork to dig into his lasagna. "How come?"

"I'm not supposed to tell you. But I'm sure you'll find out after dinner."

He quirks his head at me but shrugs. "Okay."

I stir my soup and try to think of something to talk about that isn't related to Jen's engagement and Jack's final week at Cool Beans.

The first one makes me anxious and the second one just makes me sad.

Sometimes it seems like everyone around me is moving on, growing up, and changing, and I'm staying stagnant. Jen's getting married and moving out, Jack's working at a zoo and leaving me with a new co-worker at Cool Beans, and even Zach and Kate are changing. The new baby will make three.

And then there's me. Same apartment, same dog, same job.

"Now you look depressed," Jack says, not really helping my mood.

"Thanks."

"What's wrong?"

"Are you *positive* you want to spend the rest of your life scooping manure? I mean, you could be staying at a job where the smelliest thing you deal with is the occasional spoiled milk." I blow on my soup.

Jack smiles sympathetically and reaches for my hand again. "It's not going to be so bad, Nutkin."

"Not so bad? Come next Monday, I have to spend eight hours a day with a total stranger!"

Alisha, the owner of Cool Beans and my boss, said the new guy is really nice. "He's a junior in college, and he just transferred to Cal-Hudson," she told me. "Computer software major. Seems like a neat guy."

Which is all fine and dandy, but that makes me the oldest person working at Cool Beans. Jack currently holds that position.

"It'll be fine," he says again. He squeezes my fingers. "You worry too much."

I always knew that one day Jack would leave Cool Beans. I mean, you don't get a degree in biology with an emphasis in animal behaviors to spend your days foaming milk for lattes and icing cinnamon rolls.

My major was English education. Which is why a major in English education does leave you brewing espressos and making blended-ice drinks.

"He's a computer software major," I say.

"Who's a computer software major?"

"The guy replacing you. His name is Ethan, and he's a computer software major." I chew on my breadstick. "A junior, no less."

Jack's failing to hide his grin. "What's wrong with software majors? Or juniors, for that matter?"

"Jack, I'm almost twenty-five," I say, ignoring the question.

"Maybe I should get a real job. You know, like you're doing."

"As a teacher?"

I stab my fork into my salad. "Why did I major in English?"

"If I remember right, you liked the classes," he says.

I shake my head slightly and try to come up with something else to talk about. "So, who are your new co-workers going to be?"

Jack's eyes light up at the prospect of talking about his new job. "Well, I'm going to be interning with three other people who are also graduating this year. One of the girls was in one of my classes, and then there's another girl and a guy I've never met."

"Cool."

"Yeah, I'm excited. I think the girl I know from school, Presley, and I are going to be paired together on the African exhibit."

I feel the tiniest, teensiest twinge of jealousy here. I try to snuff it out with the steaming minestrone soup.

Presley. The name even sounds sexy, and not just because she shares it with the King of Rock 'n' Roll.

Zookeeper girls aren't typically good-looking, are they?

Bad thought, Lord. I mean no offense to Your creation.

The little twinge is getting bigger, and I'm scarfing down the minestrone soup, trying to douse it. Jack doesn't even notice; he's so busy talking about Presley and Greg, the man who's in charge of the African exhibit.

"I talked to Greg on my way home today, and he was saying there's even a pregnant lioness in one of my exhibits. Isn't that amazing? Presley and I will probably be in charge of the birth, though I bet Greg will do most of it. Presley's hoping to stay on next year permanently. She's hoping to transfer to the Asia exhibit, though. She says that's more her taste in animals."

With my soup gone, I start tearing through another breadstick. How does he know all this about the hopeful Presley anyway?

"The four interns have all been chatting on Facebook," he says, answering my unasked question.

"Oh," I say. Swell.

I shouldn't be jealous. I mean, if Jack had liked Presley, he wouldn't have asked me out when he already knew Presley.

So there's nothing to worry about, right?

So what if they have the same interests, same goals, same educational background? So what if she's like the female Crocodile Hunter? So what if she's got a gorgeous tan from being outside all the time, and she's going to take my place working with Jack all day?

I look down at my pale arms and think about my useless major and my not-grown-up job. And Jack keeps droning on.

I could use some encouragement here, God.

"Which is really cool." Jack's voice cuts into my thoughts. "Greg even said that Presley and I can run the elephant rides for a few weeks."

I grab the server's arm as she passes by. "I need a tiramisu. Please."

She gives me a quizzical look, nods, and leaves. Jack's looking at me now. "You're ready for dessert already?" he asks, surprised, looking at my empty soup bowl, empty salad plate, the empty breadstick basket, and his barely touched lasagna.

"Yep. All ready." The sooner I finish, the sooner we can leave, and the sooner I don't have to hear any more sentences that have the words *Presley and I* in them.

I could just pass up dessert, but we're at Olive Garden. I

never pass on dessert at Olive Garden.

"Wow, okay. Well, I guess I'd better be quiet and eat." He starts hacking into his now lukewarm lasagna. He chews for a minute and then smiles at me. "So, what are your plans for this week?"

"Nothing much." This isn't entirely true. Once Jen gets proposed to, our apartment will probably become Wedding Prep Central. Jen's about as girly as a girl can get when it comes to weddings. She's one of those girls who cries during *Whose Wedding Is It Anyway?* on the Style Network.

I'll admit: I've gotten teary, but I've never flat-out bawled like she has, stuffing her face in the throw pillows to soak up her tears.

I decide we should probably start the wedding plans by looking for a good waterproof mascara for Jen.

"We're working the nine-to-five shift again, huh?" Jack says. I nod. "Yep."

He chews his lasagna; I watch for the server. Silence.

She finally comes, carrying my plate of espresso-soaked ladyfingers buried in sweet cream delight.

"Oh, thank you," I say, sighing, grabbing my fork.

The server looks over at Jack's half-eaten lasagna. "Dessert for you, sir?"

"Mmm. No thanks."

She leaves.

"You didn't want dessert?" I ask, swallowing. "This is amazing."

"I'll have some of yours when I'm done."

I yank my plate closer to me. "No, you won't. This is mine. I'll be working out for the next week because of this, so I'm going to enjoy every second of it. Get your own."

"Hey. Sharing is caring," he quotes.

"Hey. Get your own."

He smiles at me. "You know, the zoo cafeteria sells tiramisu. All of us interns got it at orientation two weeks ago. They call it Tiramizoo. Presley said it was a cute name." He rolls his eyes. "I think it sounds like a disease."

I down the rest of the tiramisu and slap the table. "Okay. You ready?"

"Whoa. Easy there. We still have to get the check." He quirks his head at me. "Why the rush?"

Um. Because you're sitting here talking all comfortably about your new tanned, cutesy co-worker, and me and my Swedish-decent skin and ego can't take it.

"I'm tired," I say.

"Wait until all that sugar kicks in." He waves at the server. "Can we get the check, please?"

"Sure thing." She hands him the slip of paper, and he gives it back to her with his card.

"Thanks for dinner, Jack," I say nicely. He did pay for a very nice dinner. And I was wearing a dress. So, long conversation about the co-worker or not, we were still on a date.

The ride back to my apartment is quiet. I'm busy thinking about this Presley person and if she's cute or not. Jack looks over at me a few times but doesn't say anything. I guess he can tell all is not good in the passenger seat.

He pulls into a parking space a few spots down from my apartment. "You okay?" he asks, unclipping his seat belt but staying in the car.

I'm craning my neck to see if Travis's pickup is in the lot, and I'm not seeing it. I don't really want to have this conversation with Jack. Worrying about some new co-worker of his just sounds petty.

"Mm-hmm," I hum noncommittally.

"No, you're not." He grabs my left hand before I can slide out of the car. "What's wrong?"

Oh, the ever-present Male Question.

"Nothing!" I lie. I'm trying to decide if it's better to be a liar or a petty girlfriend. Neither one sounds exceptionally amazing.

"Really." His tone doesn't imply belief.

I sigh. "Okay." Better just to spit it out. "The truth will make you free" is how the Bible put it.

I look over at him. "I guess I'm jealous."

He blinks at me. "Jealous of whom?"

I shrink to about four inches. "Presley," I mutter.

Jack's forehead creases. "Presley? Why?"

"Why? Why not?" I burst. "She's tanned and beautiful, and she has all these things in common with you, and she's going to work with you every day —"

He cuts me off. "Maya, stop."

Considering how rarely he calls me by my name, I shut up immediately and just look at him. He squeezes my hand and lets his breath out.

"Okay. First, you have absolutely nothing to worry about with Presley. She's a nice girl, but she's definitely not you. And I don't believe I ever called her tanned and beautiful, because compared to you she's not even worth looking at. And even though, yes, I'll be working with her every day, you'd better believe that I'm going to be thinking about you every second of it." Then he kisses the back of my hand.

I swallow and duck my head down. The muscles that were all tight in my stomach are now going mushy. Trust Jack to say something like that. Now I just feel stupid for ever worrying.

Jack squeezes my hand again and, instead of getting out of the car, rolls the engine over again. "How about some coffee?" he asks, backing out.

I smile thankfully at him and glance at the dashboard clock. It's nine o'clock, and Cool Beans will be open for another hour.

He drives the familiar streets to work and pulls in front of our cute little coffee shop. "Hang tight," he says when I start getting out. "I'll get it."

He walks inside.

I sit in the dead-silent car and sigh. "Good going, Maya," I mutter. "Now he probably thinks you're becoming one of those ridiculous girls who doesn't let her boyfriend talk to anyone else female."

Swell.

I'm not like that. Seriously. Granted, Jack is only the second guy I've ever dated, but even when I was dating Travis, I didn't care what he did. If he wanted to hang out with other girls, so be it. I wasn't going to guilt him into dating me. There were plenty of other guys out there who would want to spend time with me.

So why this green tint to my cheeks now?

I check my face in the mirror on the visor. Maybe my confidence is starting to slack the older I get.

My hair is holding its curl very well tonight. Typically on warmer nights like this, it starts resembling Ms. Frizzle from *The Magic School Bus* before too long.

I study my hair, frowning. Back when I was dating Travis, it was blond. I mean really blond, like Kate Hudson blond. Now, it's my natural chocolate-brown color.

Maybe all my confidence was in that bottle of bleach. I squint at the mirror. They do say blonds have more fun. Do they have more self-esteem, too?

Weird thoughts. I close the mirror and push the visor back up.

Okay, Lord. Here's what's going on. I got crazy jealous over this girl who Jack is going to work with, and I can't figure out why.

I have this sudden ache for my Bible. Isn't it weird how you can be holding that Book and feel way more secure? I think it's because I know that God loves me always. And He knows me better than I know myself—and *still* loves me.

It's bolstering my confidence just thinking about it.

Thanks, Lord.

Jack comes back to the car carrying two take-out cups. "One mocha," he proclaims, passing it over to me.

"Mmm." I inhale the spicy, sweet scent floating out from the lid and sigh. "Thanks, Jack."

"No problem." He sets his drink in the cup holder and starts driving.

"Where are we going?"

He shrugs. "I don't know. I just didn't want to talk to you about this stuff in front of Lisa." Lisa is our co-worker. She's adorable and sweeter than caramel flavoring, but Jack's right. It would be a little awkward. And at this time of night, Cool Beans is quiet and the baristas are bored. I've snooped on tons of conversations when I've worked the night shifts.

"Good thought."

"Thanks." He drives west through town, toward the interstate. Hudson is small enough that it doesn't take too long to drive from one end to the other. If it weren't for the college and commuters to San Diego, I'm not sure Hudson would exist.

"How about that little picnic area right before you get on I-8?" I ask.

He nods and pulls off on the side road that leads to it a few minutes later. I take a sip of my steaming mocha and frown.

"Is this decaf?"

"Maybe."

"Jack!"

"What? You're worked up enough without needing extra caffeine."

"Grinch."

"Tough." He pulls into a parking spot and turns off the car, reaching for his drink. "Mine's decaf, too, if that makes you feel better."

"Actually, it does," I grumble. I peer out the windows. The park is dark, silhouetted only by three dim streetlights casting an eerie glow over the picnic tables. If we weren't in tiny Hudson and if I weren't with Jack, I might be creeped out.

"So, what happened back there?" He asks it casually, but he's not looking at me, so I know he's serious.

"You got me decaf," I say, trying to lighten the mood.

"Maya."

Real name again. I bite my lip. "It was just a momentary lapse of sanity. I got it back. It was probably because I started dinner with the salad when I should have started with the tiramisu." Never underestimate the power of espresso-soaked ladyfingers.

Jack carefully sips his drink, staring thoughtfully at the creepy picnic benches. "I've never known you to get jealous before," he says.

"Me either." I grip my cup with both hands. "Look, Jack, I'm sorry. I don't know what came over me. I mean, maybe it's because she shares a name with, like, the most attractive rock 'n' roll singer ever."

Jack grins over at me. "Oh boy."

"In any case, I'm sorry. I'll try not to let it happen again. If you want to . . ." I swallow and look away from his gaze. "If you want to hang out with Presley or *whoever*, it shouldn't bother me."

The car is quiet for one whole minute, but it feels like fifteen. I gulp my mocha, actually glad he got me decaf. Which should explain the state my nerves are in.

"But it does," he says finally.

"What?"

"It does bother you."

The car is starting to feel more and more stuffy, and those spooky picnic benches are starting to look more and more inviting. I squirm.

"Nutkin?"

I clear my throat and pop open the passenger door. "Fresh air," I announce like the guy who describes the prizes on *Wheel of Fortune*. I hop out and immediately wish I was wearing something other than a cute sundress and high-heeled sandals. Note to self: Never question jeans and a nice shirt for a date again. Shrubby grass is everywhere, and those picnic benches don't look super clean, especially with me wearing a white dress. The droning buzz of cicadas fills the air.

Jack comes around the front of the car holding a jacket. He spreads it on one of the benches and points. "Don't ruin your dress."

"Thanks."

He sits beside me, and we both listen to the ugly insects singing, facing away from the table, leaning back against it.

"We don't have to talk about it anymore," he says.

"Okay." Relief is making my stomach cramp.

He turns slightly and pushes a curl back behind my ear. Whatever relief I felt is suddenly replaced by a rush of adrenaline mixed with something tingling deep in my stomach.

Jack grins. "So, you kind of like me a little bit, huh?"

"Looking for a compliment?"

"Hearing one every now and then would be nice."

I glance over at him for the briefest second. "Then, yes."

"That's good." He takes my hand in both of his. And we sit quietly.

It's nice. And it's completely weird.

Maybe I was right a few months ago. Maybe dating your best friend is definitely a not-good idea. Maybe all this emotional upheaval isn't me losing my confidence as much as God saying this isn't the right thing to be doing.

Jack drops my hand and wraps an arm around my shoulders. "I don't want you to get cold." He excuses his actions.

It's seventy-five degrees and humid. Being cold is the last of my worries right now.

I can't help feeling nestled in, though. His arm isn't slung around my shoulders like he's declaring me his property nor is it awkwardly lying there like a cold, cut-off cow tongue. Instead, it's gently curved around me, tucking me into his shoulder.

It feels natural. And very scary.

I try to shush the warring voices in my head. Part of me wants to just relax into his side hug; the other part of me wants to get up and run back to my safe little apartment, slam the door, and revert back to the goofy friendship Jack and I have always had.

I *hate* feeling so off-kilter with him all the time! It's too hard. I can't do it. I just want things to go back to how they were before. No second guessing, no worrying about him wanting to date other girls, no weird tingles in my chest whenever he grins at me.

I just have to tell him.

"Maya." He says my name so softly that I almost don't hear him over the cicadas.

I look up at him.

His arm squeezes around me. "Look, I don't want to scare you, but . . ." His eyes go all soft, and he touches my cheek with his other hand. "I'm falling in love with you."

CHAPTER SEVEN

I just look at him, my neck muscles completely freezing. I can't think, I can't breathe, I can't even blink.

He's what?

One thought makes its way through the empty space in my brain: *I guess we're not going to revert back to Just Friends.*

I guess he notices my bug-eyed look because he brushes my hair back and pulls my head down on his shoulder.

"You don't have to say anything back," he says quietly. "I just wanted you to know you've got nothing to worry about as far as me with any other girl."

I nod into his shoulder, and I have to admit, I feel a little relieved at the thought that Jack isn't going to be with any other girl. Okay, a lot relieved. I suck in a deep breath and close my eyes. Both of his arms are around me now, and my head is resting in that little dip just under his shoulder.

I fit perfectly like this. I feel protected.

There's a slight pressure on the top of my head, and I think he just kissed my hair. I swallow. I'm not a good enough girlfriend for a guy like this.

I squinch my eyes closed tighter.

This is *Jack*. Jack Dominguez, the kid who traded his lunch with me every day in the second grade because neither of us liked what our moms packed us. The guy who's been my best friend for years, who's seen me screw up more than I'd like to admit, and who's teased me, joked with me, and comforted me. I think I've talked with him or seen him every day for the last five years.

Oh, Lord, what do I do?

And then, suddenly, I *know.*

"Jack?" I whisper it, barely hearing myself over my heart thundering in my ears.

"Mmm?"

"I love you, too." I say it so softly that I bet he had trouble deciphering what I said over the droning of the cicadas.

He lets out his breath, and I realize how tense he was. "I'm glad," he says, a smile in his voice. He tucks me into his hug, kissing the top of my head. "Very glad."

We sit like that for a long time. Not saying anything, just listening to the cicadas.

Jack pulls into a space near my apartment building at eleven. "Well, it's a good thing we're not opening tomorrow," he says, grinning over at me.

"Ugh. No kidding." I look around. Travis's pickup is in the spot two spaces down from our apartment. I grin.

"What?" Jack says.

"Let's go inside." I hop out and run for the metal staircase.

"What's going on?" Jack asks, catching up to me at the third stair. Darn those tall-person legs. I swear, sometimes being short . . .

I shake my head, not answering, and keep running up the

steps as best I can in my dress and sandals. I'm again wishing for jeans.

Though Jack complimented me on the dress, so maybe I like it. I smile.

I bang open my apartment door, and Jen bounces off the couch like a yo-yo. Travis starts laughing from where he's dumping Jen's favorite snack—healthy popcorn—into a bowl in the kitchen.

"I'm engaged! I'm engaged! I'm ENGAGED!" Jen screams.

I grab her around the waist, and we jump and laugh and cry and scream. Then I step on her foot right as she leans to the left, and we go crashing down on the floor.

Our downstairs neighbors are going to hate us.

"Auuugh!" Jen screams on her way down.

"Girls, seriously!" Travis says, coming over. Jen grabs at his hands, and he hauls her off me. Jack looks at me in a tangled heap on the floor, sighs, and turns to the now-upright Jen.

"Congratulations, Jenny," he says, grinning in a big-brother kind of way. He wraps her up in a hug.

I heave in a breath and help myself up. If only one of us was going to get the chivalrous type, I guess Jen deserves it more than me. She's very ladylike. According to my mother, anyway.

I grab the back of the couch and wince. I think I tweaked my knee somewhere between the jumping and the crash landing. I bite my tongue. *Oh, no.* In high school, I had a major knee injury, and I'm hoping I didn't just twist it the wrong way and strain my PCL again.

I can hear Dr. Otero's voice from the past. *No more jumping, Maya. And no running for at least a year.*

I've been running fine for the past three years, so I don't know what happened.

"You okay?" Jack asks me. Jen's back to squealing, her arms wrapped around Travis's waist. I smile over at them, my eyes feeling wet. They are perfect for each other. And they look like a model couple, which doesn't hurt.

I rub my knee. "I'm fine." Or at least I will be once I get some ice.

Travis pushes Jen away to arm's length. "We have a lot of things to think through."

She nods. "Yes. Yes, we do. When do you want to get married?"

"How's Monday?" Travis grins.

Jen rolls her eyes. "Monday. Heh. Please. Honey, I'll need at least six months to plan this."

"Six months?" Travis's eyebrows go up. "Why?"

"Travis, it's Jen." I offer the explanation. "Does she ever do anything halfway?"

The answer is no, and Travis knows that. It's what makes Jen such an amazing legal assistant. She's thorough, detail-obsessed, and definitely in charge. Without her, Jen's boss, Wayne Davids, would most likely be wearing stained ties and have absolutely zero research done for most of his cases.

"Still . . ." Travis shakes his head. "How about four months?"

"Well, maybe. There are a lot of decisions." Jen defends herself. "The location, the clothing, the colors, the flowers, the pastor, the attendants, the registries . . ." She's ticking everything off on her fingers until she runs out of fingers. "See? A lot to do."

Jack grimaces at Travis. "Bow out now. All you need to do is show up on the wedding day."

"Baby, I think you have this under control," Travis says immediately. "This is your wedding; you do what you want."

She grins. "Okay!" Jen looks over at me, where I'm balancing on my good foot. No sense spoiling the mood, but my knee is throbbing. "Will you be my maid of honor, Maya?"

I kind of figured on this, but I'm still touched. "Of course," I say, nodding emphatically. "Definitely."

"Oh, good! We'll start looking for locations in the morning. That's the most important thing to get on the calendar quickly, you know."

"I did not know," Travis says. "But have fun." He gives Jen a quick kiss on the cheek, and then he and Jack exchange a quick look and both go sit on the couch, turning the TV to *SportsCenter*.

I limp to the kitchen, but Jen's chattering so happily about what colors she likes that she doesn't notice as I fill a Ziploc bag with ice cubes. I heft myself on one of the bar stools and stretch my leg out on the other stool, balancing the ice bag on top of my knee.

Ouch.

I reach across the counter and grab her left hand. Her ring finger is sparkling with a zillion tiny rainbows bursting from the huge ice rink that's attached to what appears to be a platinum band. I whistle in approval.

"Isn't it gorgeous?" Jen whispers. "It's huge! And it—it's all glittery." She turns her hand left to right, and the rainbows shake loose and sparkle over the counter.

"Beautiful," I say. "Wow." The ring fits Jen perfectly—not so big that it's pushy but probably close to a carat and insanely pretty.

She's back to planning mode. "Okay, stop me if you disagree, but if we get married in four months . . . so, like, August or September, I'm thinking an emerald green or a cranberry for the dresses. What do you think?"

I frown at her. "I thought your dream was to get married in June?"

"No June," Travis yells from the couch. "I'm not waiting more than a year to get married. Four months is bad enough."

Jen raises her eyebrows at me, and I lift my hands in surrender. "Fine. No June."

"Thank you." He goes back to watching *SportsCenter*.

"So. A fall wedding then."

She nods. "Yes. And it's okay, Maya, really. I know I've always said June, but now I just want to be married to Travis before Christmas."

"Your call." I mash the ice down tighter on my knee. "So, where are you thinking for the location?"

"Well, I'd pick church, but it's really not very pretty."

No arguments here. Our church used to be a YMCA. Services are held in what used to be a gym. It's very functional, but it's not pretty at all. I think one girl has gotten married there in the whole time I've been going to that church, and let me tell you: The fluorescent lights don't do anything for anyone's skin tone.

Jen's eyes are all bright, and she's smiling softly. "I was actually thinking about that church on Madison Street."

I squint, trying to remember. "What church?"

"The one with all the wood paneling and the stained glass?"

I don't remember this church at all, but it sounds kind of cheesy to me. However, Jen is the bride. "We'll check it out tomorrow," I say. I decide to broach the difficult topic. "Have you called your parents yet?"

Her face immediately loses that soft glow. She chews on her bottom lip. "No," she says finally. "I'll put it off as long as I can."

"Jen. Not informing your parents until they get an

invitation in the mail is probably poor form," I say gently.

"I know, I know." She sighs. "I'll call them tomorrow. I just want tonight to be perfect. Okay?"

"Fine." I nod. I'm not a huge fan of Jen's parents, but they are her parents for a reason. Her mom and dad got divorced when she was six, and she was shuttled back and forth between Baltimore and the DC area every year after that. Summers with one parent, school year with the other. And then they'd trade off. Which means Jen never had friendships that lasted more than a year all through junior high and high school.

There's a reason she moved to Hudson, California, for college. I've never met Jen's dad in the whole six years that I've known her, but I've spent time with her mom.

To put it kindly, Jen's mom is awful.

I try to turn her thoughts away from her parents. I'm sure they'll both make the wedding. Actually, I'm sure her mom will make the wedding. Her dad might be another story.

"When do you want to look at dresses?" I ask.

Her face immediately brightens. "Can we go tomorrow?" she asks excitedly.

I grin. "Sure."

"Oh, good!" She's back to being giddy. I like this Jen.

SportsCenter ends, and the boys stand up. Jack stretches and then frowns at the ice pack on my knee. "What happened?"

Jen notices it then, too. "Oh my gosh, Maya! I didn't even see that!"

"It's nothing," I say, rolling my shoulders nonchalantly, like it's not sending shards of throbbing pain up my thigh. "I think I just tweaked it in the grand crash."

"Holy cow." Jen blows her breath out. "I'm sorry!"

"I'm fine," I say again.

Jack comes over to look at it, and I slap my hand over the bag. If he lifts the ice, he'll see the swelling, and then he'll make me go to the doctor, and we'll ruin Jen's night.

Tonight is not about me. Or my stupid injury.

"You're still having trouble with your knee?" Travis says, coming over as well.

"It's fine," I keep protesting, holding the ice in place.

"What happened to your knee?" Jack asks.

"Maya had surgery on her PCL after a track accident in high school," Travis says, standing next to Jen in the kitchen. Far enough away that it isn't awkward for any of us.

"You ran track?" Jack is incredulous.

"Hey! What's that tone of voice?" I ask. "You knew me in junior high. I played soccer."

"Yeah, but not very well."

I roll my eyes at the insult. "Which is why I started running track instead."

"How'd you mess up your knee?" Jen asks.

"Hurdles," Travis answers. "She missed a step and screwed up her knee. And her elbow, if I remember right."

Ugh. That was not a pretty day for me. I was crying because of my knee, and I scraped all the skin off my elbow when I fell.

I shake my head. Tonight is not about me. I smile, showing everyone I'm okay.

"I didn't know you had knee problems," Jen says.

"I don't usually. Enough about me. What flavor of cake do you guys like? And are you going to have music at the ceremony?"

Good questions to switch the focus. Jen and Travis immediately hop on the Change of Conversation Train. Jack is more reluctant. He's still frowning at my hand clutching the bag of ice on my knee and gives me a look that says, *We're not finished with this discussion yet.*

"I would like Andrew to officiate," Jen says.

"Fine by me." Travis nods. Travis goes to a little church on the other side of town, but I imagine he will switch to our church soon. Plus, he's met Andrew multiple times, and they get along well.

"And, Maya, do you remember when Liz Chapman sang at Nate and Lacey's wedding a few months back?"

I scrunch my face, remembering. "She sang the one Rascal Flatts song that isn't about the girl leaving and the guy crying?"

Jack grins. Jen nods. "Yeah, that one. I think I might see if she wants to sing at our wedding. She's got a gorgeous voice." Jen pokes Travis. "Remember her?"

"Not really."

"Tall, pretty, redhead who is in love with Andrew?" I say.

Travis shakes his head. "Sorry," he says. "Maybe if I see her again."

This is the thing about Travis. Most guys would definitely notice Liz. She's beautiful, but not in a slutty, everyone-look-at-me kind of way. She's tall, long-legged, and slender, and she has this natural grace that is both charming to guys and incredibly envy-inducing for girls like me, who are short and tweak their knee congratulating their best friend.

I sigh.

Travis, however, doesn't notice anyone but Jen. Angelina Jolie could walk through the room in her bra and underwear, and Travis would only notice how blue Jen's eyes look that day. He's very complimentary, that one.

It's a nice trait in a guy.

I look up at Jack, and he's still frowning at the ice pack on my knee. Then you have Jack, who is so darn overprotective that I can barely get a paper cut without him hovering around, asking me if I'm okay.

"What song do you like?" Jen asks Travis. I hide a grin. At the rate she's going, we'll have this wedding planned by noon tomorrow. Maybe they *can* get married on Monday.

"I like lots of songs," Travis says. "What song do you like?"

Smooth move, serving the question back to his fiancée.

Fiancée.

Eyes misting over again. I fight to keep it together.

Jen's absently twirling a lock of blond hair, trying to think. "Well, we have time," she says finally, after a few minutes of silence.

"That we do." Travis nods.

"You might need a date before we do anything," I say, the excellent voice of reason.

Jen gapes. "You're right! When do you want to get married?" she asks Travis again.

"I said Monday, but that was vetoed." He shrugs. "Anytime with enough notice, so I can definitely get a week off for a honeymoon. I've been saving sick days for two years."

Jen grabs a calendar. "How's the first weekend in August?"

"Good for me. Done." Travis leans over and kisses Jen.

I politely look away. Sheesh. PDA in my own kitchen and while I'm icing my knee. Not cool. Not cool.

I frown. Actually, the icing the knee part is pretty cool. Cold, actually.

I wince. I know it's my bedtime when that degree of dry humor is reached in my brain.

"Great! August 2 is officially the wedding day." Jen grins, happiness exuding from her. "Let the planning begin!"

"Let me see it," Jack says about thirty minutes later. Jen walked Travis out to his car a good ten minutes ago, which means they are either (a) doing more wedding planning or (b) making out on the front porch.

Personally, I'm betting on choice *b*. They just got engaged. So as long as the increase in affection stays out on the front porch and keeps relatively pure, I don't care.

I'm guessing Jack's assuming choice *b*, too, because he hasn't left yet. It's almost two in the morning. It's obvious that I'm tired, and his eyes are bloodshot, which means he's really tired. We moved to the couch, and my leg is stretched out, resting on the coffee table.

"No," I say to him, smashing the ice down on my knee and trying my best to hide the wince at the quick jolt of pain.

"Nutkin."

"Jack, no. I'm fine."

"You're not fine, and you know it. Now, let me see your knee."

I glare at him as he yanks the bag of ice away from my leg. Now he's wincing.

"Oh, honey . . ."

I swallow. I'm not sure if it's from the lack of ice or from him calling me "honey." He's never called me a term of endearment before. Unless you count "Nutkin" and "Pattertwig," and I don't.

I look down at my knee, and it is a mix of jewel-toned colors that would probably be quite stunning if they were painted on bathroom walls or something. Emerald green, deep purple, some red . . . sadly, though, it's on my knee and not the walls, so I bite my lip. On the plus side, you can't tell that my kneecap isn't tanned. Always look at the positive, that's what my mother taught me.

"Dang, girl," Jack says, whistling. "What exactly did you do in high school?"

"I missed the hurdle." I shake my head. "Actually, I *didn't* miss the hurdle. That was my problem."

"I don't ever remember you mentioning a track injury."

We both grew up in San Diego. Jack and I knew each other all through elementary school and most of middle school, but then we ended up going to separate high schools. I didn't see him again until we ended up in the same fitness elective junior year at Cal-Hudson.

So Jack missed all the track-running, Travis-dating, blond years.

It's a good thing.

"Well, by the time we saw each other again, I wasn't injured," I say. I gingerly poke around my kneecap. "I think I just tweaked it. The bruising makes it look worse than it is."

"You sure you didn't tear it again?"

"Very sure." After the first time, I'm very certain I could tell if I did it again.

Jack glances tiredly at the front door, but Jen hasn't come in yet. I smile sympathetically.

"Just go out," I say, glad it's not me trying to leave.

"Easy for you to say."

"They are probably just talking about the wedding." *Or not*, I think.

"Or not," Jack voices, grimacing. "No thanks, I'll stay in here. You can go to bed though, if you want."

"What, and earn, like, the Worst Girlfriend of the Year award? Yeah, I think not." I'm already tiptoeing around being a finalist; I don't need to win.

Jack smiles. "You aren't a bad girlfriend."

"Sure." I roll my eyes. He has to say that.

"Anyway . . ." Jack says, rolling his shoulders and leaning back against the couch cushions. He turns his head and smiles at me.

I'm feeling twinges in my stomach. Either that mocha isn't sitting well or Jack is awfully close. It might be a mix of both. It was decaf, you remember.

Jen comes in right as Jack opens his mouth to say something.

"Ohhh," she sighs, closing the door behind her. "This is the best day of my whole entire life."

I angle my head so I can see her over the back of the couch. She's standing next to the door, staring dreamily at her ring. It's two in the morning, and she looks absolutely beautiful.

It's hard living with her sometimes. I think it's God's way of keeping me humble.

"I'm never going to be able to go to sleep tonight," she says softly.

I look back at Jack and try to send him a message with my expression. *Get out while you can.*

He's become too good at reading my thoughts. "Well, I'd better go," he says. He smiles sweetly at Jen. "Congrats, Jenny."

"Thanks, Jack."

He rubs my shoulder. "I'll call you tomorrow. Keep ice on that knee, and keep it elevated."

"Yes, doctor."

He grins at me, eyes softening as he squeezes my hand. "Sweet dreams, Nutkin."

"Night, Jack."

The door clicks softly behind him. Jen is still standing in the entryway, focused on the diamond.

"Come here," I say, patting the couch. "I need another look at that."

She hurries over and thrusts her hand in my face. "I can't stop looking at it!" she says. "I keep thinking that I'm going to blink and this will all be some kind of daydream."

I have to give the man credit. Travis did *very* well with this ring.

"It's not a dream, Jenny." I hold her hand in both of mine. I can feel a teary party coming on.

"I'm getting married," she says softly.

We just sit there, looking at each other, holding each other's hands. I think I start blubbering first. "I'm so happy for you," I choke out.

Tears start slipping down her cheeks. "Really, Maya?" she says, swallowing.

I nod because there is a big lump in my throat. I am happy for her, but this also means that she's going to move out. She won't be there for late-night movies or our Saturday-morning tradition of strawberry pancakes. She won't be there to give a much-needed opinion on my clothing choice for the day or to watch old cartoons with me on our days off.

I wipe my cheeks with the back of my hand and sniff. "Really happy," I manage, and we both half-giggle, half-sob. I pull her into an awkward hug, seeing how my leg is still propped up on the coffee table.

"It's almost three," Jen says finally. "We should probably go to bed."

"Yeah," I sniffle. I push myself off the couch and start hobbling to my room.

"Are you sure you're okay?" she calls out after me, flicking off the living-room light.

"I'll be okay." I smile at her though the darkness. "Love you, Jenny. Night."

"Love you, too, Maya."

I close the door behind me, push Calvin off the bed, pull off my sundress, and throw on an old T-shirt and a pair of shorts. I'm asleep before I touch the pillow.

CHAPTER EIGHT

I hear someone in my room before I see them. My eyes are closed; my face is mashed against my pillow. I blink one eye open.

Jen's standing beside my bed looking at me, grinning, and biting her lower lip. She's wearing her pajama shorts and a T-shirt from Cal-Hudson.

I grunt and clear my throat. "What are you doing?" I mumble. She's turning into a psycho roommate. Maybe it's good she's moving out.

"Maya?" she whispers.

"Mmm?"

"Are you awake?"

"Mmm."

"Guess what?"

I squint one eye up at her again. "What?"

"I'M GETTING MARRIED!"

Her scream startles me so much that I jump a half-inch off the bed before falling back down on it. I roll to my back and cover my eyes with both hands.

"Oh my gosh. Jen!"

"Sorry! I can't help it! I got up, I saw the ring, and I was so excited—and there was no one to be excited with!"

I want to be mad; I really do, but I just can't be. Not with her standing there grinning and all hopeful. I look up at her from under my hands and sigh. "I'm getting up."

"Thank you!" She skips out of the room whistling "Chapel of Love."

It might be a long four months.

I roll over and look at the clock. It's nine thirty, so it's not so ridiculously early that I have to make Travis a widower before he even gets married. I look over at Calvin, who is still snoring on his little dog bed.

Grabbing my Bible and a pad of sticky notes, I decide to go with the random passage selection this morning. I open it to Philippians. "Rejoice in the Lord always; again I will say, rejoice! Let your gentle spirit be known to all men. The Lord is near."

> *Reasons I Can Rejoice:*
> *1. Jen and Travis are engaged.*
> *2. We have Cool Beans's French roast in the pantry.*
> *3. Jack and I are . . . Jack said he . . . For Jack.*

I swing my legs around the side of the bed and gingerly put weight on my knee. It's a beautiful painting of blues and greens and deep purples, but it isn't as painful as it was last night.

There's another reason to rejoice, I guess. Even if she is becoming a psycho, I'm going to miss Jen.

Thanks, God. And, Lord, please help these next four months to go by quickly. And extremely slowly.

I limp to the kitchen and find Jen dancing around the refrigerator, singing "Chapel of Love" and whistling the parts where she doesn't know the words. She sees me standing there and dimples.

"I'm getting married!" she announces again.

"You've mentioned," I say dryly, but I smile as I slide onto one of our bar stools. I balance my elbows on the counter and my head in my hands. "Did you sleep at all?"

She winces, stopping the dance midtwirl. "Not very much. I kept noticing how the ring glistened in the moonlight." She turns her hand back and forth, and even from across the kitchen, I can see the sparkles.

"He did good," I say.

"Yeah." She smiles self-consciously. "I had to text him and tell him how it looked in the moonlight."

I grin. "You texted with him all night, didn't you?"

She clears her throat. "Not *all* night. Only until six."

"This morning? Jen!"

She blushes. "Well, he was writing back! It's not my fault!"

I laugh. "Oh, Jen." I grin at her, looking all chagrined. "At least it's Saturday, and neither of you have to work. I have a feeling someone is going to need a nap today."

"A nap? Are you kidding?" She waves her hand dismissively, sending a spray of rainbows over the kitchen. I hide my smile — she never used to gesture with her left hand before today. *Awww.*

"I couldn't sleep at all last night! I knew I was supposed to be tired, but I just kept staring at the ring." She's back to staring at it now.

"Wait until the adrenaline fades . . ." I say. I comb my fingers back through my sleep-matted curls. I suddenly have a genius idea. "Have you had breakfast yet?" I ask her.

She shakes her head.

"Let's go get pancakes to celebrate. My treat." I grin. "Unless you're going to your water-ballet thing today."

"No synchronized swimming today." Jen's forehead is all wrinkled in thought. "Pancakes?" she repeats. "I don't know, Maya. I have to fit into a wedding dress soon."

"In four months!" I say. "Come on. One morning of carbs won't kill you."

After a few more minutes of twisting her face, she agrees. "Okay. You're right." She grins, and her smile is about ten thousand times brighter than the diamond on her left hand. "I'll go get dressed!"

I slide off the bar stool and go back into my room. Calvin has migrated to the bed, and he's curled up in a little ball under my covers.

He looks at me but doesn't move.

I shake my head. "Lazy bones." I pull on a pair of faded blue jeans and a gray T-shirt from my Christian sorority's sophomore-year fund-raiser. I finger-comb my hair back into a fuzzy ponytail and tie my tennis shoes on my feet. I decide the bare minimum will have to do for makeup, so I brush on a little bit of mascara.

Jen's waiting for me when I finally come back out to the living room. She, of course, looks beautiful without any makeup. She's wearing jeans, a plain red T-shirt, and flip-flops.

"Ready?" she asks brightly, clutching her purse. "I'll drive."

I grab my keys and my wallet and nod.

We settle into a booth at IHOP. I had to pull Jen's attention from her left hand on the steering wheel back to the road seven times on our way here. A tired-looking server comes over to take our order, coffee pitcher in hand.

"Chocolate-chip pancakes," I say, handing her my unused

menu. "And a cup of coffee." She pours my coffee, nodding.

Jen's perusing the menu still. "Is there any way I can get fresh fruit on my pancakes instead of the fruit compote?" she asks.

I shake my head. Jen does not understand the point of working out is that you can eat whatever you want in the meantime. In moderation, of course. It's the whole portion-controlled diet. Doctors everywhere are saying it's the best diet out there.

Seriously.

"Uh," the server says, "I can ask."

"Thanks. And I'll take a cup of tea, please."

The server gives me a look that says, *Oh, one of those tea people*, and leaves. Um. No pun intended. You know. Tea. Leaves.

I shake my head and dump three sugars in my coffee. Obviously I did not get enough sleep last night.

Jen's back to staring at her ring. I add cream, stir my coffee, and smile.

"So, what's the plan for today?" I ask.

She jerks her attention away from the diamond and looks at me. "The dress!" she squeals.

"Okay then." I smile across my coffee at her. The tired server brings Jen's tea.

"I'll have the food out in a few minutes," she says.

When the pancakes arrive, I dig into them with a gusto that belies my small frame. This is why I work out.

Jen, on the other hand, daintily eats one minuscule bite at a time until half of her plate is gone. Then she declares she's full.

I think she's just worried about sizing that dress.

We're standing in Lionel's Bridal an hour later. Jen insisted that we go home and change first. "I do not want to try on wedding dresses without any makeup on," she said. So, we changed into nice clothes and put on makeup.

There are dresses upon dresses upon fluffy white dresses, all in plastic bags, lining every single side of the store.

A lady who looks exactly like Joan Cusack greets us in the entryway. She's wearing a blue skirt suit.

"Hi, welcome to Lionel's. I'm Janet. Which one of you is the bride-to-be?" she asks nicely.

I blink. She sounds just like Joan Cusack, too. Weird.

Jen raises her hand. "Me!" she says, like she's calling for her turn during show and tell.

Janet nods. "Lovely. Here's what I want you to do." She takes us to a small table and points to a well-used catalog. "Thumb through there and mark any dresses you like. And then we'll begin."

Jen sits down, and I pull up a chair, leaning over her shoulder to see better. "Ick," she whispers in my ear, pointing to a dress with long white peacock feathers down the front. "It looks like a dress for a Vegas showgirl."

"Be nice. Some people like feathers."

She turns the page. "That's pretty." It's long, straight, and boring, but I don't tell her my opinion.

Thirty pages later, she's *oohed* over nine of them.

"Well, let's start then. Go ahead and get changed into these," Janet says, handing her a corset-looking thing and some strappy heels. "You can wait right there," she says, nodding to a couch in front of one of the four sets of three-way mirrors around the store.

I sit on the couch and squint at my reflection in the

three-direction mirror. I changed into my cute white capris and a brown fluttery top with brown sandals. It looked cute when I put it on, but now I'm not feeling the white. Too much white around me.

Jen emerges from the dressing room, Janet right behind her. She's got on the long, straight dress.

It looks beautiful, but Jen always looks beautiful. I think she should be aiming for *fabulous*.

"Oh, this is weird," she says, voice hushed as she stands in front of the mirrors. Her eyes start to well up, but then she manages to keep the tears at bay. She looks at me, clutching her hands in front of her. "What do you think, Maya?"

Honesty time. "It's nice, but I think it's kind of simple."

"Simple is really in right now," Janet says.

"Oh," I say, hearing the unspoken *shut up*. I shrug, since my opinion is apparently not good.

Jen frowns at the mirror. "You're right," she says, but not to Janet, to me. "It is very simple." She looks at Janet. "Let's try on the next dress." They disappear back into the dressing rooms, and once again, it's me and the mirrors.

Another bride is coming in; she's with her mom and what looks like her little sister. They get her situated at the mirror next to me.

"Hi," the sister says, relegated to the couch, same as me. She's probably around fifteen.

"Hey." I nod. "Your sister?"

"Yeah. Yours too?"

I shake my head. "Best friend."

"Are you the maid of honor?"

"Yeah. You?"

She sighs. "Yeah." She picks at her already mangled nails.

"I hate dresses."

"I'm not too fond of them either."

"And I have to wear heels."

I nod again. "Hear you there."

Jen comes out then, pausing our conversation. She's wearing an off-the-shoulder A-line gown with a light lacy-gauzy thing on it. It looks staticky.

"And dress number two," she announces, stopping in front of the mirror.

Janet is giving me evil eyes. I blink innocently at her and then look at Jen. "What do you think?" I ask her.

She tries to smooth the dress down, and it ends up catching on her ring. "Oh!" she says, lightly pulling her hand away. "Yeah. Definitely not." Back to the dressing room.

The girl's sister is in her first dress. It's strapless, simple, but with a few beaded embellishments on the bodice. See? A few touches make a simple dress that much prettier.

Jen comes out a few minutes later. The dress has a halter-style top and is extremely fitted until the waist, where it then changes to an A-line with a long train. There are tiny crystals all over the bodice and scattered on the skirt. It's a slightly off-white color.

It's beautiful!

"I love this one," I say, mouth agape. "It's gorgeous!"

Jen looks tall and slender, and the color makes her seem a lot more tan than she actually is. She stands in front of the mirror, absently smoothing her long blond hair, smiling dreamily.

"Wow," she whispers.

"This dress does look nice," Joan—I mean Janet—says. "And I know we have some ivory veils to look at, too. Would you like me to grab one?"

Jen doesn't respond; she's too busy staring at the dress.

"I think that's a yes," I say.

Janet nods and leaves to go gather the veil. I stand and get a closer look at the gown.

It really is beautiful. The halter top is a thin, thin, thin band, almost as thin as a bra strap, and it's covered with the tiny crystals. The bodice sparkles almost as much as Jen's ring, and there are little random circles of crystals down the full skirt. The train is long, which is exactly what Jen needs to balance out her height.

"Wow," I say, echoing her earlier comment.

"This is it," Jen declares. "This is the one. I don't even want to try on anything else."

"Are you sure?" I ask, like the proper maid of honor. But secretly I agree with her. She doesn't need to try on anything else — this is definitely the one.

"Yep," she says, nodding. "This is it." She smoothes out the silky satin, and her ring doesn't get caught.

"That's pretty," the girl from the couch says to Jen. Her sister must be back in the dressing room.

"Thanks," Jen smiles. She looks at me. "Hair down? Hair up?"

Janet returns with the veil before I can answer.

"I brought our two basic styles so you can decide. We have the shoulder-length one." She pops it on Jen's hair, and Jen and I both tilt our heads, making that *uh* sound.

"I don't like it," I say, earning another glare from Janet. "You look like that girl in the beginning of *My Best Friend's Wedding.*"

Jen giggles.

"Then there's the elbow-length," Janet says, pinning that one to Jen's hair.

This one is classy and, paired with the dress, looks both elegant and fun. I decide which one I like the best.

"Ooh, this is nice," Jen coos to the mirror. "I'll take them both."

We leave Lionel's about thirty minutes later. The dress is going to be ordered, altered to Jen's height, and steamed.

She starts squealing the moment we climb into the car. "I'm getting married! I have a wedding dress!"

I grin, buckling my seat belt. I let her squeal for another ten minutes before interrupting, though I feel awful saying it.

"Jenny, you need to call them."

She knows exactly who I'm talking about, so she immediately quiets. She bites her bottom lip and then lets out a long sigh. "No, you're right," she says. "I mean, they are my parents."

"Yes, they are."

"And I'm assuming my dad will pay for it. I should probably ask."

I think it's a safe assumption, considering how much he pays just to salve his conscience, but I don't say anything. She looks over at me and then pulls her cell phone out.

"Mind if I call now? I just want to get it over with. Plus, I need you for moral support, and you can't go anywhere if you're seatbelted in." She gives me a little smile.

I squeeze her hand. "It'll be fine."

She dials and then starts talking a minute later. "Hello, Mother?"

I discreetly send my mom a text. *Thank you for being a nice mom.*

Jen listens for a minute, forehead creasing. "What? I . . . Mother, I never . . . Mother? *Mother!*"

Jen huffs and then gathers her Christianity back to her, as

she likes to say when she's talking to her mom. "I'm getting married. Travis proposed, and I said yes."

We stop at a red light, and I watch as Jen's shoulders fall closer and closer to the brake pedal. I can hear the slight chipmunky sound of her mom berating her about her choice in a future husband.

"Regardless," Jen finally answers, "I love him. He loves me. We both love God. So we're getting married."

More chewing out occurring on the other end of the phone. My cell buzzes, and it's a text from Mom.

Thx hn i <3 u. u R nic 2. Dad sayz hi.

Mom really needs to learn how to text proper words.

We pull into our apartment complex, and Jen parks, then sits with her head against the steering wheel, phone to her ear. "Mm-hmm. Mm-hmm," she hums over and over.

I reach over and gently pull the phone out of her hand. "Let's go inside," I whisper. We get inside our apartment, and I set the phone on the kitchen counter.

We look at each other, then look at the phone where you can still hear Mrs. Mitchell jabbering, then back at each other.

And then we plop on the couch and turn on the TV, leaving Jen's mom to talk to the empty air separating us and her.

CHAPTER NINE

The week goes by much too quickly. Before I know it, it's Friday, Jack's last day at Cool Beans. By this point, I've cried four times—once when I was ringing up a customer.

"Want to take your lunch break?" he asks me gently. Probably because he knows I'm this close to crying again.

I nod mutely and go to the back. Alisha, our boss, came by this morning and dropped off a big basket of chocolates for Jack. They sit on the table, like a friend in the midst of a huge crisis.

"I'll still probably see you every day," Jack said to me this morning as I plugged my eyes with both thumbs, keeping the oncoming tears behind my eyelids.

"It won't be the same," I said back.

I look around the empty kitchen and bite the inside of my cheek. Now I have to work with Ethan or whatever his name is, the young and upcoming software major.

He's coming in from two to nine today for training. That means my last day with Jack is going to be crowded with trying to explain that customers here want coffee without the beans floating on the top, which happened with one person before we hired Lisa. That guy didn't last more than two days. I guess he liked his coffee crunchy.

I pull my peanut-butter sandwich from the fridge and sit at the table, staring at Jack's chocolate basket.

What if Ethan is all geeky and likes video games and won't talk about normal stuff with me?

"Hey, Nutkin," Jack says, coming into the kitchen.

"Who's watching the front?" I ask.

"We'll hear the bell over the door," he says, shrugging nonchalantly. "I want to enjoy my last lunch break at Cool Beans with you."

He digs one of those microwaveable pizzas from the freezer. Unwrapping it, he pops it into the microwave and sits down next to me.

I'm again blinking back tears. I hate the word *last*.

"Nutkin, if you cry, you'll make the bread all soggy. And that's just gross," he says, trying to make me laugh.

It doesn't work. Tears spill over my cheeks, almost like in the cartoons where the character's tears look more like a juice box is exploding. I put the sandwich down, because Jack is right. Soggy peanut-butter-and-jelly sandwiches are kind of gross.

He sighs and scoots his chair closer to me, pulling me into one of those awkward seated hugs. "Maya, seriously."

"What if we end up being one of those couples where the only thing we had in common was work?" I say, sniffling in between each word.

"Please. We have way more in common than just straining coffee grounds. And if we don't, we need to work on that now because that's not a healthy relationship."

I manage a small smile.

"We both like movies," he continues.

"Not the same kind."

"We both like to eat out."

"Which is expensive."

"We both go to the same church."

I give him that one.

"We both love dogs."

"So does half of America."

He sighs again and pushes me away. "Look at me, Maya. We aren't going to be one of those couples. Okay? And besides, you can come visit me at the zoo anytime you want."

I can't help it. I bust out laughing.

He frowns until he realizes what he just said, and then he grins self-consciously. "Okay. All right. It's not that funny."

I giggle.

"I'm going to ask the other zookeepers how they manage any sense of pride after being the brunt of every joke," he says.

I rub his shoulder. "It cheered me up."

"True."

"And I'll be sure to visit you at the zoo. I'll even bring you a snack."

He grins. "Well, thank you."

"Maybe peanuts."

"Nutkin."

"The fear of the LORD is the beginning of wisdom, and the knowledge of the Holy One is understanding."

I'm in Proverbs 9:10. It's almost one o'clock in the morning on Friday night, or, well, Saturday. Jack and Travis were both over watching the Food Network with me and Jen and just left fifteen minutes ago.

Jen and I have a thing for Bobby Flay.

I'm not sure what it is. Something about a man who knows

his way around a grill, I guess. Maybe it's the charm of knowing you would never starve with him around.

Travis fell asleep halfway through the first show. Jack had the decency to stay awake through that one but was long gone before the end of the second show.

Just tragical.

"Bobby would never fall asleep during this," Jen whispered to me at one point.

"That's because it's his show," I whispered back. "It's poor form."

Travis left first. While Jen walked him out to his car, Jack leaned over, kissed my cheek, and whispered again that he loved me.

I think I could get used to that.

I look down at the Bible in my hands and reread the verse. *Understanding.* That would be nice right now.

Things I Need Understanding About:
1. Jack. Momentary thing or Diamond on the Finger thing?
2. Jack. Do I love him like a future husband or like a great friend?
3. Jen. Three months and three weeks until she's in wedded bliss.
4. Why both boys don't like Bobby Flay. Seriously.
Man and grill. That should be guy language.
5. Jack. Jack. Jack.

It's Sunday morning, and I'm pulling on yet another dress, thanks to Jen's constant nagging.

"You never wear anything feminine around Jack," she told me again yesterday when we went for a jog. "All he ever sees you in are jeans and T-shirts."

"Not true. I wore a dress for a date last week," I told her. It was for the Infamous Date, but I haven't worked up the nerve to tell Jen that we're officially in the He Said I Love You stage.

So, I pull the dress over my head. It's a yellow mock-wrap dress that pretty much screams summer. I have no idea what to wear for shoes though. Calvin is standing by, waiting to give advice.

"Black sandals or brown?" I ask him.

He looks at both and then looks up at me. I swear he shrugs. "Jenny!"

She appears, looking like the most adorable engaged girl ever, wearing a bright white skirt and a red top. "What's up?"

"Brown or black?" I show her both shoes.

She purses her lips. "Brown."

"Done."

"I'm meeting Travis for lunch at a potential caterer after church, so we'll need to take separate cars," she says.

I nod, slipping on the brown sandals. Jack has an orientation thing at the zoo today after church. And I'm supposed to meet Ethan, the new guy, at Cool Beans to give him a key at two o'clock. Then, I'm heading over to Mom and Dad's for my weekly Sunday-night dinner.

Ethan seems nice enough. He made it through training without pouring coffee beans in someone's drink. He's rusty on the cash register, but he'll get it. He seemed overwhelmed on Friday, but I guess I would be too if the woman training me was bursting into tears and then apologizing every hour.

I pet Calvin on the head and run for the door. Being late to Sunday school again is not an option, especially when I'll be getting enough attention already wearing a bright yellow dress.

"Good morning, ladies," Andrew says as Jen and I walk through the door.

"Hey, Andrew," I say. Jen smiles.

"How's the soon-to-be Mrs. Clayton?" Andrew asks. "We're starting premarital counseling in a month, by the way."

"I'm good. And okay," she says. She goes to find a seat in the third row back.

Andrew slaps me on the arm. "And how are you doing since Jack joined the circus?"

"It's the zoo, Andrew," Jack says, appearing in the doorway behind me.

"Same basic idea. Exotic animals. Weirdly dressed adults. Overpriced tickets." Andrew shrugs. "I went to the circus once. They made an elephant carry an umbrella like it was pretending to be Dumbo. And the whole time I kept wondering if the poor elephant realized that the umbrella was way too little to shield it from any actual rain."

I just look at Andrew. "Really?"

"Really, dudette, I swear." He holds up his fingers like a boy scout.

"You got hit with the hockey puck too many times," Jack says.

Andrew grins. "You're the one spending his days in a zoo." He clears his throat loudly. "Time to start!" he yells, turning to the class.

I look at Jack and shrug. We take a seat next to Jen.

Andrew sits on his rickety stool and faces the class. "I have an announcement," he says, voice booming off the walls. There are probably twenty-five people here this morning. Most are pouring coffee in their mouths as if they are going to perish without it.

"After much resisting and gnashing of teeth, I have agreed to host a barbecue in my backyard this coming Sunday afternoon," Andrew says. "Now, before you praise me for my kind and generous hospitality, I'm going to warn you that the only thing I know how to grill is steak so rare, it looks more sunburned than cooked."

I grin. Andrew is one of my favorite people in the whole world, false pride and all.

"So, if you want other food than that, you are going to have to bring it yourself," he finishes.

Liz raises her hand. "Actually, since it was my idea, I'll organize the food collection. If everyone who thinks they can make it will just write down what they can bring, I'll make sure we have everything."

"And if you don't think you can make it, then don't promise to bring anything," Andrew says.

"I thought that might be self-explanatory." Liz grins.

I mash my lips together as Andrew smiles affectionately at her. It might only be a matter of time before our friendly Viking of a pastor gets married.

"Now," he says gruffly, looking back at the class, "pop open those Bibles to the first chapter of 1 Corinthians, and we'll get started on why you shouldn't follow theologians, but only the gospel of Christ."

He teaches for forty-five minutes and finishes with a verse from the second chapter of 1 Corinthians: "For I resolved to know nothing while I was with you except Jesus Christ and him crucified" (verse 2, NIV). "Don't pay attention to whatever the latest and greatest preacher says. We should resolve to know Christ and Christ alone."

He prays, and then there's the gentle rumble of people closing Bibles, gathering belongings, and starting to visit. Liz is
making her way around the room with a piece of paper, gathering everyone's promised food items for next Sunday's barbecue.

"Hi, Maya," she says, smiling sweetly at me. Liz is way too
beautiful for Andrew. I hope he doesn't take that for granted.

"Hi, Liz."

"Think you'll be able to make the barbecue?"

"I don't see why not," I say, shrugging. "What do you need
me to bring?"

She squints at the list. "How about a dessert?"

I nod. "Sure."

"Great! Thanks! I'm really glad you are going to come," she
says, all friendliness.

I smile at her. Liz Chapman would make a great pastor's wife.
She's even got all the organizational skills a guy like Andrew
would need in a wife.

She gets a promise of chips from Jack and another dessert
from Jen. "Will your fiancé be coming?" Liz asks Jen.

"I'll ask him," Jen says. "But I'm sure he'll come."

"What church will you guys go to when you're married?"
Liz asks.

I look oh-so-subtly at Jen.

She shrugs. "Guess we'll see!" Noncommittal answer. I
frown. Jen's been coming here since her freshmen year at Cal-
Hudson; she and Travis are doing their premarital counseling
here; and I just assumed they would go here.

But I guess Travis has been at his church for a few years, too.

Jack elbows me in the side, so my frown must have been
pretty evident. "Sorry," I whisper.

He gives me a hug a few minutes later. "I'll see you tomor-row night," he says.

And so the changes have begun.

I drive home to my quiet apartment and change out of the yellow dress. Calvin is happily running circles around the room because he knows it's Sunday and he gets to go see Mom and Dad.

I eat lunch by myself, clean up the kitchen by myself, and drive to meet Ethan.

By myself.

I can almost hear Celine Dion crooning that depressing song in the background of my life. "All by myyyyselfffff . . ."

Ethan is waiting beside his car at Cool Beans. I have Jack's old key in my hand, and I'm reluctant to give it to him. It seems so final.

So I drive three miles an hour across the parking lot and finally stop beside his little red Civic.

Ethan is a nice-looking guy. He's about average height with dark hair and green eyes, and he already has a nice summer tan. Therefore I hate him. By the tightness of his sleeves around his biceps, I can tell he works out.

Either that or he needs to buy larger clothing.

I squint at his bicep as I climb out of the car. No, definitely works out.

"Hi," Ethan says. He doesn't remark on my snail's pace across the parking lot. "Thanks for meeting me today."

"Sure." I grip the key tighter in my palm. "So, I guess I didn't scare you off Friday since I'm giving you a key today."

He shrugs. "Nah. I have two sisters. I'm used to tears."

Humph. I do not cry all the time, and I feel led to tell him this. "I'm not usually that emotional," I say. "I've just worked with Jack for the last four years."

"No, I know. Alisha told me. Sorry you have to work with me now. Though it is pretty cool that Jack is going to be in the zoo now." Ethan pauses, then realizes what he just said and busts into a huge grin.

He has a nice smile.

I grin at him. "Working *at* the zoo. Not in the zoo." I hand him the key. "Welcome to Cool Beans."

"Thanks." He slides it on his key ring. "Well, I guess I'll see you tomorrow. Nine o'clock, right?"

I nod. "Nine to five."

"What a way to make a living," he mutters under his breath. I almost don't hear him except that the Dolly Parton song was going through my head as I told him the times.

Maybe Ethan is gay.

"What?" I ask politely, trying not to assume.

He growls out a breath. "My mom made me watch it with her and my sisters. I needed a brother." He pauses. "Or a dad who didn't work eighty hours a week."

Hmm. Family issues. "Got it," I say, again politely ignoring the self-disclosure. "See you in the morning."

"Okay. Bye, Maya."

I get to Mom and Dad's at five on the nose. Zach and Kate's car is already here. I open my passenger door, and Calvin leaps from the car as if he's in an ejection seat and races for the front door, yelping excitedly the whole way.

I follow him, more slowly and not as loudly.

Mom opens the door before I knock and about gets bowled

over by Calvin. "Hi, Calvin!" she coos excitedly.

"Roo! Roo!"

She laughs and rubs his ears, then turns toward me. "Hi, honey."

"Hi, Mom," I say.

Dad, Zach, and Kate are in the kitchen. Kate has probably put on five pounds in the last two weeks. She's eating a package of Oreos as she complains.

"I feel like such a chub," she's saying as Mom and I walk in. She smiles sadly at me. "Enjoy tankinis while you can, Maya."

"Hi to you, too, Kate." I give Dad a hug and wave at Zach.

"It's just so frustrating!" Kate shakes her head. "I saw this woman I haven't seen in about a year at the grocery store, and she told me she gained weight in the first few years of marriage, too."

I look at the Oreos, at Kate, back at the Oreos, then at Zach, who has his lips mashed together staring at me and is slowly shaking his head.

I keep my mouth closed.

Mom rubs Kate's shoulder. "It's okay, honey. It happens to all of us."

Kate sighs. "I have to go to the bathroom. *Again*. I'm either eating, sleeping, peeing, or throwing up."

"Funny how similar that is to the first five months of your baby's life," Dad pipes up.

I grin.

Kate leaves, going down the hall to the bathroom. I wait until I hear the door close before I look at Zach, raising my eyebrows.

"I know," he says, sighing. "Pregnancy hormones kicked in major this last week. The only thing she can keep down is

Oreos and Sprite."

This just makes me laugh because Kate used to be all into natural foods. Organic veggies, cage-free chicken, all-natural fruit juice.

"How did she find that out?" Dad asks.

"She just had this craving at midnight for Oreos after she'd been throwing up all day," Zach says. He rubs his eyes. "So, I went to a twenty-four-hour Walgreens and bought her a package. She finished it by six the next morning. I think she's becoming nocturnal."

"Shhh," Mom hushes us, hearing the bathroom door open. "We're having a variation of Thanksgiving meal tonight," she says brightly as Kate comes back in. "Turkey, dressing, cranberries." She pulls a bowl of cranberry sauce from the fridge.

Kate suddenly slaps a hand over her mouth and runs back to the bathroom. I wince at the sounds coming from down the hall.

Zach is wincing with me. "I'll be right back." He walks down the hallway. "Honey?"

I look at Mom and Dad, wide-eyed. "She gets sick at the thought of a Thanksgiving meal?"

Mom's panicking. "Oh, I didn't know!" she bursts. "I loved turkey when I was pregnant!"

"I'm sure it's not a big deal," Dad says. "Poor Kate."

Zach comes back a few minutes later. "Would you guys mind if we didn't have cranberries on the table? Or on our plates?"

"Nope," I say.

"No," Dad says.

"Of course not!" Mom says, obviously relieved it wasn't the turkey causing the problem. She shoves the cranberries in the back of the fridge, and Zach nods.

"Katie, they're gone!" he yells down the hall.

She comes back, looking embarrassed. "I'm so sorry, Mary," she says to my mom. "I wish I could control it."

"Don't you worry about that," Mom says. "We don't mind at all."

We sit down to turkey, dressing sans cranberries a few minutes later. Kate is happily crunching away on Oreos again, taking swigs from a can of Sprite in between cookies.

"So," Mom says, passing me the green beans, "how was Jack's last week at Cool Beans?"

"Oh yeah, this was his last week, huh?" Zach says.

I sigh. "Fine." I ladle the green beans onto my plate and pass the bowl to Dad.

"Just fine?" Mom prods.

"I cried eight times this week."

Kate grins. "Now you are starting to sound like me."

"And I have to work with some guy named Ethan now. What kind of name is Ethan?"

"A nice one." Kate says. "I like that name."

"Is he friendly?" Mom asks.

"He's fine. He wears shirts that are too small."

Zach makes a face. "What does that mean? Like a cropped-top type of thing? Like what Britney Spears used to wear?"

I shake my head and point to my sleeve, since my mouth is full. "I think he works out," I say after I swallow.

"Oh," Zach nods. "So how are things going with Jack?"

The whole table looks expectantly at me. I chew my cornbread dressing carefully, considering my options.

Option A: *Jack and I are in love.*

Option B: *Jack has said he loves me twice now.*

Option C: *Jack and I are fine.*

"Things are fine," I say, going with the third choice.

"Boring," Zach announces.

"What? We're fine."

"How come he's not here?" Kate asks in between Oreo crunches. "Did we scare him off?"

"He's doing orientation at the zoo," I say. I turn the conversation away from me and Jack. "How are things going with picking a baby name?"

Now, Mom and Dad are looking back at Zach and Kate. I grin at Zach triumphantly. He concedes my victory with a slight smile.

"Actually, we really like the name Kenzington," Kate says.

I try to make my face void of emotion. *Kenzington Davis.* Definitely an interior-designer name. I glance at Dad and notice he's become very interested in his green beans.

Mom is curious. "For a boy or a girl?" she asks.

"Probably for a girl," Kate says.

"Would you call her Kenzie?" I ask.

"I hate nicknames," Kate says. "Remember?"

"Yeah, but Kenzington is going to seem awfully long when you are cheering at her soccer games," I say.

"Soccer games, huh?" Zach says.

"That's such a brutal sport," Kate says. "But you do bring up a good point, Maya. Okay, well, what do you think of Alexander?"

Alexander Davis. Attorney at law.

I deflect the question to Dad. "I don't know. Dad, what do you think?"

He clears his throat, still focused on the beans. "Um. Mary?" He passes the question to my mom.

"I think people will shorten it to Alex," Mom says. You might have to pick shorter names if you don't want a nickname."

Kate sighs. "I don't know. It's such a huge decision! I mean, this kid has to live with that name for the rest of eternity."

"It's true, because God keeps records of our names in the book of life," Zach says, ever the theologian.

"You could do what the Native Americans used to do and just name it after the first thing you see when the baby is born or something you see a lot when you're pregnant," I say.

Zach immediately starts shaking his head. "No, no, no. Then the baby's name will be Nabisco."

Kate's eyes fill with tears.

Zach winces and reaches for her hand. "I'm sorry, Katie, honey. I didn't mean anything by that."

She shakes her head, swiping at her eyes. "No, it's just that you're right," she chokes out, staring at the half-eaten cookie in her hand. "I'm going to become a fat slob of a mother." Now the tears are coursing down her cheeks, and it's getting more and more awkward at the table.

I decide to follow Dad's cue and study my green beans.

"You aren't going to be a fat slob of a mother," Zach says in his soothing doctor tone of voice. "I was just kidding about Nabisco. You're going to be a gorgeous mother. All of our kid's friends will be jealous."

"We'll never find a good enough name." Kate sniffles.

"Yes, we will." Zach says, deep and in a monotone like a psychiatrist. "We'll find the perfect name. We still have more than five months. Okay? All right, honey?"

I only hear sniffling, but I'm assuming she's nodding. My green beans are getting colder the more I push them around.

I peek at Kate, and Zach is leaning over, kissing her tear-streaked cheek.

I hope when I get married, I marry someone who is as nice

about pregnancy hormones as Zach is.

Kate looks down at her plate of Oreos and starts eating again. Zach looks up at me, raises his eyebrows, and sighs.

Okay, maybe I hope I marry someone who just seems as nice as Zach is.

CHAPTER TEN

It's Wednesday morning, and I've been working with Ethan Benson for two whole days.

And I have not seen Jack for two whole days.

He had two more orientations both Monday night and last night. "I'm so sorry, Maya," he said, all hurried last night on the phone. "I've got an orientation in the Asia exhibit tonight."

I could hear the safari-themed music in the background, and his breath was short, meaning he was running as he was talking to me.

"I'll talk to you soon. Love you, bye."

He hung up before I had a chance to say anything.

I unlock and open the door to Cool Beans with a sigh. It's dark and dank in here, the air conditioner squealing in the silence.

I go to the back, turn on the lights throughout the store, and hang my purse on its little hook. I pull on my cherry red apron, loop the strings around my waist, and tie it in the front.

Ethan is coming through the door as I come back to the front. "Good morning, Maya," he says, all cheerful in the morning.

Here's what I'm learning about Ethan: He is a morning person.

This does not bode well when I usually utter only the bare minimum of decipherable words before noon.

"Hey," I say.

He disappears into the kitchen and reappears with his apron on. "It is such a great day outside today! I'm definitely going bike riding as soon as we get off."

Here's the other thing about Ethan that I'm learning: He is obsessed with working out. Biking, hiking, lifting weights, running . . . you name it; he loves it.

"Mmm. Not me," I say.

"Oh, come on. I know you're a jogger. Go jogging. Actually, why don't we go jogging together tonight?" He's rubbing his hands together, eyes sparkling with the thought of physical exertion.

"Well," I say, getting my list of reasons ready.

"Maya, you like to jog. You told me so yourself. Look outside!" He waves his hand toward outside, and I have to admit that it's a beautiful spring day.

Okay, this is awkward. I don't think Jack would take too kindly to me jogging with the cute and very fit Ethan. Regardless of the fact that Jack is spending all of his time with zoo animals instead of me.

Not too flattering, huh?

"Ethan," I say, turning on the computer that doubles as a cash register, "I'm not too sure Jack would like that."

"Why not?"

"We're dating."

"I know. You told me. I just don't understand why he can be gone doing orientations all night long and you can't go jogging with a friend."

Ethan isn't a Christian. So maybe he doesn't get the basic

respect associated with dating.

"So, if you had a girlfriend, you would still go do something one-on-one with a different girl?" I ask.

"Sure. Why not? It's not like I'd be dating the other girl. It's just a jog, Maya."

He starts grinding a batch of Breakfast Blend, and I work on the dark Italian roast while I think about what he just said. Sure, it's just a jog. But would I care if Jack went on "just a jog" with Presley, the female Crocodile Hunter?

Heck yes, I would.

"Sorry, Ethan," I say, when the noise level dies down. "You'll have to find another jogging partner."

He gives me a weird look and then smiles. "Is this because of that faith thing we were talking about yesterday?"

Ah, yesterday, when I patiently tried to explain that no, Christians are not all the sanctimonious crutch-users that people tend to describe them as.

"No, Ethan. It's your basic dating courtesy." I dump the Italian roast grounds in the coffeemaker. "I mean, yes, it's probably tied back to my faith somewhere along the lines, but it's really just me respecting Jack."

"Ah, but those lines are blurred, aren't they? You said so yourself yesterday."

Auuugh.

Ethan clearly likes playing devil's advocate.

Lord, why couldn't I be paired with someone else who is a Christian? Or at least someone like Lisa, who is so close to becoming a Christian that I can already see her name on the list for the next baptism service? Why not her? Why this guy?

I think he takes my silent prayer as a concession because he grins triumphantly. His teeth gleam against the summer tan of his face, and I dislike him all the more.

And seriously, God. Swedish background notwithstanding, I would have appreciated at least the capability to tan.

I start working on the medium blend. I already do not like working with Ethan. Jack and I always had a good time picking out the day's roasts together. Ethan doesn't care. Jack would see what needed to be done and do it. Ethan does the bare minimum. Jack would joke around, let me wake up slowly, and always make me a mocha first thing in the morning. Ethan doesn't do any of that.

More like the opposite.

I start the medium blend in the coffeemaker and go flip the open sign over. Lately, a group of cute young moms have been meeting here every Wednesday morning around nine thirty. They all have babies and toddlers and cute haircuts, and it gives me hope that moms can still be stylish.

"The cinnamon rolls need to be put in the oven," I say nicely, trying to remember that it's only Ethan's third day at work and he might not remember the morning routine yet.

"Oh, I thought you did that," he says.

"We both do. There's not really a split," I say slowly. Third day, it's only his third day.

"Maybe we should split the chores," he says. "It might save from confusion. I can make up a chart in an Excel file. We could create it based around the time each task requires and how quickly it needs to be done."

I'm seeing why Ethan is a computer software major. But there is actual work to be done, not just theories to be made.

I pull the batch of cinnamon rolls from the fridge and put them in the oven. I mix the frosting, pull out the pan of frozen scones, and find the cookies that Kendra left in the fridge for today.

She stuck a note on the plastic wrap covering the perfect little balls of chocolate-chip cookie dough.

Maya—*Bake these at 350 degrees. And I'm praying for you, sweet girl! I know you'll miss Jack, but keep your chin up! Call if you need anything. Love, K.*

I turn the sticky note over and find a pen.

Reasons I Miss Jack:
1. His laugh
2. His good-morning hugs
3. His daily mochas with the little cinnamon shavings on top

I hear the bell ring over the door in the front, and a minute later, Ethan is calling into the back.

"Maya? Can you come out here please?"

I add one more to the list. "On my way," I yell back.

4. I miss being called Nutkin.

I get home at five fifteen. Bible study starts at Cool Beans at eight o'clock.

"See you in a few hours, Maya!" Lisa waved as I left, then turned to start giggling over something with Pam, our other co-worker.

I want to work with Lisa instead.

I take a quick shower to get the smell of coffee out of my hair. Tonight will be the first time I've seen Jack since Sunday morning, and I'm going to help him remember why I'm his girlfriend.

Jen gets home as I'm putting on my makeup.

"Maya?" she calls, knocking on my bedroom door.

"Come on in," I say carefully, halfway through my eyeliner

application. You should not make sudden movements with eye-liner; it can be ugly.

She comes in and leans against my bathroom wall. "Ohhh, I love that shirt!" she says, all giddy.

I'm wondering how long the giddiness is going to last. All four months of the engagement? Just the first?

"Thanks," I say, smiling. It's a brown lacy top that makes my curves look like assets instead of the other way around.

"So, I think I found the reception site," Jen says.

"Oh yeah? Where is it?"

"Well, I was driving home today, and there was construction on Central, so I took Madison Street instead. There's the cutest park ever with this huge community center thing and a gazebo, and I think it would be just gorgeous. So, I stopped to ask about it, and it's actually cheap and they have an opening on our wedding day."

"Did you tell Travis?" I ask, moving on to eye shadow.

"Yeah, and he liked the idea, so I went ahead and reserved it."

"Great!"

She pushes off the wall and takes my eye-shadow brush without asking. "Yeah, so I just need to figure out decorations now," she says, taking over the application. "Close your eyes."

"Um. Okay." I can't help but grin.

"What?" she asks, seeing it.

"Nothing."

"I can style your hair for you, too," she says.

I thought my hair was already styled, but evidently not. I shrug. "Okay." Jen's better at this stuff anyway.

She finishes my hair and makeup a few minutes later.

"You are good," I say, giving her a hug. "Thanks!"

"Why all the fuss? Got a date tonight?"

"Bible study. I'm finally going to see Jack again."

She nods. "Dinner before?"

I sigh. "No." That was my initial hope, but I got a text at four thirty today. *So sorry, I've got a training with the giraffe exhibit at five. I'll be at Bible study though. I miss you. Jack.*

Jen's watching my expression. I try to put on an "it's okay" face, but it's too late.

"Hey," she says slowly.

"What?"

She smiles gently at me. "You love him, don't you?"

I bite my lip. "Yeah," I say, after a minute.

"Well, it's about time!" she bursts. "How long have you known him? And how long has he been, like, amazing for you?"

I smile at her.

"Gosh, Maya!"

I laugh. "Anyway. Do you have a dinner date tonight?"

She shakes her head. "Travis is working late tonight and tomorrow so he can take Friday off. So he'll just make Bible study. We're supposed to meet with Andrew at ten on Friday morning, then I want to show him the reception place, then we've got to get the caterer figured out. We have meetings with three potentials."

"Fun," I say dryly.

She brightens. "The catering part will be. We get to plan out the meal, and we might get to taste some of it."

"Isn't it a little early for that? I mean, you've got three and a half months."

"Maya, some caterers were saying you need to have the food ordered a *year* in advance."

While I'm busy gaping, she's back in planning mode.

"Which reminds me, I need to order our "save the date" cards."

I'm never getting married. It's too much work.

She switches out of planner mode just as quickly. "How was your day with Evan?"

"Ethan," I correct.

"Sure."

"Frustrating. He's annoying! And he's obnoxious. He's all into splitting the workload in half, so he's making an Excel spreadsheet for it. He's . . ." I shake my head.

"Not Jack?" Jen finishes.

"No. He's not Jack."

She rubs my shoulder. "It'll be okay. Though I have to admit, the spreadsheet thing is a little weird."

"A little? He has it organized down to the time it takes to do a task." I suddenly feel very tired. "He asked me if I wanted to go jogging with him today."

"You're here with a cute shirt and makeup on, so I assume you said no," Jen says, proving once again why she's a legal assistant. Deductive talents.

"I said no."

"Good. That's weird."

"I know."

"You're dating Jack."

"Jen, I know. I said no."

"I'm just saying. I don't think that's very nice."

I just sigh.

I follow Jen to Bible study. She's changed from her skirt and blazer to jeans and a white tank top with a chocolate-colored jacket over it. She looks amazing, but she always does. We had a dinner of Lean Cuisine for her and frozen Bertolli dinner for me in front of *Friends*.

I love that show.

We walk inside Cool Beans, and I immediately spot Jack across the room. He's talking with Andrew. He looks like he's gotten some sun in the last few days. He's using his hands as he talks.

Man, I miss that guy.

He looks over at me then and grins, his whole face lighting up. He says something to Andrew and comes over.

"Hey, Nutkin," he says, sweeping me up in the hugest hug ever. He lets go and pulls me outside by my hand.

"Wait, where are we going?" I protest.

"I just want to talk to you for a minute," he says. "Just the two of us."

We stand on the sidewalk outside, and he squeezes my hand. "You look beautiful."

I think I'm happier than I've ever been.

"You look like you've gotten a tan," I say.

He touches a slight sunburn on the back of his neck. "Yeah. Nutkin, I love this job! I've learned so much in such a short period of time. I'm dead tired when I get home, but it's the best job in the whole world. I got to watch a little kid with Down syndrome feed a peanut to an elephant today. It was amazing."

His eyes are so bright when he's talking. I can see how excited he is.

It's good. Right?

He leans over and kisses my cheek. "I miss seeing you every day though."

Okay, it's definitely good.

"How is it? Working with Ethan, I mean," he says.

Now is not the time to complain. "Fine," I lie. "I miss you." That part is true. I don't add that I would be on my knees begging him to come back if he even hinted that he didn't like working at the zoo.

He squeezes my fingers. "I'm sorry I've been so busy. Let's go out to dinner."

"Okay. When?"

He stares into the starry night as he thinks. "Um. I can't do tomorrow. And Friday I've got an exhibit training." His expression squinches. "How about Sunday?"

"I go to Mom and Dad's on Sunday night." He doesn't remember this? I've only been doing it since I moved out to go to Cal-Hudson seven years ago.

"Oh, that's right," he says, shaking his head slightly. "Sorry, I can't believe I forgot that."

"I mean, you can come with me. They were asking where you were last Sunday," I say.

He nods. "I'd like that, but I still want to see just you. Maybe Saturday night? I have to fill out some paperwork during the day, but I could probably be at your apartment by five."

Who knew being a zookeeper was such a time-consuming job? "Okay," I say. "I guess that's fine."

"I'm sorry, Nutkin."

I shrug, like it's no big deal. I'm not sure why, but I sort of feel like I'm more of a burden to him than anything right now. It's not a good feeling. "We'd better get back inside."

I walk back to the door.

Andrew's gearing up for announcements as I grab a seat in the back, next to Jen and Travis. Jack sits next to me.

"All-righty, ladies and gents, we're going to get started,"

he says, planting a chair in the front and settling down on it. "Barbecue, Sunday afternoon, my house. Be there, or don't and have your steak consumed by someone who wants it more."

Jen giggles. Travis is holding her hand, while his other arm is settled around her shoulders. He looks at her and smiles like he's holding the most beautiful thing he's ever seen.

It is really hard not to be envious.

I look away and meet Lisa's gaze, who is standing behind the counter, holding a dish towel. She smiles at me like she knows what I'm thinking.

What if Jack only thought he loved me? Before he discovered that he really loved working at the zoo? I mean, wouldn't he be making more of an effort to see me if he felt the same way Travis feels about Jen? Travis drops everything if Jen even breaks a nail. It's sickening in one sense, sweet in another.

"Tonight, we are going to talk about jealousy." Andrew breaks into my thoughts.

I gulp a breath of air and look up at him guiltily.

Of course.

I'm convinced it's only me who has this issue. Every time I'm struggling with something, Andrew ends up teaching about it on Wednesday nights.

Lord, seriously. Could I just wallow? For a minute at least?

"Open your Bibles to Proverbs chapter 14 and take a look at verse 30. 'A heart at peace gives life to the body, but envy rots the bones' (NIV)."

This must be God-speak for "no wallowing."

Andrew makes a face. "This is not a pretty picture with the whole rotting-bones thing, but we're going to do a little digging into this. What is envy or jealousy? What are the side effects?"

I sit there and listen for forty-five minutes straight about how envy causes you not to love fully, live fully, and serve fully. I shrink further into my chair with each point. I try the best that I can to keep my eyes focused straight ahead on Andrew and not even glance at Jen and Travis still holding hands.

Andrew prays, but I'm too busy having my own conversation with God to pay attention to his.

Lord, I'm sorry. I get it; I shouldn't be envious. God, I'm jealous of an elephant because at least Big Ben got to see Jack today.

I think this brings me to a new low in my spiritual walk.

Jack leaves right after Andrew finishes praying.

"Sorry, Nutkin, I have to be out the door by six tomorrow morning. I'll see you Saturday," he says, kissing my cheek and walking out the door.

Everyone else starts gradually trickling out. Lisa and Pam are working at light speed to try to get out of here at a decent hour.

I start pulling tables and chairs back into their regular spots, even though I'm not working tonight. Jen and Travis have left to go have ice cream at Dairy Queen, and soon it's only Andrew and me in the front of the store, while Lisa and Pam clean up the kitchen.

"So," Andrew says, sliding the couch back to its regular place, "how you doing, Maya?"

I open my mouth to say the word *fine* and lie twice in one night — and at Bible study, no less — but Andrew starts in before it comes out.

"And if you say the word *fine*, I'm going to throw this cup at you. You are not fine. I could tell the whole time I was teaching."

These darn pastors and their intuitiveness. The few counseling classes they have to take in seminary really pay off.

I slide a chair next to a table and huff my breath out.

"Not fine."

"What's eating you, kid?"

"Honestly? Jealously."

Andrew grins. "And isn't it cool when you hear a fabulous lesson taught by a rather stunning man on that exact topic right when you are struggling?"

"Do I need to teach a lesson on pride?"

He blows on his knuckles and rubs them across his shirt. I roll my eyes.

"Okay. Who are you jealous of?" he asks, plopping on the relocated couch and nodding to the other end of it.

I sit on the sofa crisscross-applesauce style, as my mother would say. "It's more of a what, I think."

"What?"

"Yeah."

"No, I mean, what are you talking about?"

"I think it's more of a *what* than a *who* that I'm jealous of."

Andrew visibly thinks about that and then nods. "Okay. Back on the same train track. Keep going."

"It's just . . ." I use my hands to try to find the words. "Jack has only had this job for what . . . three days? And already I'm crazy jealous of the time he spends there. And I have to work with this software guy, and he's just not Jack. I mean, an elephant gets to see Jack more than I do. And it's just—I don't know. . . . Travis drops everything whenever Jen needs him, and Jack doesn't do that with me."

Andrew nods through my whole confession. "Mm-hmm. Mm-hmm." He rubs his chin in a way-too-old action for him. "So, you are jealous of Jen."

"No, I'm jealous of Jack's time."

He shakes his head. "I think you're more jealous of Jen. I

think you look at her and Travis and expect your relationship with Jack to look like that. When it doesn't, you get envious of Jen and how Travis treats her."

I look at him, eyes wide. "Those counseling classes are really something."

"Yeah, well, it's mostly just my finesse with this kind of stuff." More blowing on the knuckles.

"Seriously, Andrew. Major lesson on pride."

He smiles. "I think what you need to realize is no one's relationship is going to be like yours and Jack's, because you are not other people. And, yes, I realize that was incredibly deep."

I roll my eyes. "Very deep."

"You could have used a diving board for that one."

I can't help the grin. I love Andrew. "So how do I not get frustrated when he's busy all the time with the hippos or whatever?"

"Well, one, remember that he's starting a new job and those first few weeks of any new job are just killer. Two, try to remember that Jack is just as committed as you to this, so you need to trust that he's missing you as much as you're missing him. And, three, keep in mind that even if Jack isn't the right guy, you have put your trust in a God who has already written the future and knows everything that is going on."

I nod. "I guess that makes sense."

"Like I said, finesse."

I sigh and smile at him. "Thanks, Andrew."

"You're welcome, kid. Let me know how it's going, okay?" He reaches over and knuckles my head like a brother would do.

"Ow."

"You have a bony head."

"Everyone has a bony head!" I say, rubbing my noggin. "It's the skeletal system that God created."

He grins and pushes himself off the couch. "Get home, young lady."

"Yay. Off to my apartment, where it's me and my dog," I say without enthusiasm, also standing.

"Spend some time hanging out in Romans. You'll see what I mean about God writing the future."

"Speaking of the future," I say, "how's Liz?"

Andrew the Pastoral Know It All Viking suddenly morphs into Andrew the Awkward Twelve-Year-Old. "Uh," he says, clearing his throat and looking down at his shoes. "Fine."

"*Fine*, huh? You like her," I say, grinning.

He smiles at me.

"A lot," I tack on.

"Yeah, well . . ."

"Yeah, well, does she know?" I ask, copying his tone.

Back to looking at his shoes. "I think she probably guesses. She's very smart. She's got a master's in science."

"You haven't said anything to her?" I gasp. "Andrew! What happened to all that stuff you used to tell me about the guy needing to be the strong one, asking the girl out, and girl not taking the initiative and blah blah blah?"

Andrew grimaces. "It was easier when it wasn't me."

"Look, Liz is gorgeous, sweet, and funny, and you already mentioned she's smart," I say, ticking her attributes off on my fingers.

"I know, I know, I know," Andrew says, holding up a hand. "You don't have to continue."

"I'm just saying. You need to whisk her away into Unavailable Land before someone else does."

He sighs.

"Where's all that false pride you had on earlier? Put it back on and go ask her."

"Ask her what?" Andrew says. "Hey, will you, the gorgeous, smart, sweet, funny woman, go out with me, the goofy, over-grown ex-hockey player who saves his toenail clippings?"

"Ew," I say.

He spread his hands. "See? Why would she possibly be interested?"

"Andrew, you're nice-looking, you're smart, and you've got the whole lonely-pastor-guy thing going." I rub my cheek. "I just wouldn't mention the toenail thing until after the honeymoon."

He grins.

"Just ask her, you scaredy-cat."

"Just trust Jack, you doubting Thomas."

We both smile at each other, and he pulls me into a ginor-mous hug. Anytime Andrew gives me a hug, I feel like I'm going to get lost somewhere in his chest and they'll never find me again. He's huge; I'm little.

He shoves me out the door a minute later. "Get lost, Maya."

"Bye, Andrew."

He winks, and I walk to my car, unlocking the door, sliding in, and pulling it closed behind me.

God, help me to trust You. And Jack.

I turn the ignition and sigh.

And, Lord, do You think You could maybe make the zoo less busy? I'd appreciate that a lot.

My phone buzzes with a text at four fifteen on Saturday. I took Calvin for a jog and just finished with a relaxing shower.

From where I sit on the bed, Bible in my lap, I look at my phone on the dresser. I was right in the middle of Romans chapter 4. Abraham believed that God had the power to fulfill His will.

I set the Bible on the bed and reach for my phone. I'm certain it's Jack, canceling on our date tonight.

Trust God, trust God, trust God, I say to myself as I open the phone.

It's from my mom.

Is J cmng fr dnnr tmrw? <3 M

She seriously needs to discover the amazing world of complete words in text messages. I write her back. *Maybe.*

I haven't been able to confirm with him about the family dinner yet. Last time I talked to him about it, it was Wednesday. I thought he said he was coming, but these days you never know.

He called me at eleven o'clock last night. Jen was on a date with Travis, so it was me and Calvin cuddling on the couch, watching *27 Dresses* and sighing over sweet men like James Marsden. Actually, I think Calvin was sleeping. I was sighing over James Marsden.

He's adorable.

I talked with Jack for three minutes before he said he was exhausted and was falling asleep on the phone.

I hung up and put in *Hairspray* next. Feel-good musical, funny cast, and again, James Marsden. I fell asleep with "Welcome to the 60's" playing through my brain.

I close my phone, slide off the bed, fix my hair, and pull on a T-shirt and jeans. Since Jack is evidently exhausted, we will probably spend tonight watching a movie and eating pizza on my couch. Not exactly a dress-up date.

The doorbell rings at exactly five o'clock. I open it and find an overwhelmingly huge bouquet of daisies, roses, and lilies attached to a pair of jeans.

"Oh," I sigh, being a girl. "They're beautiful."

"Thanks for putting up with me this last week," Jack says from behind the flowers. He comes in, sets them on my kitchen table, and pulls me into a hug.

He's wearing a button-down shirt and nice shoes, and I slap his arm. "Why didn't you tell me to wear something nice?" I say.

"So go change real quick. I'll get a vase for these."

Calvin is ecstatically greeting Jack while I run to my room and shut the door. I pull on a cute brown skirt and a bright pink top.

Brown and pink has to be the girliest color combination ever, and if we are going out, I want it to be very obvious that I am not an elephant, hippo, rhino, giraffe, or orangutan. I am a girl.

I come back out to the living room, and Jack whistles at me. I blush.

"I was thinking we could go to Outback, then maybe catch that new Sandra Bullock movie, and then get dessert somewhere. And I need to go to the grocery store and pick up a bag of chips for that barbecue thing at Andrew's tomorrow," he says, grinning.

"Better late than never," I say.

"Ready?"

We are sitting at a table in Outback twenty minutes later. The server comes with our drinks, and Jack orders a twelve-ounce steak. I raise my eyebrows and order the kebab with a few shrimp thrown on there for fun.

"Hungry?" I ask, after the server is gone.

"I'm starving. Half the time, I never get lunch anymore. I'm usually running from one exhibit to another, or I'm having to answer questions guests ask, or I'm working the elephant ride."

I grin.

"And no zoo jokes, or I won't take you to dessert."

I mash my lips together.

He grins at me and reaches across the table for my hands. "Man, I've missed you. I promise it won't always be like this."

"I hope not." Better to be honest about how much I hate it.

"It won't." He squeezes my hands. "Okay. We aren't going to talk about my job anymore tonight. How's Ethan working out?"

"I think he works out a lot, actually."

Jack rolls his eyes.

I grin. "He's not you."

"Because I don't work out a lot?"

"Right."

"Well. It's probably because he's not as good-looking as me."

"No, he's nice looking; he's just—"

"Maya," he interrupts, raising his eyebrows.

"I mean, no, he's definitely not as good-looking as you."

"Better." He smiles. "So, he's learning the ropes at Cool Beans?"

I butter a piece of bread. "He made a spreadsheet," I say dully.

Jack frowns at me and gets his own piece of bread. "What kind of spreadsheet?" he asks.

"The Excel kind. He has our jobs all organized. I have the dark and medium roasts coffees and making the frosting for the cinnamon rolls. And I have cash-register duty from ten until one, and then we switch."

Jack chews his bread and swallows. "Wow. Your job is more organized than the zoo now." I open my mouth, and he holds up his hand. "Remember how precariously balanced dessert is on this conversation." I mash my lips closed again.

The server sets our meals in front of us. "Enjoy."

"Thanks." Jack holds out his hands to me. "Let me pray." He bows his head. "God, I just thank You for this amazing girl." He pauses, thumbs rubbing the back of my hands. "I don't deserve her company. Thank You. Please bless the food. Amen."

I look up at him. Who is this romantic guy?

He smiles at me, squeezes my hands, and reverts back to the Jack I know. "All right, so how is the wedding planning going?"

I dig into my shrimp and steak. "Fine, as far as I can tell. They have the sites booked, and they met with the caterer yesterday."

"Wow. They might have to shorten the engagement."

"No, knowing Jen, she'll find enough stuff for us to obsess over for the next four months."

"Did she ever tell her parents?"

"Yeah, she called her mom. I'm pretty sure she left a message for her dad. Her mom didn't take to it too nicely. And I don't think her dad has called her back."

Jack makes a face. "I didn't think her mom would be very happy, but that's sad. Poor Jen."

"Don't feel too bad. Travis has sent six tulip bouquets in the last week to make her feel better. And Mrs. Clayton called and told Jen that she was officially adopting her." I smile about that last one. Travis's mom is one of the nicest ladies I've ever met. One of the hardest parts about our breakup was when I realized I wouldn't see Mrs. Clayton anymore.

"That's good," Jack says.

"Yeah."

We lapse into a comfortable chewing silence. Jack swallows and looks up at me. "So."

I copy his tone. "So."

"Am I still invited to dinner tomorrow night at your parents' house?"

"Of course," I say. Mom can't wait to have Jack over again. She's pulling out the fatted calf. "You get to witness firsthand the scary pregnancy hormones affecting my poor sister-in-law." I squinch my face. "Actually, maybe they are affecting my brother more than Kate."

Jack grins. "Oh fun."

The movie is hilarious, and we get dessert at Olive Garden, my favorite place for dessert. By the time we are driving back to my apartment, two bags of Fritos for tomorrow's barbecue in the backseat, I've decided it's one of the best nights ever.

Jack grins over at me in the car and reaches for my hand, holding the steering wheel with his left hand.

"Have a good night?" he asks.

"Awesome night. Thanks, Jack."

"We needed a nice night out after this last week." He squeezes my hand, weaving his fingers between mine. "It'll probably be busy for a few weeks, just to warn you. I'm sorry."

"That's okay. Maybe Ethan can make a spreadsheet for me of what to do while you're busy with work." I grin.

"Funny, Nutkin."

"I try."

"Not very hard."

"Hey!" I protest. "I'm very funny! I'll prove it. What's the difference between a duck?"

"A duck and what?"

"Nothing. One leg is shorter than the other."

Jack purses his lips, and his forehead creases. "What?" he says finally.

Maybe telling my dad's jokes isn't the best way to prove to Jack that I'm a funny person.

"Never mind," I say.

He pulls into the parking lot. We climb the steps to my apartment, and I open the door. Calvin greets me with an enthusiastic doggy dance.

"Hey, baby," I say, rubbing his ears.

Jen looks over from where she sits next to Travis on the sofa. They're in the middle of watching *Runaway Bride*, and Ike is about to have blue hair. I watch him buy a hat off the kid on the bike and smile.

Travis is a sweet guy for watching this with Jen.

"Hey," she says, waving.

"Hi," Travis says around a mouthful of popcorn. He holds the bowl above his head to us. "You guys want some?"

"Sure," Jack says, reaching for it. He grabs a handful and pops it into his mouth. His expression changes from one of anticipation to one of slight disgust.

"Low-fat popcorn," I tell him.

"What?" Jen asks, pulling her gaze from the television again.

"Jack forgot that you guys don't eat real popcorn," I say.

Travis puts the bowl back in his lap. "This is real popcorn." He defends his bowl of Styrofoam. "It's a healthy snack."

Two words that should never meet: *healthy* and *snack*.

I motion to the kitchen and open the pantry. I stashed a box of Kettle Korn behind a big bag of rock salt that I'm not sure how we ended up with.

I pull the box out of the pantry and show it to Jack.

"I knew there was a reason I loved you," he whispers.

I grin. I put the popcorn in the microwave and go back into the living room. "So," I say, "*Runaway Bride*? Is this a foreshadowing of what's to come?"

Travis snorts. "No, but that threat is exactly Jen's way of making me watch these movies. We already watched *Music and Lyrics*." He closes his eyes. "I think Hugh Grant scalded my retinas with that dancing."

Jen grins over the back of the couch at me. I hold up my hand, and she gives me a big high-five.

"Hugh Grant is adorable in that movie," I lecture Travis.

"Maya, he shook his rear end at me. *Shook* it."

I start laughing. "I don't think he was specifically aiming for you, Travis."

"I'm pretty sure he was."

Jen pokes Travis's temple. "It was not that bad. Sheesh."

He grins sweetly at her, crunching on popcorn. She kisses his cheek, and I go back into the kitchen, feeling awkward about observing their moment of affection.

"What's up?" Jack says, standing by the microwave, the smell of the nearly done Kettle Korn filling the kitchen.

"Hmm? Oh. Nothing."

The microwave beeps, and Jack pulls out the steaming bag of sweet and salty goodness and pours the popcorn in a bowl. "So. You want to go watch the rest of the movie with them or hang out in here?"

I'm considering how many times I've seen *Runaway Bride* and how little I've seen Jack lately. "Hang out in here," I say.

He grins. "I was hoping you'd say that." He nods to the table and we sit, popcorn bowl on the table between us.

"What are you doing tomorrow?" I ask, crunching on a handful of popcorn.

"Not working, thank goodness. Not much. Church. Barbecue. Dinner at your parents' house. Spending all of that with you." He shrugs. "It'll be a good day."

I can't help the smile. "Good."

"I've got one more week of orientations, but after that, I'm hoping I'll have a normal shift schedule like everyone else who isn't new."

"I still want to come see you in a safari hat."

He sighs. "It's really not that cool, Nutkin."

I highly doubt this. I've never seen Jack in any kind of hat, so going from his normal short, slightly gelled hairstyle to a huge "welcome to the jungle" kind of a hat has to be sort of funny. If not hilarious.

I grin.

He sighs again and throws a kernel of popcorn at my head.

"Want kind of shirt do you wear?"

He immediately averts his eyes. "A khaki button-down shirt."

"Nice, Indiana Jones. Does it have your name on it?"

He hedges around the question. "Does it matter? I'm not the focus, the animals are. People don't come to the zoo to see me."

I look at him and open my mouth. He holds up a hand. "What?" I protest. "You can't threaten me with no dessert now."

He growls and chomps on the popcorn.

I watch him for a minute. "It's got a goofy saying on it, huh?"

More chomping. "Yes."

I grin. "What's it say?"

"I'm not going to tell you. You'll mock me."

"Then I'll just come Monday to see it." I gesture to him with a kernel of popcorn. "Want to be mocked in private at the table here or in public next to the sea-otter exhibit?"

"I don't work with the sea otters."

"Jack."

He sighs and throws another popcorn kernel at my head. "It says, *Save the Animals — We Can Zoo It.*" He ducks his head and winces.

"Well, that's not too bad," I say.

He lifts his head and squints at me. "What?"

"I mean, it's not like *We're Just Zooing Our Job* or *We Zoo This So You Can Zoo That* or *Zoo Days Are Better Than One.*"

He's laughing now. "Nutkin."

"Saving the animals is a noble cause, and I think you can zoo it," I say, keeping my expression very serious.

He snorts. "Nutkin."

"I mean, if you guys weren't going to zoo it, who would?"

"Maya!"

I start giggling. "Or if you — "

"Hey!" Jen yells from the living room. "We are trying to watch a very romantic scene where Ike and Maggie are finally falling in love, and you are ruining it!"

"Sorry, Jen."

"Sorry, Jenny."

She's still frustrated. "I mean it. Keep it down in there!"

"We will, Jen," Jack says, his voice all pacifying.

"We'll zoo our best," I holler back.

Jack loses it. He snorts loudly and busts into gut-wrenching laughter. He's trying to hold it in, but it's spilling out as he leans back in the kitchen chair.

"Hey!" Jen yells again.

"Sorry, Jen," I say nicely. "Jack's being loud."

Travis rubs Jen's arm. "He does work in a zoo."

I have to bite my thumb to keep from laughing.

CHAPTER ELEVEN

"Okay. How does everyone want their steak cooked? I can do pink or crispy," Andrew says loudly. It's Sunday afternoon, a gorgeous day, and there are probably thirty of us wandering around his backyard and house.

"I would like mine medium well," I say.

"Crispy, got it."

Everyone gives their orders, and he goes out to the smoking grill and starts laying the steaks on. Feeding steaks to thirty people has to cost a small fortune. I follow him outside.

"Do you need me to take up a collection for those?" I ask, pointing to the steaks.

Andrew gives me a look. "They're that pathetic looking?"

"What?"

"Why are you giving them a collection?"

I grin. "No, for you, dork. Steaks are expensive."

He flips a steak over and turns to me, gesturing with his gargantuan spatula. "I will have you know, Maya Davis, that I do not offer things for free without thinking through the ramifications."

"Is that a no?"

"That's a definite no."

"Is one of the ramifications impressing Liz?"

"That's a definite yes."

I grin and pat his arm. "Then be sure to tell Liz I said thank you for the steak." She's busy in the kitchen organizing the side dishes everyone brought. She's so obviously going to be a great pastor's wife.

"I probably won't pass that along." Andrew smiles all cute and shy. He visibly shakes off the cuteness though. "Don't go saying stuff like that while I'm grilling, Maya. A man has to feel like a man when he's grilling."

"You don't feel manly?"

"Not when you're making me look all desperate."

I look at him. "You're holding a spatula the size of my refrigerator. I think the desperation factor is low."

"Like this, huh?" he says proudly. "My father gave me this spatula. It has been in my family for six generations."

I'm getting a mental picture of a Viking carrying it on a warship, but I blink away the image. "Huh. Cool."

He rolls his eyes. "Code for you aren't interested. Hey, I noticed Jack is here. Things are better?"

I nod. "Yeah. Sorry for the freaking out."

"Nah," he says, shrugging off my apology. "You're a girl. You're entitled to freak-outs. At least, that's what my mom tried to convince me of."

"Smart woman."

"She survived raising three boys, so yeah, I'd say so."

I smile.

Jack pulls his car into my parents' driveway at five that evening. It was a nice marshmallow cloudy day in Hudson, but in San

Diego, the clouds look more like angry dryer lint.

"We will probably get rain," Jack says, opening the passenger door for me.

"Yep." I nod. Calvin leaps from the car after me and races up the steps to the front door. Zach and Kate drive up right then. Jack and I wait for them to get out of the car before heading inside. We're polite like that.

"Jack!" Kate says, getting out of the car. "I'm so glad we didn't scare you off two weeks ago." She smiles nicely at him and then gives him a huge hug.

My eyes widen to half my face. Who is this? I look around Kate to Zach, who just sighs at me and shakes his head.

Kate is not a hugger. She usually goes for the brief side-hug squeeze, and that's only when a hug is absolutely necessary. Like Christmas or something.

She pulls away from Jack and then grins at me. "Hi, Maya!" Suddenly her arms are around my shoulders, and she's squeezing me so tightly that I can feel those extra pounds called Mini-Davis pressing against my ribs. Kate is quite a bit taller than me.

I hug her back, because I am a hugger and I'm not wasting a good hug from Kate, and then grab Zach's arm as we all file toward the front door.

"What is going on with her?" I whisper in his direction. Zach is also quite a bit taller than me. Whispering in his ear is not going to happen.

Another sigh. He looks so melancholy that I nearly laugh.

"Maybe your baby is going to be a hugger, too!" I say excitedly. This will mean that whatever recessive genes I got, this little Davis kid is going to have them as well. Maybe he'll be short like me.

I frown. I don't think I would wish that on Zach and Kate's

baby. He'd feel like a munchkin whenever he was around them.

We walk inside, and Kate is hugging Mom before Mom even knows what's going on. Then Kate moves on to Dad, and I guess she feels like Zach got left out, because she scoots under his arms next.

I think everyone is thrown a little off balance by this new Kate. Meanwhile, Calvin is going nuts around everyone's feet. It's chaotic.

"Hi, Jack," Mom says a few seconds later, gathering herself. "I'm so glad you could come again."

"Thank you for having me, Mrs. Davis."

Here we go again.

I give my mom a hug and a kiss on the cheek, leaving my arm around her shoulders. "What's for dinner? It smells amazing in here!"

Mom looks worriedly at Kate. "Pancakes, actually." I think she's remembering the Oreo incident.

Kate's eyes light up. "Really? Mary! I love pancakes!"

I can feel the relief in Mom's posture. "Oh good!" she says. "I called Zach to try to figure out what you liked eating other than Oreos lately."

Zach squinches his face right as Mom says the word *Oreos*, and Kate gets very pale.

"Uh," Zach says, "we don't like those anymore. Not even mentioned." He smiles apologetically at Mom while Kate does some Pilates breathing. *In through the nose, out through the mouth.*

I can wait a very long time before I get sick even hearing the word *Oreo*. I look over at Jack, and he's failing miserably to hide a smile.

"Well, pancakes are getting cold," Dad says, leading the way to the kitchen. Calvin is happily chewing on yet another new toy.

He gets spoiled rotten here.

Dad flips the pancakes on everyone's plates, and we settle at the table. There are strawberries, raspberries, and blueberries, each in their own little bowls in the center of the table, along with my grandma's famous maple syrup.

Dad passes a small bowl of chocolate chips to me, and I grin at him. "Thanks, Dad!" I say. Dad and I both love chocolate-chip pancakes. Mom and Zach think they're the grossest thing they've ever heard of.

They're weird.

"Let's pray real quick," Dad says.

Jack takes my hand under the table. Everyone bows their heads.

"God, thank You for this meal and for all my kids being home, and we pray a special prayer for the little one You are creating. Amen."

Dad's prayers are always short and sweet. I think he sounds more sincere than someone saying an eloquent ten-minute prayer. I remember reading a verse one time that said something about not babbling on when you pray. I thought of Dad when I read it.

Jack holds my hand for a second or two longer than necessary and then drops it while we dig into the pancakes. I sprinkle a healthy coating of chocolate chips on top of the steaming pancakes and then add a few raspberries and some syrup.

"So, how's the zoo, Jack?" Mom asks nicely. And just as nicely, I bite my tongue.

Jack flashes me a warning look. "It's going fine, ma'am. Thank you for asking. I'm learning a lot."

"Maya said you've been really busy," Mom continues.

Jack nods, sprinkling some blueberries on his pancakes.

"I've had orientations like crazy. Once I get through next week, though, it should calm down quite a bit."

"Good!"

Zach chews a bite of pancake, but he's polite enough to swallow before he starts talking. "I think we came up with our official baby names," he says.

"What?" Mom asks excitedly.

Kate smiles at Zach and then looks at everyone. "If it's a boy, his name will be Zachary Evan, and we'll call him Evan. If it's a girl, we like Rachel Maria."

I grin. "I like those!"

"Those are good names." Jack nods.

"Much better than the last several," I say.

Dad is nodding, finally smiling at the thought of being "Gramps." "I like Rachel Maria." He looks at Mom, the original Mary, and smiles sweetly.

She blushes, so I'm assuming it's one of those references to the past when my parents were young and romantic.

I hide the smile with a forkful of chocolate-slathered pancakes.

"Well, our ultrasound is next week, so we'll bring pictures," Kate says in between shoveling pancakes into her mouth.

"Will you find out whether it's a boy or girl then?" I ask.

Zach nods. "We're debating about telling you guys though."

"Hey!" I protest.

"What?" Mom asks him at the same time.

Jack looks over at my dad, and they both shrug. "That's fine," Dad says.

"It is not fine!" I say. "You can't keep a secret like that."

"Sure we can. We kept the pregnancy a secret for three months," Zach says. "You guys didn't even guess."

True.

"I just don't want everyone to be all prepared for a girl, and it ends up that the ultrasound was a mistake and it's a boy," Kate says.

"So what are you going to do? The gender-neutral green and yellow thing? Because that's always reminded me of a bruise," I say.

Kate shrugs, still chomping the pancakes like this is her last earthly meal. "I haven't really thought about it. We'll probably tell people; I'm just worried is all."

Mom waves her hand. "Don't worry, honey. I didn't know with Zach or Maya. Those were preultrasound days. I just used all the pink dresses I got for Zach's shower when Maya came."

Kate nods. "I could do that. I'm hoping this isn't our only child."

"How many do you want?" I ask.

Zach pipes up immediately. "Three."

Kate says, "Two," and gives Zach a dirty look.

Mom and Dad smile again. "Bring back memories, Mary?" he says.

"Since there are only two of us, I take it Mom won?" I ask, smiling.

Mom nods. "My uterus stretching out, my final say."

"I like this rule," Kate says.

"And it's officially awkward," I add.

Jack stops in front of my apartment at eleven o'clock. I'm still full from the pancakes, and I'm tired after three games of Cranium.

We tried to play a game of Jenga, but it was a lot faster than we had anticipated. Calvin ends all Jenga games very early.

The girls whooped the guys at Cranium.

I unbuckle my seat belt and yawn, glancing at him as he unclicks his. "You don't need to get out, Jack."

"I'm going to walk you to the door."

"Well, you don't have to. I can get there myself."

"I know I don't have to. I want to."

"But then you'll have to walk all the way up the scary metal stairs and all the way back down, and I know you have to be at work at seven tomorrow." I find my purse.

"Maya." He sighs and glares at me. "I want to. Now shut up and let me be a gentleman."

He comes around to the passenger side of the car, opens my door, helps me out, then opens the back door and lifts a sleeping Calvin out.

He carries my little beagle up the stairs and sets him on the landing by the front door. I dig in my purse for my keys. Jen's car is in her parking space, Travis's car is not here, and all the lights in the apartment are off, so she's probably in bed.

I find my key, open the door, and Calvin waddles in, yawning.

I smile up at Jack. The light beside the door is on, giving Jack a weird orangey-yellow halo.

"So, I probably won't see you tomorrow," he says, lingering. "I have orientations tomorrow night."

I nod. "Will you make Bible study again?"

"I'm going to try. I have to learn the emergency evacuation plan on Wednesday afternoon, so it will depend on how long it lasts." He shrugs. "We'll see." He reaches for my hands. "Definitely dinner on Friday though. Okay? Wear a dress — we're going somewhere nice."

I know he's just trying to give me something to look forward to so I won't be sad all week, but I'm still bummed I won't see him.

"Good night, Maya," he says gruffly. He leans in and kisses my cheek softly. "I love you."

It's only been a couple of weeks that he's been saying it, so it still makes my stomach do weird things that feel like tiny needles poking me.

I pull him into a hug. "Love you, too. Have a good week, Jack."

"Bye."

I drag my Bible over onto my lap a few minutes later, teeth brushed, face washed, my pajama shorts and tank top in place. I'm sitting on top of my covers, leaning back against a few pillows I propped against the headboard.

I open my Bible, and it flips right to the first chapter in Philippians.

"I thank my God every time I remember you. In all my prayers for all of you, I always pray with joy because of your partnership in the gospel from the first day until now, being confident of this, that he who began a good work in you will carry it on to completion until the day of Christ Jesus" (1:3-6, NIV).

I close my eyes.

Thank You for continuing to work on me, Lord.

I can feel a smile making its way across my face. *And thank You for Jack.*

CHAPTER TWELVE

I wake up at seven Monday morning to someone talking loudly in the kitchen.

I blink groggily, push myself out of bed, and stumble down the hall, trying to squish my straggly hair out of my face.

Jen's standing in the kitchen, growling at her cell phone, which is lying on the counter four feet from her.

"What's wrong?" I mumble, looking between her and the phone.

"Mom." One word, but it explains everything.

"Oh." I scuttle over to Jen and wrap both arms around her waist, laying my head against her shoulder. "I'm sorry."

Jen slumps against me, and we stand there quietly for a few minutes. Jen's wearing her blue yoga pants and a white T-shirt that I'm pretty sure she stole from me and I stole from Zach.

It's made the rounds.

"What happened?" I ask when I feel her start to straighten.

"More lectures. She doesn't think Travis is 'Mitchell Material.' I said good, because I'm not Mitchell Material either. So then she got mad and said she didn't want me settling for someone beneath me." She growls again. "Seriously. It's like we still live in the time of *Gone with the Wind* or in India with the caste system or something. I've told her that Travis is my perfect match in every way, especially in my faith, but then she launches into the whole 'I didn't raise you to need a religious crutch' talk."

"I'm sorry." I feel like I'm always apologizing about her mother.

"It's not your fault. She's not your mom." She huffs out her breath and pushes away. "Well. More to pray about, I guess."

"What's that verse you were memorizing about her?"

"Be thankful always." Jen says it like a mantra. "Be thankful always, be thankful always, be thankful always."

"We think this is bad — imagine the persecution Christians were experiencing in those days, when Paul wrote that," I say.

"True." Her voice is so melancholy. I take on the role of the Official Cheerer-Upper.

"And it could be worse."

She rubs her cheek. "I guess."

"She could be calling and telling Travis all of this."

"True."

"Or she could be living in Hudson."

Jen makes a face. "That's true."

"Or with you, for that matter."

"You're right."

I can tell she's starting to cheer up. I pat her shoulder and start measuring six teaspoons of coffee into the coffeemaker.

Jen's stretching now. "Work at nine?" she asks me.

"Yup. You?"

"Yup. Hey, do you want to go look at bridesmaid dresses with me today?"

I look over at her, grinning. "Did you have to ask?"

"I guess not," she says, smiling at me. "We'll go after work. Want to meet here, and then we'll go to Benjamin's Bridal at, say, around five-fifteen? Does that give you enough time?"

I nod and flip the On switch on the coffeemaker. "Plenty of time."

I get to work at nine on the nose. Ethan is two minutes behind me.

"Good morning." I greet him, turning on the lights in the back and pulling on my apron.

"Hey," he says, yawning.

I start grinding the medium roast, true to my assignment on the new spreadsheet taped to the cabinet under the computer.

There's a little sticky note on there, and I pull it off.

What the heck?—*Lisa*

I grin.

Ethan comes in from the back, pulling his apron over his head and logging into his time card on the computer.

"How was your weekend?" I ask, being nice. I might have to work with this guy, but I'm not going to just sit here in silence all day.

"Fine. I just studied. I'm taking two night classes starting next month, and I'm trying to clep out of the first one."

"Oh yeah? I thought you graduated. What classes are you taking?" I move on to grinding the dark roast, and Ethan starts working the other grinder on the light roast of the day: Breakfast Blend.

Again.

Our poor light-roast customers are going to get awfully tired of his lack of creativity. Jack and I always experimented with the flavors. Sometimes a light hazelnut, sometimes an Italian blend, sometimes a Colombian light roast with a sprinkle of cinnamon.

"I'm trying to clep out of a class introducing ancient Roman history, and then I'm taking a class on comparative religions," he says, surprising me. I was assuming they would be about computers or software or something else I have no desire to learn about.

"What religions?" I ask carefully, trying not to sound too excited that he's interested in religion.

"I think it covers everything: Islam, Buddhism, those weird African tree-god religions, Chinese stuff."

"Christianity?" I ask, starting the espresso machine. Time for a morning mocha. I'm going to make it a Mexican mocha. Cinnamon, whipped cream, and chocolate shavings. The perfect way to wake up in the morning!

Ethan shrugs nonchalantly and moves on to grinding the decaf house blend. "Maybe. I really don't know. I'm mostly taking it because I have to take at least two summer classes to stay on my scholarship. It seemed easy."

"Oh." So maybe no interest in religion.

"I've heard the professor isn't into tests or anything. He's supposed to be one of the best teachers there."

Zilch interest in religion. "Best because he doesn't give tests?" I ask.

"Heck, yeah!"

"Oh." I go to the back and pull the cinnamon rolls Kendra made last night out of the fridge. They've risen to palm-size and look amazing. I turn the oven on and pop the rolls inside.

It's Monday, and the retired men's group will be here in twenty minutes. They will want the cinnamon rolls.

I start whipping the cream cheese for the frosting and think about Jen's mom. Candace Mitchell is one of the most critical women I know. Every time I have to interact with her, I try my hardest to find something good about her to focus on instead of her meanness, but I can't ever find anything.

If she's not ragging on me about the size of my hips, she's making snide comments about my curly hair or my lack of a tan.

"You should at least look into a gym," she always says, looking me up and down. "And straighteners will do wonders for that hair. And, Maya, really, they did invent tanning salons for a reason."

Hard to believe that sweet, innocent Jen came from a family like that.

The bell over the door jangles just as I pull the pan of piping hot cinnamon rolls from the oven. It's Mr. O'Neill, and I wave from the back.

"Hi, Maya." He waves back and looks at Ethan. "So you're the new guy."

"What can I get for you, sir?" Ethan asks politely.

"A decaf and a cinnamon roll," Mr. O'Neill says, dropping his weekly dollar tip in the jar.

I'm slathering the frosting on the steaming rolls as quickly as I can. "Leave room for plenty of cream," I call out quietly to Ethan. Mr. O'Neill always assumes we know, since he's been coming here for years.

"Right. Lots of room," Mr. O'Neill says, apparently hearing me. He grins at me as I bring the pan of rolls to the front. "How are you, Maya?"

"Doing well. And you?"

"Doing fine. I'm leading the study today, so I have a valid excuse to be here first this week."

I smile at him. "Sure, sure. You are just one of those early people. Admit it."

"Well . . ." He shrugs.

Mr. Patterson walks in the door then. He's got his Bible under one arm, and he's digging his wallet out of his pocket as he walks over. "Hey, Maya. Lindy said to tell you thanks so much for the cinnamon roll a few weeks ago."

"You're welcome," I grin. "This is Ethan."

"Hi, Ethan." He nods. "How's Jack faring at the zoo?"

I can't help the laugh.

The day flies by, and before I know it, it's after five and Jen and I are on our way to the bridal store. Jen climbs out of the car and skips to the front of the store. She's grinning ear to ear, and she's pretty much jumping up and down.

"You're going to try on bridesmaid dresses!" she squeals when I get out of the car.

I start laughing. "You're so cute."

"I'm getting married!" She's doing a happy dance. "I get to wear a wedding dress!"

"Well, then quit stalling, and let's get in there!" I grab her arm and start walking to the door. "I want to see some lace!"

I push open the door and a nice-looking older woman looks up from a bridal magazine. "Can I help you, ladies?"

The store is little, much smaller than the place where Jen got her wedding dress. But it's cute, and there are racks and racks of bridesmaid dresses in every possible color.

"I'm getting married, and this is my maid of honor, Maya," Jen says, pointing to me, even though it's fairly obvious I'm the maid of honor because I'm the only other person there.

"Hi," I say.

"We're looking for bridesmaid dresses."

The woman nods. "Wonderful. I'm Sylvia; I'll make sure

you are taken care of. Was there a particular style you were looking for?"

Jen looks at me. "Since mine is a halter, does yours need to be a halter too?"

I shrug. "I don't know. I've never been married. Or a bridesmaid. And, honestly, I've never paid that much attention at previous weddings."

Sylvia pipes up. "Not necessarily, no. Why don't we have her try on a variety of styles, and you can pick the one you like the best?"

Jen nods. "Sounds good."

"What colors are you wanting to look at?"

"Greens and cranberry colors. It's a late summer wedding."

Sylvia nods, and we follow her back to a long rack of dresses. "Maya, why don't you go ahead into the dressing room?" she says. She hands me two different dresses, one fuchsia and one sort of the color of Coke. You know, that artificial caramel coloring?

Maybe Sylvia is hard of hearing.

"Try them on for size and style. Both of those come in a beautiful cranberry color," Sylvia says, reading my mind. Or maybe just my confused expression.

She slaps a cranberry color swatch in Jen's face.

"That's pretty," Jen says.

I push the dresses ahead of me into the dressing room. Maybe they look pretty on the swatch, but I can guarantee she's not going to like the fuchsia color on me. I hold the dress up and frown.

It's like a prom dress from the eighties. Loads of ruffles. That line from *27 Dresses* about the bride making the bridesmaids wear horrific dresses so they don't steal the attention from her goes through my brain.

erynn mangum

I pull the dress on as best I can and walk out.

Jen's face is picture-perfect.

"Oh my," she gasps.

"It looks like this one comes in cranberry and a sea-foam green," Sylvia says, reading off a catalog, mistaking Jen's horror for amazement, I guess. "This is by far our most popular choice for bridesmaid dresses."

She nods and stands, coming closer, away from Sylvia. She pokes a ruffle, and it pops right back into place, adding six inches to my hips. "You look like a fuchsia Michelin Man," Jen whispers.

"Please don't make me wear this," I say. "I feel like a 1985 Barbie doll."

She clears her throat. "Let's look at some other styles."

I hurry back into the dressing room.

The artificially colored caramel dress isn't too bad. It's cut on a bias, so I'll need to do a bunch more running before the wedding if Jen picks this dress. It's sleeveless and has a cowl-neck, which I'm not a fan of. A bunch of loose, drapey fabric around my chest isn't usually my idea of attractive. More like a higher probability of some kind of malfunction.

Jen likes it though. "That's cute!"

"Again, this comes in both cranberry and a sapphire green," Sylvia says.

"Oh, this would be so pretty in green!" Jen coos.

And so, the bridesmaid dress is chosen.

I change out of the dress and follow her out of the store a few minutes later. "Who else are you asking to be a bridesmaid?" I ask her.

"Travis's sister, Megan, and my cousin, Lacey."

"Have I met Lacey?" I tag along behind her back to the car

180

like a little lost puppy. I know Travis's sister from when Travis and I were dating.

Suddenly, I realize how awkward this could get.

Jen's busy telling me that no, I've never met Lacey because she lives in the Seattle area and has never made it out to Hudson, but she's Jen's closest cousin. I'm busy worrying now. Weddings mean family, and that means family I've met and hung out with and gone to reunions with before.

"Um. Jen?" I ask, sliding into the passenger seat.

She looks over at me and then sees my expression, which, judging by her reaction, is pretty pained. She frowns. "What?"

"Is this going to be awkward?"

"Is what going to be awkward?"

I just look at her. She gives a slight nod and then slides the key in the ignition.

"I thought about that. Maya, it's been six years. I think it's been long enough. It will only be awkward if we let it be awkward."

So the story goes. I happen to believe that is not true. Right after Travis and I broke up, I ran into his mom, Mrs. Clayton, at Kohl's. Trust me, I was trying not to let it get uncomfortable. I gave her a hug, like I used to before. I tried to talk normally, but you could just tell things had changed and both of us couldn't wait to leave.

"Stop opening and closing the console," Jen says, pushing my hand away from where I was fiddling while I thought. She pulls the car out of the parking lot.

"Oh. Sorry."

"That wears out the spring. It could break before the rest of the car now," Jen gripes.

"I didn't realize I was doing it. I was thinking. Sorry." I look around her newer sedan and roll my eyes. "Like you'll keep this thing for much longer. First comes love, then comes marriage, then comes — "

Jen whacks my arm. "Hush!" she shouts before I finish the age-old nursery rhyme.

"You're going to need a car that fits a few booster seats in the back." I grin, rubbing my arm where she hit me.

"Shhh," she says, covering her lips with one finger. "I don't even want to go there yet."

I give her a look. "You might want to consider going there. You're getting married, after all. Things happen. Didn't your mom get pregnant with you while she was on the pill?" Jen's mom and dad probably wouldn't have had kids except for that little incident four years after they'd gotten married. Jen has told me she sometimes wonders if they would have stayed together if she hadn't been born.

Honestly? I doubt it. It's awful, but I seriously doubt it.

Jen's chewing on her bottom lip now. "Travis and I want to wait at least four years before we even think about kids."

"Why? So you can be thirty and trying to potty train? Almost fifty at graduation? Nearly crippled as grandparents?"

She rolls her eyes at me. "So we can have a nice-size nest egg before the kids come. And so we can travel together and get to know each other."

"Well. From one surprise baby to another . . ."

"Shhh."

I grin. My mom and dad were totally content with one baby. I think the doctors had even told Mom that she would never have any more children.

And yet, here I am.

Jen pulls the car back into the apartment parking lot and turns it off. We sit there for a second, and then she smiles at me. "Oh, Maya."

"Oh, Jen."

"It's so weird to think about."

I know she's talking about marriage, kids, the whole lot of things. I reach over for one of those awkward car hugs. "You guys will be fine."

"I know. It's just weird. This is for the rest of my life." She squints out the windshield. "The *rest* of my *life*. Forever and ever."

"Amen," I finish, smiling at her.

She doesn't laugh. She's back to worrying. "What if we have some horrific fight?"

"Then you'll make up."

She's nibbling on her lip again. I can just picture the scar tissue building up. "What if we buy a house and it burns down?"

"Then you'll collect the insurance and buy a new one."

"What if we have a baby, who is also a surprise, and the baby cries and cries and cries in the middle of the night—"

I stop her before she finishes. "Jen."

"What?"

"You guys will be fine. Travis loves you. You love him. You both love God. What else really matters?" I quote from her previous conversation with her mom.

She sighs, and her posture relaxes slightly. "You're right."

"I know." I pat her arm. "And if the baby won't stop crying, you can call her favorite Aunt Maya to come watch her while you try to sleep."

Jen giggles. "Yeah, right. A truck carting logs could collide with a steamroller in your bedroom, and you wouldn't even change REM cycles."

"Not true. I think I'd notice the trucks in my bedroom."

She grins. We exit the car and climb the metal staircase to our apartment.

The blinds in the front are open, and I peer at them, mouth pursed.

"Hey, Jen?" I question slowly as she flips through her keychain to find the key to the apartment.

"Yeah?" she says distractedly.

"Did we leave the blinds open?"

She looks up and frowns at the blinds. "I didn't open them. I never open them on weekdays when we're gone."

"Me either."

We exchange a long look and then both look back at the door.

"What do we do now?" Jen asks.

I frown. "I'm sure one of us just did it before we left for the bridal store without thinking. It's not like someone is going to break in and open the blinds."

She looks at me worriedly but nods. "You're right."

I get my mace out though, just in case. She nods at the can in my hands. "Good thought."

"Thanks."

She pushes open the door, and I step in. I take one whiff, smell expensive perfume, and almost whirl around and run back down the steps.

I'm not fast enough.

"Jennifer, this disgusting mutt has peed all over the carpet, and I cannot believe this is the way I am greeted after flying all the way out here to see you."

I close my eyes and open them, hoping it's a nightmare or some kind of freaky *Manchurian Candidate* mirage.

Nope. There she stands in the flesh. Pointing a long manicured finger at my quivering puppy. Jen's mom.

Candace Mitchell.

CHAPTER THIRTEEN

"Mom!" Jen gasps.

At least she can speak. I just gape wordlessly from Mrs. Mitchell to my shaking dog. Calvin's cowering under her pointed finger, little wet puddle patches on the carpet.

"What are you doing here?" Jen demands.

"What am I doing here?" Mrs. Mitchell repeats. "Jennifer, I told you this morning that we would continue our conversation. Well, I am here to continue our conversation."

This is Mrs. Mitchell. Who else agrees that's clear for "I'm flying out there to visit you"?

Probably no one.

I pick up my freaked-out dog and sigh at the carpet. Without fail, every time Mrs. Mitchell walks into the apartment, Calvin makes a puddle.

I don't blame him.

Mrs. Mitchell is scowling at him. "He is disgusting. I do not see how you put up with that mutt."

I cuddle Calvin closer and walk back to my bedroom without a word. She doesn't say hi to me; I don't say hi to her. Especially if she's invading my house without permission. And insulting my dog.

Calvin is not disgusting or a mutt. He is very clean, and he's purebred, according to the beagle shelter I got him from as a three-month-old puppy.

I drop Calvin in the tub and bend down, scratching his ears. "Don't worry, buddy. You're a good dog."

He licks my hand pathetically. I turn on the water to a nice warm temperature, and he cheers up.

Calvin loves baths. He's one of those weird dogs.

I grab the carpet cleaner and a clean rag from the laundry room and go back into the living room.

"Mother. You can't just come here and expect to stay until the wedding!" Jen shouts right as I walk in.

I drop the bottle. "Until when?" I gasp.

I don't even get a discarded look. Mrs. Mitchell is glaring at Jen, eyes on fire. "If you are going to make the biggest mistake of your life, then I'm going to be here reminding you of it until that day comes!"

The wedding, the wedding. I do the math in my head. That's like ninety-plus days.

She is *not* staying here that long.

Jen's arguing back, and I bend down to get the cleaner, suddenly noticing the huge pile of suitcases stacked around the recliner.

I squeeze my eyes shut.

Oh no.

"Mother, I'm sorry. I don't mean to be disrespectful, but this is my house and my rules. If you come to visit, you are going to abide by my rule of calling before you come. And you are going to adhere to our rule of a three-day-only stay." Jen holds up a hand, silencing her mom's comeback. "And that is all we are going to say about it. If you would like to stay for three days and *three days* only, then you are welcome to."

Mrs. Mitchell is glowering. "You are the most ungrateful daughter I have ever known," she declares. "After everything I have done for you, you won't even allow me the joy of helping you plan your wedding."

"You don't want to help me plan. You want to break us up."

"He isn't Mitchell Material," Mrs. Mitchell says matter-of-factly, not arguing with Jen's assessment. "However, this seems to be a theme in your life. Neither is this apartment or that mutt or your roommate."

She knows I'm in here and can hear her. I bristle but shut my mouth and scrub at the carpet.

God. Please.

"Maya is my best friend. Her dog is one of the best behaved dogs I've ever known. And this apartment is in a good area of town, it's close to my work, and it has every amenity I could ask for." Jen is amazing. She keeps her voice calm and level. Her hands are shaking, though.

I finish scrubbing the carpet and go back to the bathroom. Three days. Three days in the apartment with that woman.

Calvin is sitting in the water with his head bowed so low that his ears are getting wet. He looks so cute and sad.

"Awww, poor puppy," I coo, kneeling beside the tub and rubbing his little head. "She doesn't know what she's talking about, Cal. Don't take it personally."

"Roo," Calvin sighs.

"If it's any consolation, she doesn't like me either."

Calvin licks my hand, and that's that. We're in this together, as Troy Bolton would say on *High School Musical*.

I squeeze my eyes shut.

God, please . . . please just keep me patient.

I need more than a little prayer right now. I scoop Calvin out of the tub, set him squarely on a big ratty towel, and wrap him up. I carry him to my bedroom and plop him on his little dog bed. He starts licking himself dry.

I grab my Bible and flop on the bed. I remember Andrew quoting from some verse in Ephesians when I was complaining about Mrs. Mitchell before. I finally find it, starting in chapter 4, verse 31.

"Let all bitterness and wrath and anger and clamor and slander be put away from you, along with all malice. Be kind to one another, tender-hearted, forgiving each other, just as God in Christ also has forgiven you. Therefore be imitators of God."

I put the Bible down as it moves on to chapter 5. I blow out my breath slowly, counting like the too-calm yoga instructor at the gym does. "One . . . two . . . three . . . four . . ."

Time for the inner checklist. Bitterness toward Mrs. Mitchell? Check. Wrath toward Mrs. Mitchell? Check. Anger? Big check. Clamor reminds me of cymbals, but if that's referring to the loud bongs going off in my brain any time I'm around her, then check, check, check.

Okay, God. I'll try to be all tender-hearted around her. But this is going to be the hardest thing I've ever done. I squint at the ceiling. *Yep, even harder than Travis dating Jen.*

You know those commercials with the Staples Easy Button? Yeah, I want one of those right about now.

Breakfast Tuesday morning does not go well.

"No fat-free milk, Maya?" Mrs. Mitchell greets me as I walk into the kitchen. I'm aiming for the coffeepot, focused on getting my caffeine and getting out, and I'm repeating "be kind, be kind, be kind" in my brain like some kind of cult mantra.

"Good morning! I think it's 2 percent," I say, trying my best to instill some cheer in my voice. I end up sounding like a squeaky prepubescent Jonathan Taylor Thomas from *Home Improvement*.

Mrs. Mitchell sighs and tilts her head at me. She's showered and is wearing khaki-colored silky slacks and a muted blue top that compliments her blue eyes. Mrs. Mitchell would be very beautiful if she weren't so mean.

"Two percent is not fat-free milk, Maya." She looks pointedly at my waist. "You would do well to switch to fat-free. It will do wonders for those hips."

Be kind. Be kind.

I don't respond. I just pour a cup of coffee.

"Well, both Jen and I are going to work at nine," I say. "What are you going to do today?"

Mrs. Mitchell flips her blond hair over her shoulder. "I told Jennifer she needs to take the day off so we can get some things settled for this wedding, if indeed it happens. That reception place she booked. Have you seen it?"

"Yeah, isn't it beautiful?"

She rolls her eyes. "Clearly, settling runs in this apartment. Maya, a Mitchell does not settle. Not for a man, not for a wedding location."

I'm taking this to mean she doesn't like the park with the gazebo. When Jen took me there, I thought it was probably one of the most beautiful places to get married ever. It's set way back from the road and is surrounded by tons of gorgeous pine and aspen trees. The gazebo has just been repainted a shiny white, and it's almost like a replica of the one in *The Sound of Music*. Can we say romantic?

Plus, there's this huge community center set a ways back from it where Jen wants to have the reception. The ceilings are tall, and the whole building is this light maple-colored stone with white accents. It's gorgeous.

"I think it's beautiful," I say, quietly. "And I think that if Jen likes it — and she's the bride — then she should get her say."

"You would think that. You do not have a reputation to upkeep, Maya. Jennifer does."

I sip my coffee slowly, trying to figure out how to politely leave the kitchen. "Well, I need to go shower," I say loudly and leave.

By the time I'm out of the shower and dressed, both Jen and her mom are gone. Calvin's relaxing on his doggie bed, and I grab a bagel as I run out the door for work.

Ethan beats me there. "Morning, Maya," he says, yawning behind the counter. "You're a little late."

"Jen's mom is staying with us," I say, flipping the sign on the door to *Open*. "Sorry."

"Who's Jen again?"

"Roommate."

He nods. "Oh yeah."

After exchanging my purse for my apron, I wash my hands and go back out to the front.

"Breakfast Blend?" I ask, noticing him pull the beans from under the counter.

"Yeah."

"Maybe you could try a light Italian roast today," I suggest nicely, trying not to step on his toes. I'm not his boss, so I don't want to be the mean one. But seriously, a little variation!

Ethan gives me a quizzical look. "But the Breakfast Blend is the light roast."

"It's one of the light roasts."

"There are more?" He's aghast.

It appears that Jack and I did a horrible job training this guy. "Lots more," I say nicely. "There's Italian, there's a Colombian Blend, there's our light House Blend. Lots of them. You can even use a strong French roast and mix it with our decaf Cinnamon Pecan Blend." That one is amazing. I'm not a light-roast person, but I flip for that one.

"Wow," Ethan says. He puts the Breakfast Blend back under the counter. "So which one would you recommend for today?"

"Cinnamon Pecan. Lower shelf on the right."

"Thanks."

I nod and start on the medium roast. The phone rings and I answer it, popping it between my shoulder and my ear as I measure the medium roast. Tuesday mornings, for whatever reason, can be busy.

"Cool Beans, thanks for calling, this is Maya. May I help you?" I recite.

"Morning, Nutkin."

I hear the familiar gravelly voice, and my heart jumps. "Jack!" I say, suddenly feeling myself grinning ear to ear. "Why are you calling here?"

"I heard there was a beautiful girl working there, so I decided to try my luck at getting dinner with her tonight."

I can feel the blush working across my cheeks, and I turn away from Ethan's smart-aleck grin. "Really? You don't have any trainings?"

"Not tonight. I was told I have an option to do one with Esmeralda, but I told them no."

"Who is Esmeralda?"

"A gorilla."

"Awww, you picked me over the gorilla?"

Ethan evidently hears me because he's now snorting.

"Babe, I will always pick you over the gorilla. Let's go eat. Somewhere swanky where I can show you off. Wear a dress."

"Yes, sir."

"And heels."

"Jack . . ."

"I'll hold you up. I just need to see a human girl who looks like a human girl. None of this camo, khaki, almost-combat-boot thing."

"I'll do my best." I grin and push the On button on the grinder. Jack or not, customers will be here in less than five minutes. The coffee needs to be ready.

"Perfect. I'll see you at six, beautiful. I love you." The phone clicks in my ear, and I set it back on the hook slowly.

"You've got a really goofy look on your face right now," Ethan says. I jump.

"What?"

"Sort of all squishy looking. Like a lovesick sponge." He grins at me and snaps a towel at my leg. "You never told me you liked Jack like *that*."

Here comes the blush again. "Well . . ."

"This explains a lot. All those tears you cried on his last day? I thought you were just one of those super-emotional girls who cries at everything."

Only during a certain time of the month. I don't tell Ethan this, though. Ever noticed how if it's all girls you can complain about periods and cramping, but when there's a guy around you don't know too well, it's suddenly the Forbidden Topic?

"Not usually," I say instead.

"So . . . Maya really likes Jack." He's still grinning as he finishes up on the light roast and our first customer walks in.

It's a lady who comes in at least once a week, so I now know her name. "Hi, Maya," she smiles, pulling a $5 bill from her pocket. "Can I get a medium decaf cappuccino, please?"

Ethan starts making the cappuccino.

I ring her up. "How's it going, Katrina?" I ask, handing her the change. She plunks all of it in the tip jar, as is her custom.

"Very well." She smiles sweetly. "Kevin and I just found out we're pregnant."

"Oh my gosh!" I say, genuinely excited. She had told me awhile ago that she and her husband had been trying for the past two years.

My mom got pregnant with me without even trying, and she always said she wasn't sure how people who had to wait so long did it. "Nine months is hard enough," Mom always said.

Katrina is one of those people, though, who is optimistic about everything. "I wouldn't trade these last two years alone with Kevin for anything," she told me last week.

"When are you due?" I ask, passing over the decaf cappuccino.

"Next February. Try to help me come up with girly names," she says, smiling. "I'm thinking I like Violet."

"Like in *The Boxcar Children*?" I ask.

She laughs. "You and everyone else have that answer!" She waves. "I'm meeting Kevin for brunch. I'll see you later!"

"Bye, Katrina. Congratulations!"

Ethan watches her walk out. "Thus the decaf, I guess," he grins.

I watch him smile to himself as he wipes down the counter. Here's what I'm deciding: Ethan is not half bad.

I get a text from my mom at three fifteen.

Cn U ask JM re srprs dnr?

I stare at it for the next ten minutes. There's a group of giggling junior highers at the bar, three men in suits at a table, and two guys who look about my age doing a Bible study at another table.

Ethan is in the back, making another bowl of frosting for our third batch of cinnamon rolls today. They still have about five minutes in the oven.

What? I write Mom back quickly. Even though Alisha Kane, my boss, doesn't mind if we have our cell phones out while we're working, I think it doesn't look very professional.

Cn U ask JM re srprs dnr?

I think she just hit the resend button. I sigh.

I'll call you after work, I text back.

Ethan comes out with the bowl of frosting. "So, I've decided that I'm officially going to gain twenty pounds working here," he says, inhaling. The sweet scent of cinnamon, sugar, and yeast is lacing the air.

I only laugh.

I call Mom as I'm driving home.

"Hi, honey," she answers the phone. "How are you doing?"

"Fine away from home," I say. "Not so fine at home. Mrs. Mitchell is moving in."

"I'm sorry?"

"Me too."

"No, I mean, she's what?"

"She's moving in. Or she wants to. Jen told her she could stay for three days, and then she had to go."

"Why is she wanting to move in?" Mom is in shock. She has met Mrs. Mitchell before.

"She's wanting to break up Travis and Jen, and I guess she thought it would be easier to do that if she were living in our apartment." I sigh.

"Wow."

"I know."

"I'm sorry, honey."

"It's not your fault; you're not moving in." I rub my forehead. "What were you texting earlier?"

"Oh. Can you ask Jen if Sunday night works for her to come have a surprise dinner at our house?"

I think about this question while I make a right onto my street. "Mom," I say, "if I ask her, won't it ruin the surprise?"

"You don't have to tell her it's a surprise dinner," Mom says. "Just see if she and Travis want to come to my house for dinner. And you and Jack, too, of course."

"What about Zach and Kate?"

"We're going to have carrot cake."

Apparently this is code for: *Yes, they'll be there.* Not sure why carrot cake means that.

"Kate's craving carrot cake like nothing else these days," Mom continues.

"Oh. Even more than Oreos?"

"Even more than Oreos."

"Wow."

"I know," Mom says. She starts giggling. "It's so cute, Maya! I saw her yesterday, and she has the tiniest little tummy showing! Just a little chubbiness."

I'm thinking my sister-in-law does not like this aspect of being pregnant. Kate has always been the perfect-swimsuit-model kind of girl. She's one of those people who works out beyond the recommended workout times. One time she told me that she wakes up just itching for a nice long run.

I have nothing in common with Kate.

I pull into the apartment parking lot and see Mrs. Mitchell's rental car is back. *Swell.*

"Well, Mom, I need to go. I'm home. Pray for me."

"Will do. Love you, Maya."

"Love you, too, Mom." I hang up, grab my purse, take a deep breath, and climb out of the car. I won't be here long. Just long enough to take a quick shower, do something with my curling-out-of-control hair, and put on the dress and heels Jack asked for.

The apartment is deathly quiet as I unlock the front door. No voices, no TV, no radio. Nothing.

I'm hoping Jen didn't take matters into her own hands. I've heard weddings held in jail can be on the tacky side. Orange jumpsuits don't look good on anyone.

I peek over at Jen's closed door. Mrs. Mitchell slept there last night because, and I quote, she "cannot sleep on a flimsy sofa pullout mattress." Evidently, though, Jen can. Let the one who is working forty hours a week and trying to plan a wedding sleep on the flimsy pullout mattress.

I don't want to knock on Jen's door, just in case Mrs. Mitchell is taking a nap. I'm thinking she would not react well.

Calvin is not around either.

As I walk into my room, I find him and Jen snuggled up on the bed, watching *Whose Wedding Is It Anyway?* on my tiny TV. Jen's wearing navy blue sweatpants and a long-sleeved gray thermal shirt. On the TV, the bride is walking down the aisle, the groom is grinning ear to ear, and Jen is blubbering into a very soggy Kleenex. Calvin's half-watching the screen, half-staring at Jen.

"You okay, Jenny?" I ask.

"Oh," she says foggily. "Hi, Maya. Sorry for stealing your TV."

"No problem." I sit next to her on the bed and pet Calvin's head. "What are you doing?"

She dabs at her eyes. "Taking a sanity break. And crying. I hope Travis looks at me like that guy looked at her."

"He does."

"I mean on our wedding day." More sniffling. "What if he hates my dress?"

Personally, I find this a dumb question. But you don't say that to someone who is on the verge of matrimony. Emotions take over. It's better to be understanding.

"He's not going to hate the dress," I say, my voice all monotone like my sophomore English teacher. "Even if you came down the aisle in a dress made completely out of rubber bands woven together, he'd still find you insanely attractive."

She giggles.

Mission accomplished. I hate it when Jen cries.

I rub her hand. "How'd it go today?"

She knows I mean with her mom. Jen's eyes fill again. "Well, she hates the reception place, she hates the restaurant that's catering, and she thinks my dress is unattractive. So, not good."

"Oh, Jenny."

"And, on top of that, I can't get ahold of Travis, and I need to talk to him. He doesn't even know Mom is in town." She swipes at her eyes with her knuckles and lets out her breath. "She's taking a nap. So, I'm going to sit here and watch *Whose Wedding Is It Anyway?* and be thankful that at least my life doesn't have three kids from a previous marriage, a drunken ex-husband, or a mother of the groom who wants to wear an all-white dress to the wedding."

"Way to be optimistic." I applaud her.

"What are you doing tonight?"

"Jack is picking me up at six for a dinner date. I have to wear a dress." I grin.

She perks up immediately. "Maya! Go get in the shower right now—it's almost five thirty!" She pushes me off the bed and clambers off as well. "I'll start looking through your clothes. Go!"

I do as she says, and when I come back into my room in my huge terry-cloth robe with a towel wrapped around my head, Jen has five different dresses laid out on the bed, three of which are hers.

"Like I can fit into these," I say, pointing to the three on the end.

"Please. Maya, you definitely can. And they are my shorter dresses, so they'll be just the perfect length for you—right at the knee."

I'm still dubious, but I try them on for her. She ends up liking one of hers the best, an all-white eyelet lace dress.

"Wear those woven strappy wedge sandal things of yours, and you're set!" she says.

I agree, blow-dry my hair in record time, then slap on some mascara, eyeliner, and eye shadow. The doorbell rings at six on the nose.

I can hear stirring in Jen's room, but we don't even go near her door. Jen gives me a hug. "Have fun tonight, okay?"

Her cell buzzes as I reach for the door. "It's Travis!" she says, relief filling her voice. "Have a good time, Maya." She disappears back into my room, phone to her ear.

I open the door, and Jack whistles. "Wow!"

I'm pretty sure I blush. "Thanks," I say. "You look nice, too." And he does. He wearing on nice jeans and a button-down shirt. His hair is all spiky and perfect, and he's grinning at me.

"How does Alejandro's sound for dinner?" he asks, leading the way down the metal staircase. I close and lock the apartment door behind me, praying that Travis will come take Jen away from her mom.

"Sounds great," I say. Alejandro's is this adorable little Mexican restaurant, and all the tables are lit by candlelight.

Jack opens the passenger door for me and then walks around to get in himself. "So, how are you?" he asks, starting the car.

"A little frazzled, but that's only natural since Mrs. Mitchell moved in."

"What?" he gapes.

"She wants to help 'plan the wedding,'" I say, using my fingers for quotation marks.

Jack snorts. "Yeah, right! I bet she just wants to break them up. Doesn't she hate Travis?"

"Well, he's not Mitchell Material," I say. "I can understand why she's upset." I roll my eyes. "Apparently, Jen has poor taste in roommates, too. Mrs. Mitchell was kind enough to point that out."

"She's insane. Jen has great taste in roommates!" Jack looks over at me as he pulls to a stop in front of a red light. "And here's a question I've always wanted to ask: Why does she still go by Mrs. Mitchell and refer to Mitchell Material if she is no longer a Mitchell?"

"Maybe in her mind, she is still a Mitchell." I frown. "I don't know. I've never thought about it." I'll have to ask Jen later.

Jack sighs. "Well, let's just forget Mrs. Mitchell and enjoy dinner, okay?"

"Can do." I nod.

He pulls into the restaurant parking lot, and we get out of the car. Alejandro's is crowded tonight. He holds my hand as we navigate through the group of people waiting around the hostess booth.

"I have a reservation for six fifteen under Dominguez," he tells the hostess, who looks like she's around fifteen. She's thin as a rail, and I almost want to tell her that she might need to eat more of Alejandro's amazing sopapillas.

She checks her list. "Okay. Right this way, sir." She leads us to a quiet little corner table. The candles in the center of the table are flickering, and all around us are couples out on dates.

This is definitely a dating restaurant. I don't know if it's the risk of a child catching on fire from the candles or what, but I've never seen any kids here. It keeps the decibel level down.

We sit, and the hostess hands us our menus and leaves.

I look over at Jack. He isn't looking at his menu; he's grinning at me. "What?" I say self-consciously. I haven't even started eating, so the odds of there being something on my face are low.

"Nothing. I'm not allowed to look at you?"

"You look like the Cheshire Cat."

"That's because I'm happy." He grins even wider.

I hold up my menu in front of my face. "Well, I'm glad you're happy, but seriously. You're weirding me out."

He laughs.

I decide I'm getting the rolled enchiladas. California Mexican food can usually leave something to be desired in the way of spice, but Alejandro's is pretty good about going that extra chili mile.

"What are you getting?" I ask Jack.

"Tacos."

"We come to the best Mexican restaurant in town, which is code for the most expensive, and you're going to order something you could get for eighty-nine cents down the street at Taco Bell?"

He shrugs. "Why not?"

Jack Dominguez has, as you would guess by his name, a Hispanic background. His mom makes the best homemade salsa I've ever tasted. Jack's mom used to send him to school every day with homemade tamales in his lunch. My mom sent me with tuna fish.

I hate tuna fish. And for all of Jack Dominguez's Spanish name, he just doesn't get into Mexican food. Which is actually how we met, way back in the second grade.

We were lunch-swapping buddies.

I just shake my head at him getting tacos. Seems like a waste of good money spent on Mexican food.

"So, how's the zookeeping?" I ask, grinning. "Still zooing well?"

He sighs. "Yes, Nutkin. It's all good."

"Thanks for skipping out on Esmeralda the Gorilla for me."

"Thanks for coming out with me." His brown eyes are sparkling at me. He reaches across the table and picks up my hand. "I miss seeing you more."

"Me too."

"It won't always be this bad. How's Ethan doing?" Jack asks.

"Really well. He's actually a nice guy. He's taking a religion class this summer, so I'm hoping to talk more about Christianity with him."

"Good," Jack says, nodding, as our server comes over. "I'll be praying that goes well."

"Good evening, folks, can I get your orders?"

We tell him our orders, and he leaves. Jack is still holding my hand across the table. "So," he says.

"So," I echo.

"How are Jen's wedding plans going?"

"Good, I think. She's got her dress, the bridesmaid dresses, and the reception place picked out." I scowl. "Unless Mrs. Mitchell convinces her otherwise."

Jack lifts up a hand. "No talk of Mrs. Mitchell, remember?"

"Fine." I rub my forehead. "It's better this way. I'm trying to be kind."

"New Bible verse?" he asks, grinning.

"Be kind to one another, tender-hearted, forgiving each other, just as God in Christ also has forgiven you" (Ephesians 4:32), I quote to him. I've been working on that verse all day.

Jack nods. "Very impressive. How's the application coming?"

This is how Jack is: He isn't afraid to ask me tough questions about my walk. I think it's a good thing.

Mostly.

"Well, I'm just trying to keep my mouth shut around her," I say, referring to Mrs. Mitchell.

"So being kind is the lack of being rude?"

I quirk my head. "Uh . . . sure."

"You don't think it's an action in itself?"

"Kindness? Uh . . . sure." I frown. "What do you mean?"

"Is doing someone else a favor being kind?"

"Uh . . ." I stop myself before I sound like one of the mimicking parrots at the zoo. "I guess so."

"So kindness is an action."

This is what I hate about Jack: He won't just come right out and tell you his point; he has to take you in seven different circles before you finally just tell him, "Okay, I get it!"

"Okay, I get it!" I say.

He leans back in his chair. "Good. I like that verse, by the way."

"Thanks. I used to, too."

He just laughs.

We're back at the apartment by nine. Jack's already yawning as he pulls into the parking lot.

"Is that supposed to be a reflection on our date?" I ask.

"What? Oh, no, Nutkin, I'm sorry. I'm just still getting used to these early mornings. I didn't know there were earlier work days than our old seven o'clock shift." He yawns again. "I had a great time with you tonight."

"Mm-hmm." I smile nicely at him. "Thanks for dinner. Go to bed."

"Yes, ma'am. Right after I walk you up."

"You don't need to walk me up," I say, grabbing my purse and opening my door. "Go home to bed, Jack. I'll see you soon."

He yawns again at the steering wheel. "Hang on, Nutkin." He gets out and comes over to give me a hug. He pulls me in tightly and kisses the top of my head. "I love you."

"Love you, too. Thanks for dinner! Sweet dreams, Jack." I grin.

Instead of taking the hint and leaving, he climbs the stairs with me and waits until we hear my key make the little click that means the door unlocked.

"Good night, Pattertwig," he says, grinning at me, kissing my cheek, and then going back down the stairs. I wait until he's back in his car, wave, and walk in the apartment.

Jen is sitting in the living room, arms crossed over her chest, eyes bleary when I walk in. Her mom is standing in the kitchen, griping about our low-fat, versus nonfat, cottage cheese.

Is there such a thing as nonfat cottage cheese?

"Hi," I say, walking in. Jen looks at me and brightens a smidge.

"Hey, Maya. How was the date?"

"Fun. We went to Alejandro's." I hold up the plastic grocery bag I am carrying. "And we stopped and got nonfat milk for your mom."

Jen's eyebrows go up. "Wow. That's really sweet of you, Maya."

I walk in the kitchen and put the half gallon in the fridge. Mrs. Mitchell is now slicing an apple on our cutting board.

"Back from your date already?" She says this like I'm a horrible date. Not that I'm disagreeing, considering Jack's mountainous yawns just now, but she doesn't have to rub it in.

Be kind.

I keep my mouth shut.

"What did you guys do this evening?" I ask a minute later, washing my hands and pulling out a bag of popcorn. Popcorn is a favorite snack food of mine. Especially that Orville Redenbacher's Kettle Korn stuff. Delightful.

I peel the plastic off the bag and shove it in the microwave.

Mrs. Mitchell watches disapprovingly. "Do you know how many saturated fats are in bagged popcorn?"

"Guess I'd rather they be saturated and all stick together than be unsaturated and stick to me," I say cheerfully.

"I do not think that is how it works, Maya."

I watch the bag slowly inflate in the microwave. "Hmm. Oh well. So what did you do this evening?"

"Mostly argued with Jennifer's father over the wedding," she says bitterly, hacking away at the apple. "Tightwad. I remember why we got divorced."

Jen pipes up from the other room. "Mother, he is not being a tightwad. Seventy-five thousand dollars is a ridiculous amount of money to spend on a wedding."

"You say this because you have never gotten married," Mrs. Mitchell retorts. "She has no idea how expensive it is," she says to me in a low voice. "When I got married, just between our photographer and our reception venue, it cost $20,000."

So, it was worth this exorbitant amount of money to get divorced? I pull the bag of popcorn out of the microwave silently. The whole kitchen is filled with the mouthwatering scent of salty sweetness.

I feel like Elizabeth Bennet on *Pride and Prejudice*. "If I could love a man who would take me for a mere fifty pounds, I shall be very well pleased."

Isn't that in Proverbs somewhere? Something to the extent of "Better to live like church mice where there is love than to have a castle in Austria where there is hostility?"

Something like that.

I pour the popcorn into a bowl and carry it to the living room. Mrs. Mitchell is right behind me with her butchered apple. Jen's got both knees pulled up to her chest and a wan look on her face.

"Popcorn smells good," she says when I sit next to her.

"Good. We can share. I can't eat this whole bowl."

"Saturated fats," Mrs. Mitchell sing-songs under her breath, crunching on her apple.

It's to both Jen's and my credit that we don't say anything.

I get home Thursday afternoon from work and bust into the apartment excitedly. "Jen!" Mrs. Mitchell's flight was supposed to leave at three o'clock this afternoon, which means we've been free for two whole hours.

"She's not home."

I nearly drop the two congratulatory "We Made It" lattes from Cool Beans. Mrs. Mitchell appears from Jen's bedroom, holding a copy of *Big Budget Brides*. She's got her reading glasses on.

"She's . . . uh, not? Um, I thought your flight left today." I'm trying really hard not to scowl, but I imagine my expression looks like I ate a pair of cranberry-scented candles for lunch.

"Yes. It was canceled." She says this matter-of-factly, squinting at me through her reading glasses. I'm amazed Mrs. Mitchell has reading glasses. They say money can buy happiness, and while I disagree with that, it evidently can buy you the body of a twenty-year-old. And Mrs. Mitchell bought it.

Except LASIK for her eyes. Weird.

"Canceled?" I repeat. "By you or by the airline?" The words come out of my mouth before I can stuff them into the back of my throat. I blame my hands being full.

Oh, no. Not good. I'm sorry, Lord!

"Sorry," I say quickly, while she's gathering steam into her posture. She's slowly straightening. "I didn't mean that. It was uncalled for."

"You have that right, Maya Davis. Completely uncalled for! If I say my flight was canceled, then it was canceled. Do you hear me?"

I wince. She's not screaming; she's not yelling. But that false calm monotone is almost scarier. "Yes, ma'am."

"Thank you. Jen is not home yet. It is after five; I have no idea where she could be."

"She must be running late at work. I'm going to go change."
I hightail it to my room.

Calvin is huddling on his dog bed, most likely scared to
come out of my room. I set the lattes on the dresser and bend
down in front of my puppy. "Hi, buddy."

"Roo," he huffs.

"I know." I stroke his silky ears. "She's definitely not our eas-
iest houseguest." I would give that award to my cousin, Ashley.
She came for one night on her way to Los Angeles, slept on the
sofa, didn't eat my favorite cereal, and left by ten o'clock the next
morning.

Easy.

My phone is vibrating in my pocket, and I pull it out. It's a
text message from Jen.

*Hi, Maya! Travis and I are going out for dinner, just to let you
know. I'll be home later! Love ya!*

I'm assuming, by the happy exclamation points everywhere,
that she doesn't know about her mother's flight being canceled.

Canceled, my foot. I bet she called the airlines this morning
and cashed in that ticket.

I sigh. I look at my big queen bed and think about Jen sleeping on that crappy sofa pullout for the next three and a half
months before the wedding.

I don't want her posture to be ruined for the pictures, right?
Or for there for be huge dark circles under her eyes in every pose.

After one family reunion in the fifth grade, I swore I'd
never share my bed again, or at least not until after marriage.
The adults all thought it was a great idea to pile all the girls in
one room on two queen-sized mats. First off, there were nine
girls, and, second, my cousin Megan kicks like an old Western

showgirl in her sleep. She gave me two cracked ribs at three o'clock in the morning. I didn't completely heal for a month.

So, there was only one thing to do.

Jen doesn't get home until almost eleven. I hear the lock click right as I'm spreading out my old lilac-colored quilt my grandmother made for me on the sofa bed. Mrs. Mitchell went to bed a long time ago, claiming she had a headache.

I think she just didn't want to face her daughter.

Jen comes in all happy, her eyes shining for the first time in three days. "Hey, Maya!" she says. She looks at me, looks at the sofa bed, looks at her closed bedroom door, and the sparkle in her eyes disappears as she collapses on the love seat. "What. Happened?" Calvin slinks over and nudges her leg.

"Her flight was canceled," I say quietly.

"Canceled," Jen repeats dubiously. "Right."

My thoughts exactly, but I don't say anything. "I think we might just need to recognize that she's going to be here for a while," I say, again quietly. You never know who is pressed up against the door listening.

"Ha!" Jen says, standing suddenly. She scares Calvin so badly that he dives under the sofa bed. "She is not!"

"Jen. Decibel level," I remind her, jerking my head back at her closed bedroom door.

"I don't care! I can't spend the rest of my engagement in a near-breakdown!" Her hands are shaking as she wrings them together.

I finish with the quilt and go put my arm around Jen. "It'll be okay. Don't worry! Maybe she won't stay that long."

I hope Jen is seeing my point. Until Mrs. Mitchell is

convinced it's time for her to go, she's not going to leave. And with today's airport-security measures preventing us from making 100 percent sure she's on the plane, we'd drop her off at the airport, and she'd just get a taxi to bring her right back here.

Jen sits back down, and I sit beside her. She rubs her eyes with her fists. "How come I wasn't born into a family like yours, Maya?" she asks softly.

I don't think she's wanting an answer. I just wrap my arm back around her shoulders, and we sit quietly like that for a long time.

She finally pulls in a deep breath. "Well, we have to work tomorrow."

"Yeah." I point to the sofa bed. "I already made it up for me. You can have my bed. I changed the sheets. And you can just move in there if you want. I made some room in the dresser, too."

Jen is shaking her head. "No. My mom, my reason for the sofa bed."

"You're getting married, Jen. The least I can do is let you get a good night's sleep before then." I give her a hug and stand. "Night, Jen."

She hugs me back. "Thank you, Maya."

I flick the overhead light, and the living room pitches into blackness. I feel my way to the sofa bed and climb in.

Creee-akkkka! The whole bed shudders as I climb in. Maybe there is something to that saturated-fat thing Mrs. Mitchell was talking about.

I pull the covers up to my nose and try to lie very still. There's just something creepy about sleeping in a living room, regardless of whether or not it's yours. One time, when I was a little kid, I had the worse case of bronchitis ever, and my mom made me sleep on the reclining chair in the living room. I slept about two hours the whole night because I kept dreaming that a stick figure was trying to break in the window.

I hated that tree for a long time after that.

I'm finally drifting to sleep when the fridge kicks on. *Vvvvvrrrrrr!* I jump, realize what it is, and fall back onto the bed, which then creaks like a rusty garage door going down. There's a spring digging right between my vertebrae.

It could be a long night. I think I know why my cousin Ashley only stayed one night with us.

CHAPTER FOURTEEN

"Maya? Maya, are you okay?"

The time: 8:55, Monday morning.

The place: Cool Beans.

The person interrupting my sleep on the couch in front of the fireplace: Ethan.

I crack one eye open at him. I got here at seven because I couldn't sleep; I figured at least I could get some work done. So I got the coffee all ground, the counters all cleaned, and the fireplace crackling.

Which is when my head found the pillows on the sofa.

I clamp my eyes shut again. "Mmfpg."

"What?"

"Leave me alone."

"Maya, it's almost opening time." He pokes me in the arm. "You might want to get up. Doesn't Alisha come in on Mondays?"

My boss does come in on Monday mornings. I groan and roll to my back, stretching my arms up. I finally open my eyes and focus on Ethan, who is standing right above me.

"Good morning," he says, grinning. "You have the lines from that pillow imprinted on your face."

Swell.

I rub at my cheek, and, yup, it does feel oddly accordion-like. I push myself up to a sitting position and stay there for a minute, legs dangling off the couch, head bowed.

"What's wrong?" Ethan asks. "I thought you didn't drink."

Ah, a reference to our heated debate on alcohol consumption last Friday. I learned something about myself last week: I should never have heated debates when I'm running on a grand total of two and a half hours of sleep.

"We need a new sofa bed," I mutter.

"Why are you sleeping on a sofa bed?"

"So Jen can look pretty in her wedding pictures."

Ethan quirks his head, but he doesn't say anything. Instead, he holds out his hands. I grab them, and he hauls me off the sofa. "What time did you get here this morning?" he asks, noticing that all the coffee prep work is done.

I yawn. "About seven, I think."

"Seven," he repeats, shaking his head. "Buy a new sofa bed, for Pete's sake. They are only a couple hundred bucks."

Only a couple hundred bucks. Spoken like a true nonbudgeter person, whom I used to be. But one week of groceries for an extra person who has expensive taste in food and looking ahead to three months of groceries, water, and electricity from this same woman who also likes thirty-minute showers, and I can't afford a couple hundred dollars replacing something we shouldn't need to replace.

"Ugh," I say.

"Or you can just buy the mattress. I've heard those are cheap," Ethan says. "I once had a roommate who slept on his sofa full time after they replaced the mattress because he thought it was so comfortable."

"I thought we agreed that your taste in roommates was weird," I say, going to the back. I splash some water from the sink on my face and wince at the coldness. Dabbing it off with a paper towel, I check my reflection in the tiny mirror above the sink that Kendra put there so she could check her makeup before she goes home.

"Never underestimate the power of a good mascara on the man you love," she told me one time. I laughed.

"On the man you love?" I grinned.

I'm not sure the man I love would wear mascara.

My face has very vivid imprints of the pillow. I sigh and swipe at the eyeliner smear under my eyes.

I didn't even get to see Jack this weekend. His boss made him work since it was apparently going to be extra busy for no reason at all. So, I went to Jen's nonsurprise dinner thrown by my mom with Jen and Travis, Zach and Kate, Mom and Dad. Then there was me. Maya and No One.

I wanted to spontaneously burst into "All by Myself" like Renée Zellweger does on *Bridget Jones's Diary*, but that seemed a little flashy, considering the party was not for me.

Jen was surprised by the gifts, though, so that's all that matters. My mom and dad have considered her their second daughter since we moved in together after college. And considering Jen's own parents, I don't think she could be happier.

And Zach and Kate got to show off the pictures of Mystery Gender baby. They aren't telling. Cruel. Just cruel.

Mrs. Mitchell stayed home. Mom said we needed to extend the invitation to her, so I reluctantly did. But she said she was not a fan of homemade chicken pot pie because of the calories.

"It's like eating straight fat," she said, shuddering.

More for me, I say. My mom's chicken pot pie is legendary

in these parts. Jack couldn't believe he missed it when I talked to him Sunday night.

"I miss you more than the pot pie, though," he said sadly on the phone at midnight.

"I miss you, too," I repeated like a good girlfriend. But really, I just miss not saying those words every time I talk to him.

I walk back out to the front of Cool Beans, pulling my apron on. I loop the strings in the back and then tie it in the front.

We already have two customers. Ethan's making a cinnamon latte. "Can you get the medium mocha MixUp?" he asks me. He's put the cinnamon rolls in the oven, so in twenty minutes the whole room will smell amazing.

As messy as it is to make a MixUp, it's also my favorite drink to make. "Sure," I say, smiling at the lady in front of the counter. "Did you want whipped cream on top?"

"No thanks," she says.

Such a shame.

I blend the ice and the drink together and pour it into a cup. I snap a lid on top and pass it across the counter to her. "Here you go."

"Thanks."

Ethan finishes with the other lady's latte at the same time, and the two of them settle with their drinks at a table, chatting about husbands and kids.

Alisha walks in right then, pushing her sunglasses up into her dark hair. "Good morning, kids," she says to us. She frowns at me. "What happened to your face?"

"A pillow was sleeping on me," I say.

She laughs. "Hard morning, I take it?"

I smile at her and start making her favorite drink, an americano.

I pass the americano over to her, listening to her chat with Ethan. "Glad to hear classes are going well," she says. "Let me know if you need fewer hours to get homework done." She sips the coffee and nods her approval. "Or you can even bring it here and study on the downtime, if you want. As long as it doesn't bother Maya."

I shrug, because it doesn't bother me.

"Great. Good," Alisha says. She takes another sip of her coffee. "Very good americano, by the way, Maya."

"Thanks." I grin. "Does this mean I get a raise?"

"No. But you are a valued employee of Cool Beans, and for that, I thank you," she grins.

I fake a sigh.

"Okay. Let me get the list from Kendra," Alisha says. Every Monday our chef, Kendra, leaves a grocery list of supplies that we need. I go find it in the back.

It's a long list this week.

"Here you go." I hand it to Alisha, and she tucks it in her enormous purse.

"Thanks, Maya. All-righty, you two have a good day!" She picks up her americano, slides her sunglasses back on her face, and leaves with a wave.

Jen sends me a text at one fifteen. *Have a late meeting tonight at six with Wayne because he forgot about it this morning. Just wanted to warn you so you're not home alone with Mom. <3*

I click my phone closed and sigh. Swell. So I need to burn at least an hour if not more. I get a great idea right then.

I'm in the middle of my lunch break, so I log on to the computer in the back. Really, it's there for Kendra to look up recipes because she never remembers them and for the employees still in school to do their homework on breaks.

I'm neither one, but I figure I should get some computer time, too.

I go to Google and type in "Hudson Zoo." It immediately brings up a list of related links, and I click on the zoo's website.

It's open until eight tonight.

Perfect! I finish eating the peanut-butter sandwich I brought from home and set the computer back into sleep mode. I'll go visit Jack at the zoo after work today.

Never mind the jokes that immediately flood my mind.

Even though Hudson, California, is a relatively small town, the Hudson Zoo is fairly large. We attract a lot of the surrounding cities because of the easy commute to San Diego and the beach. Plus, there are a lot of bed-and-breakfast type places here, so most of the older crowd drives to Hudson, stays the night, visits the zoo and the little touristy shops around, and then drives to San Diego in the evening when it is cooler.

And since Cal-Hudson is here, we have a lot of college kids roaming around on the weekend with nothing to do. So, they go to the zoo.

It's a good plan.

I pull into the parking lot of the zoo at five thirty. I think I remember Jack saying he was working with the African exhibit. If I can't find him, I'll give him a call.

I pay the exorbitant price for a ticket and walk inside. The first smell that hits me?

Flamingos.

I never knew they were such stinky birds. I wrinkle up my

nose and frown at the sign that tells me it's breeding season, so it's the water that stinks because the zoo can't change it right now.

Too Much Information.

"Need a map, miss?" a guy in a camo shirt and khaki shorts asks me. He's sporting hiking boots and a safari hat, and he's got a name tag that says, "Hi, I'm SAFARI MIKE." There's the little *We Can Zoo It* patch on his shirt as well.

I try my best to hide a smirk.

He hands me the map and sighs. "Kills me every time," he mumbles as he turns away.

"What?" I ask.

"This stupid outfit. The hat, the patch, the boots." He sighs again. "I see a pretty girl, and I think, *Oh, I'll go give her a map, and maybe we can start talking*, but nope. Women can't see past the uniform."

I smile nicely. "I wouldn't be too upset. Some women are attracted to guys in uniform."

"Yeah, but zoo uniforms?"

I have to give him that one. "Do you know where Jack Dominguez is?" I ask.

"Jack?" Safari Mike's eyes change subtly. "So you're Maya."

"What?"

"Are you not her?"

I nod. "I'm Maya."

"Jack talks about you all the time. To the point where I thought he was making you up." He grins.

I feel a blush coming on. "Really?"

"Really. And yeah, he's in the African exhibit." He takes my map back and opens it, pulling a green highlighter from his pocket and uncapping it with his teeth. "You want to go past the flamingos, make a right at the Asia exhibit, and then follow the signs that say 'To Africa.' Shouldn't take you more than ten minutes." He folds the map back up and hands it to me.

"Okay," I say. "Thanks, uh, Safari Mike."

"I actually prefer Caravan Mike, but that's okay." He grins again. "Nice to meet you, Maya." He moves on to the next group coming in the gate.

I hold my map in both hands as I walk through the zoo. I pass the stinky flamingos, who are squawking out their apologies to the public about the smell. I make a right when I see the big, rough-hewn wooden sign for Asia. I pass the pandas that are lazily crunching on huge bamboo sticks.

I haven't been to the Hudson Zoo since freshman year at Cal-Hudson, when my professor had us all go for a class trip.

I finally make it to the African exhibit. There are tons of bright, happy colors everywhere and little trading-post type stores along the path to the animals. I see about ten people in the camo and khaki uniform, but no Jack.

"Excuse me," I say to one of them, who's name tag says, "Hi, I'm SAFARI TIM."

"Yes?"

"Do you know where Jack Dominguez is?"

"Giraffe exhibit. Pass the cheetahs. If you come to the antelope, you've gone too far," he says.

"Thanks." I pass the cheetahs and decide that for being the fastest animal, they sure are lazy during the day. Finally I find the giraffes.

And Jack.

I can't help the smile. Because our Friday date was canceled, I haven't seen him for a week now. He's wearing his camo shirt and khaki shorts, and a safari hat is smashing down his typically gelled hair. He's raking big bushels of grass over a section in the exhibit. Two giraffes are watching him curiously.

I step up to the fence and cup my hands around my mouth. "Here, Giraffey! Here, Giraffey! I have some nice wheat for you!"

"I'm sorry, no feeding the . . ." Jack looks up and then bursts into a grin. "Maya!"

Considering how rarely he says my name, I'm thinking he's glad I came.

"Surprised?" I call over.

He swipes at his sweat-moistened forehead with the back of his hand. "And very happy! How late can you stay?"

I shrug. "Whenever."

"Great! Stay until I get off. It's only two hours. There's plenty to do!" He points to the map in my hands. "Go look at the pregnant lioness. She's gotten really big this last week."

"Okay."

"And the monkeys are always fun," he grins. "Gosh, Nutkin, I'm so glad you're here!"

A couple of the people looking at the giraffes give me a weird look when Jack says my nickname, but I don't care. I smile. "I'll see you in a little bit," I say.

"Okay. And stay away from Safari Mike. He's on the hunt."

"I noticed."

Jack just sighs and then waves and gets back to raking the grass bushels.

I wander over to the pregnant lioness and feel bad for the poor girl. Not only is she in captivity, not only is it extremely hot today, but she gets to be hugely pregnant on display in front of everyone.

She is lying in the corner, huffing in the heat.

There's a zookeeper girl standing in front of the exhibit,

informing everyone that, no, Sasha the Lioness doesn't have a tumor, but she's about to have a baby. "Probably sometime in these next two weeks," the girl tells one older man.

Her name tag says, "Hi, I'm SAFARI PRESLEY."

Aha. Presley.

I try not to make it obvious that I'm looking at her instead of the lioness. For all of Jack's love of zoo animals, I'm not the biggest fan. They're smelly, loud, and mostly they just sleep. And I feel bad that they are behind bars. It's like going to a jail and looking at all the inmates.

So, I look at Presley out of the corner of my eye instead.

She's pretty in a nature-girl kind of way. She's got really short, straight blond hair poking out from under her safari hat, and she isn't wearing any makeup. She has brown eyes and fair skin.

And now she's looking at me. "You look familiar," she says with a friendly smile. "Have we met?"

"I don't think so," I say.

Then she snaps her fingers. "Wait. Are you Jack's girlfriend? Maya, right?"

"Yeah."

She nods and smiles again. "He has a picture of you in his locker."

It sounds so high-schoolish.

I again try to hide my smirk, but Presley sees it.

"I know, I know. It's lame. Just like these name tags." She rolls her eyes. "Anyway, it's nice to finally meet you, Maya!"

"Nice to meet you, too," I say.

Fears have been set aside. I blow my breath out as I make my way over to the Arctic exhibit. Why do I always worry so much?

Sorry, Lord. It's ingrained in me.

So is sin, but that doesn't mean I stop chipping it out of my life.

True. Help me to stop worrying then.

I spend the rest of the two hours wandering around the zoo, looking at the animals, and the last thirty minutes alone watching the penguins. They're so funny! There are a few babies in the bunch, toddling around with their little fluffy gray feathers.

They're cute.

"Hey, Pattertwig," Jack says, coming up beside me.

"I want a penguin," I say, pointing to a particularly animated little guy. "Can I have him for my birthday?"

"You don't want a penguin," Jack says. He rubs his forehead. "They are messy and smelly and loud."

"Oh."

He grins at me and gives me a brief hug. "I'm all sweaty, so you don't want a long hug." He excuses himself. "This is a nice surprise!"

"I hoped you'd think so."

He grins. "So, have you had dinner?"

I had a cinnamon roll before I left Cool Beans, but I'm thinking this isn't a good dinner. "Not really."

"Let's go get a hamburger or something. I'd take you somewhere nicer, but these are the only clothes I have, and I smell like giraffe."

I giggle.

We end up at Ed's, a little burger place near my apartment. They're open late, and they're renowned for their bacon cheeseburgers.

Jack orders one of those, but I'm a purist. Just a regular

cheeseburger for me, no frills like bacon or avocado and definitely no mayo.

"Well, you're boring," Jack says after they set our burgers in front of us at our table.

"Thanks."

"Let me pray." He grabs my hand. "God, thank You for this amazing girl and this great surprise. Help us to honor You with our lives. Amen."

His prayer kind of rhymes, but I've always heard it's poor form to poke fun at people's prayers, so I fill my mouth with hot, greasy cheesiness and stay quiet.

Jack swallows and smashes a napkin on his lips. "So, what have you been up to, Nutkin?"

"Sleeping on a sofa bed." It doesn't make me excited to go home.

Jack gapes. "She's still here?"

"Yep. A week now. She's going to stay until the wedding—I just know it." It's depressing to think about. There is a reason sofa beds were created to be uncomfortable. It's so guests won't stay past the three-day mark.

My mother taught me that rule. Three days was the maximum you ever stayed with anyone, otherwise you risk outstaying your welcome.

"So, is Mrs. Mitchell succeeding, then?" Jack asks.

"I don't think so. I don't think Travis has come by the apartment since she's been in town. They've been meeting places."

"Poor Jen," Jack says. Then he brightens. "You know what we should do?"

"What?"

"Have dinner just the four of us. We've never gone on a double date with them before. What do you think?"

I grin. "Great idea!"

"Let's do Friday. I should get off about six. We could meet at a restaurant at seven, so I have time to go home and shower. A little bit of a late dinner." He finishes his burger and starts on the fries.

Jack must be ravenous. I'm only about a third of the way through my cheeseburger.

He gives me a hug fifteen minutes later outside Ed's. "Love you, Nutkin. I'll see you on Wednesday, I hope."

That means he won't, so I hug him a little tighter. "Bye, Jack. Love you, too."

I get home, and all the lights in the apartment are off. "Hello?" I call out, feeling a little creeped out.

I flip on the living room light, and there's a note on the kitchen counter.

Went to meeting with DJ with Travis. —Jen

Her bedroom door is closed, so I'm going to assume Mrs. Mitchell was not happy and went to bed.

It's almost ten, so I pull the sofa bed out, straighten the sheets, and put the quilt that is stashed in the hall closet back on the bed. I walk into my room and find Calvin crashed out on his doggy bed. He's been sleeping a lot lately. I think Mrs. Mitchell makes him agitated.

So he sleeps.

I dig my pajamas out of my closet and go brush my teeth. By the time I'm climbing into the squeaking bed, it's ten thirty. And I'm exhausted!

I think Mrs. Mitchell makes me agitated, too.

I drag my Bible over to my lap and open it to Ephesians

again: "For you were formerly darkness, but now you are Light in the Lord; walk as children of Light (for the fruit of the Light consists in all goodness and righteousness and truth), trying to learn what is pleasing to the Lord" (5:8-10).

This is just an assumption, but I'm thinking God isn't pleased by my being agitated by Mrs. Mitchell.

CHAPTER FIFTEEN

By the time Friday night gets here, I'm limping. I got up in the middle of the night on Wednesday to go to the bathroom and forgot I wasn't in my own room.

I slammed into the wall and jacked up my knee again.

Jen's engagement is proving to be quite painful for me.

We all decide to meet at Luigi's, the Italian restaurant right by Hudson's pointless boardwalk. Both Jack and Travis are meeting us girls there, so Jen and I ride together.

Mrs. Mitchell is reading yet another bridal magazine as we get ready. I wave as we leave. "Bye, Mrs. Mitchell!"

She looks up at me, and I see the faintest glimmer of surprise in her expression. "Good-bye, Maya." She looks back down at her magazine. "Have a good time, girls."

Jen raises her eyebrows at me as we close the door behind us. "Did she really just say that?" she whispers.

"I think so." I grin. Maybe Mrs. Mitchell is softening.

I follow Jen to her car. She's wearing a flowy, cranberry-colored, knee-length skirt and an off-white, lightweight sweater over a chocolate-colored cami. She looks adorable.

I broke down and am wearing yet another dress. And heels. I found a chocolate cotton, short-sleeved dress, and I'm wearing gold heels.

Heels. On a boardwalk. When my knee is killing me.

Jack owes me big-time.

Jen drives the ten minutes to the restaurant and parks in front of Luigi's. I haven't been down to this area since they redid it and added the boardwalk.

It looks nice, but it's still a little weird. Isn't there supposed to be a beach by a boardwalk?

The guys are waiting outside Luigi's. Jack is wearing nice slacks and a white button-down shirt. Travis has on khakis and a cranberry shirt, and once again, I see he's been tipped off to Jen's color choices.

I grin. She's really into this whole coordinating-with-her-date thing.

"Hey, honey." Travis greets Jen with a light kiss. "Hi, Maya."

I wave at him and give Jack a hug.

We're sitting at a table for four within a few minutes. "So, how's the wedding planning going?" Jack asks as the hostess hands us our menus.

Jen sighs. "Okay, I guess."

"Okay?" Travis says. "I think it's going great! We've got the location, the DJ, the dress. . . ."

She shrugs. "I guess. We haven't found a caterer we like yet."

I look over my menu at her. "I thought you liked one of the ones you met with," I say.

Jen nods. "We did. She just called yesterday and told us she wasn't going to be able to do it."

"I'm sorry."

"Me too," she says. "Her sushi was amazing."

I see Jack's mouth tighten at the mention of *sushi*, but to his credit, he doesn't say anything. Jack is not a sushi fan. "Meat needs to be cooked," he's always saying.

"So how long until the wedding?" Jack asks.

"About three months," Travis says. "Can't get here soon enough. We should have gone with a two-month engagement."

"Two months?!" Jen bursts. "There's no way we could have pulled that off! We would have had to get married in front of a justice of the peace."

"I'm kidding," Travis says, his voice all soothing. "I'm just kidding."

"Evening, folks," says the server, notepad out. "You guys ready to order?"

I order the lasagna. It comes with the breadsticks I'm drooling over. Jen ends up with the spinach ravioli; Travis orders the chicken parmesan; and Jack orders some kind of pasta bowl with chicken, sausage, and lemon.

The server nods and tells us he'll be right back with our drinks and some breadsticks.

Jack is the first one to bring up the taboo topic. "Is your mom still staying with you guys?" he asks Jen.

She sighs.

He nods. "I'll take that as a yes."

"She won't leave." Jen rubs her temples. "I've tried begging, pleading, crying. . . . Nothing works. She told me she's not going to buy a plane ticket, so I know that even if we drop her off at the airport, she'll just get a taxi and go back to my house. She's not going to leave until after the wedding."

Travis wraps his hand around Jen's on the table. "It'll be okay, sweetie."

She squeezes his hand.

I watch them and feel a smile on my face. Only a year ago, I would have been a tense mess watching them right now. Proof that God does heal all wounds, I guess.

"Well, does she at least have good ideas about the wedding?" Jack asks.

"Other than there shouldn't be one?" Jen says sarcastically.

"Oh," Jack says.

"Yeah. Not really," Jen says.

I pipe up. "But she did tell us to have a good time tonight."

Travis's eyebrows go skyward. "Really?"

Jack looks at Jen. "Has she ever said something like that before?"

"When I was going out with someone she didn't like?" Jen shakes her head slowly. "Nope. Never. I think she told me to have a good time once when I was on my way to SAT prep class."

Jack starts laughing. "Does anyone have fun with SAT prep?"

The server shows up then with the drinks and breadsticks. I snag one right away. I bite right into it, using the hot bread to soak up the drool.

So good!

We spend the rest of the night talking about Travis and Jen's wedding plans and laughing over Jack's new job.

"What?" Jack protests a little later as the three of us are in tears. "It's not that funny!"

"The Zoo-per Pooper Scooper?" I say, through a fit of giggles. "You don't think that's funny?"

"Not so funny I'm crying about it. You should meet this guy. He doesn't find it funny at all."

Travis snorts. "I imagine."

"I hope he at least gets paid a lot," Jen says, still grinning. "I don't even want to imagine what he smells like when he gets home."

"Ew." I grimace. "I hadn't even thought of that. Yuck!"

"And he's married with three girls," Jack says. "I bet they definitely don't appreciate the smell."

"Eww." Jen's nose wrinkles up.

"That's like one of those World's Worst Jobs or whatever that show is called," Travis says.

Jack grins. "No kidding."

We leave a little after nine. I'm stuffed and getting sleepy as we walk back down the boardwalk to our cars.

"Hey, Maya, you go ahead and drive home with Jack. I'll take the car home," Jen says, grinning.

"That's silly. You're going home. Jack's going in the opposite direction," I say.

Jack tugs on my arm. "It's not a problem."

"See?" Jen says. "You guys never see each other. Spend a few more minutes together." She gives Travis a hug and a kiss, while Jack and I politely look away.

"Bye, Trav," she waves, grinning. "Thanks for dinner, sweets."

"Night, honey." Travis climbs in his car and waves at us. "Thanks for joining us for dinner! Great idea!"

They both pull out of the parking lot, leaving Jack and me standing there on the boardwalk.

Jack smiles at me. "You look beautiful tonight, by the way."

"Thanks." I can feel a blush coming on, so I'm glad it's dark out.

"Want to walk for a little bit? It's nice out," Jack says, holding his hand out to me.

A few important things to remember: I'm in a dress, and I'm wearing heels. And the slats between these boards are not exactly airtight. I guess in a plan to go for the most authentic-looking fake boardwalk, our mayor decided it should appear beaten down by wind and waves.

Since we have neither.

I look at the boards, look at my shoes, look at my knee, look at Jack's hand and take it. I'd better get Best Girlfriend of the Night award.

We start off at a slow, easy pace. There are now little window shops up and down this boardwalk. There are big yellow lights high above us every few feet that do a horrible job of illuminating anything, but it's okay because between the lights are strung tiny white Christmas lights all the way down the walk.

The shops have their window displays lit up, and we're definitely not the only people taking advantage of the gorgeous evening.

"Why haven't I come here since they finished it?" I ask myself out loud.

Jack smiles. "Because you said you thought it was stupid that we have a boardwalk and no beachfront."

Trust him to remember. "I won't ever judge anything before I see it again," I vow.

"Want to go to Andy's Amazin' Amusement Park with me sometime?" Jack asks, grinning a little smart-alecky grin.

I don't answer right away. Andy's Amazin' Amusement Park is halfway between here and San Diego, and I kid you not, people have been maimed there. I've heard people coming into Cool Beans say the coolest thing about that park was the ambulance ride to the hospital.

By all accounts, it's rickety, cheesy, and dangerous all rolled into one horrific roller coaster.

"Well," I start, swallowing.

Jack starts laughing. "Oh, good grief, Nutkin! I was kidding. Do you think I want to break my arm and leg in one trip?"

"I don't know," I say, defending my easy belief. "Boys do all kinds of stupid things."

Jack shakes his head. "I like to consider myself one of the safer people in my demographic. I'm one of those dorky bike riders who always wears a helmet; I have never nor do I ever want to taste, lick, or eat anything that I'm not sure what it is — even for money; and I always look both ways before crossing the street." He says the last one all proud, chin up.

"Yeah, but you work in a zoo around dangerous animals; you went skydiving for your twenty-first birthday; and you once drove from your apartment to Cool Beans entirely in reverse." I let out a little *ha* type of laugh. "So, I would think again before you call yourself a safe person."

He's quiet for a minute. "First off," he starts, "it was four thirty in the morning when I drove to Cool Beans. There was no one on the roads."

I grin. It happened back in the day when our boss, Alisha, had thought it would be good for Cool Beans to be open at the crack of dawn. When we noticed that we consistently didn't get more than two customers until nine, she changed the shift.

And won our sleepy hearts.

"And, second, I know how to defend myself while working with the animals," he says. "Half of my training involved that knowledge. And, third . . ." His voice trails off, and he looks toward the beach that should be there but isn't. "We have known each other way too long."

I start laughing. "Oh, Jack." I squeeze his hand. "It's fun to tease you."

"Yeah, well, the receiving end isn't as fun as the giving end, I bet." But he smiles and squeezes my hand back. "So, was tonight awkward?"

And now we've transitioned into deep questions only old

friends can ask.

I think about it. I know he's asking because of my history with Travis. We dated most of high school and part of college. We were always "Travis and Maya"; if you invited one of us, the other had to be invited, too. There was a point in time where I thought I would marry him.

Obviously, that's not going to happen.

It took me a very long time to finally let him go, but now that I think about it, dinner was fun. No awkwardness.

"No, it was fine," I say. "I don't think it was awkward at all."

I've seen Travis at the apartment enough over these last many moons that I've gotten used to the whole "Travis and Jen" thing. It even sounds better than my name linked with his.

"Good," Jack says.

"Yep," I say. "That book is closed."

"Well, I didn't think it wasn't," he says, weaving his fingers in between mine. "Otherwise, I probably wouldn't be dating you." He grins. "Just wondering if there were any lingering uncomfortable feelings going on."

I shake my head. "None."

"Very good."

We pass a little store that makes me stop walking. It's a store dedicated entirely to coffee cups. Cups and mugs of all sizes, shapes, and colors decorate the window display.

"Hey!" I burst, pointing. "We have that mug at Cool Beans!" It's one of my favorites, a bright blue oversized mug, hand-painted with tiny little daisies.

Jack frowns at it. "We do, don't we?"

I gape. "This is where Alisha gets all the mugs? Why didn't she tell me about this place before?"

"Maybe she didn't think you'd care," Jack says.

"What?"

"Maybe it slipped her mind. You never asked, so she never brought it up." Jack rolls his eyes. "It's not like you guys have heart-to-heart talks every Monday when she asks for the supply list."

"Still," I say. I step back and look at the store name. *Mug Fetish.* I grin at the little slogan printed underneath: *Cup-ling people with mugs since 2008.*

I decide I'm coming back here when the store is open. Christmas gifts for everyone are probably in there.

We keep walking. My knee is starting to throb again, but I don't say anything. The evening is too perfect to spoil with something like that. The night air is still warm; there's the tiniest breeze. As dumb as a boardwalk with no beach sounded, it's really kind of cute.

And Jack's holding my hand.

So I keep my mouth shut and try not to focus on my knee.

"You okay?" Jack asks a minute later.

"Fine."

He looks down at my feet. "You could take those heels off if you want," he says.

"And risk a splinter from the manmade, water-damaged pier? I don't think so," I say.

Jack grins. "It's not so bad at night. You can kind of imagine that the ocean is out there somewhere."

I look around. Parking lot on one side, window shops on the other. "Where?" I ask.

He waves his hand. "I don't know. Somewhere though."

I laugh.

A week later, it's Sunday morning. I am once again late to church. This time I'm not too upset though, because I convinced Mrs. Mitchell that it would be more fun to come with us than just sit at home by herself again.

"Just go to the service — at least you won't be bored to tears here," I said to her last night.

She made this horrific sigh, but finally she agreed.

So, we send her down the hall to the service while Jen and I try to sneak into our Sunday school class. Andrew is already tottering on his tiny little stool as I carefully and quietly pull the door open.

"Well, thanks for joining us today, girls!" Andrew announces loudly.

I'm sure I blush, and I drop into the first seat I find. Jen sits beside me and waves at Andrew. "Sorry we're late," she says.

"Sure," Andrew says, drawing the word out. He winks at me and then turns back to the class. "So, Wednesday night, Bible study, be there. I think that's my only announcement. Open on up to 1 Corinthians."

I plop my Bible on my lap and turn to the New Testament. I did not dress up at all today. I'm wearing jeans and a yellow lightweight sweater thing that I'm pretty sure I stole from my sister-in-law the last time I was at her house.

Hey. She won't be wearing it anytime in the next few months.

"First Corinthians," Andrew's voice booms across the room. "Chapter 9. Verse 23 to the end. Jen, will you read for us?"

She nods and starts reading. "I do all things for the sake of the gospel, so that I may become a fellow partaker of it. Do you not know that those who run in a race all run, but only one receives the prize? Run in such a way that you may win. Everyone who competes in the games exercises self-control in all things. They then do it to receive a perishable wreath, but we an imperishable. Therefore I run in such a way, as not without aim; I box in such a way, as not beating the air; but I discipline my body and make it my slave, so that, after I have preached to others, I myself will not be disqualified."

Andrew teaches for almost forty-five minutes. "Do you do all things for the sake of the gospel?" he finishes up. "Let's pray."

We're dismissed a few minutes later. "See you guys on Wednesday," he says, and the general hum of people stretching, talking, and getting more coffee starts.

He comes over a minute later. "Good morning, Maya."

"Hey."

"Sorry to call you out again." He pokes me in the shoulder. "Stop being late, and maybe I won't."

Jen is off talking to Liz and a few other girls who are slobbering over the ring yet again and asking about wedding details.

"We brought Mrs. Mitchell to church with us," I say quietly.

Andrew's eyebrows go up. He knows about Mrs. Mitchell. "Wow. Good for you guys! Let me know how it goes. See, that's a great way of doing everything for the sake of the gospel." He leaves to go talk to Liz, and I stand there, convicted.

One thing. She's been living with us for almost three weeks, and I've done one thing to show her the gospel.

Some things might need to change.

Jack comes over, raking a hand through his spiky hair. "Morning, Nutkin."

"Morning, Jack."

He wraps an arm around my shoulders and yawns. "How are you?"

"Good. We talked Mrs. Mitchell into coming." I look around. "Actually, we should probably get over to the auditorium so that she's not lost coming out."

Jack nods. "I'll walk over there with you." He looks at Jen surrounded by girls and waves a hand. "Let her be fawned over. Come on."

We walk down the hallway. Service isn't out yet; our Sunday school class always ends a little earlier.

Probably because we start so punctually.

"So, are you coming to dinner tonight?" I ask, smiling.

Jack grins. "I was planning on it. Am I still invited?"

"Still invited." Mom sent me a text last night that said this: *Pls ak J re: Dnr. Hvng Rbs.* I deciphered it to mean: *Please ask Jack about dinner. We're having ribs.*

"We're having ribs," I tell him. "So here's my disclaimer. I get a little . . . uh, messy eating ribs." Actually, my dad makes me wear an apron. Has since I was a little kid.

"Sounds amazing!" Jack says, rubbing his hands together. "I love ribs. Don't worry; I'll get messy with you." He grins at me.

I don't think he fully understands how messy I get. One time, I found enough sauce to dip an extra rib in right on top of my collarbone.

I guess it's entertaining to watch, though. My dad always gets a kick out of it.

The sanctuary doors open, and the crowd spills out. Jack and I stand against a wall opposite the doors in the foyer.

I don't see her.

I frantically scan every head I see, but no bleach blond wearing Armani and about $50,000 of plastic surgery walks past.

The crowd is starting to thin, and I frown at Jack. I poke my head in the door and look around our auditorium. It used to be a gym, so everything feels white and bleached, like a gym post-workout. The room has two floors, the main area and the upper bleachers. The bleachers are empty save for one couple trying to give their infant a diaper change.

The main area has people wandering around, little groups chatting together, kids running circles around the chairs.

Finally, I see her.

She looks very uncomfortable, but two of the nicest ladies in church, Charlene and Karen, are over there talking to her.

I grin.

I walk back out to Jack, who is waving at a cute little boy wearing tiny slacks and suspenders.

"Charlene and Karen are talking to her," I tell him.

He grins as well. "Nice. Let's let them talk then." He wraps an arm around my shoulders and pulls me over beside him against the wall. "So."

"So," I mimic.

"What are you doing the rest of today?"

"Lunch first. I'm starving. After that, I don't have plans until four-ish, which is when we need to head to Mom and Dad's."

Jack nods. "Well, I'm off today."

My eyes widen. "The whole day?" I just assumed that he would have to go in for more trainings or something after church today.

"The whole day." He grins at me. "So, I was wondering if I might monopolize some of your time, missy."

"I think that could be arranged. What do you want to do?"

"Actually, I thought maybe we could take Canis and Calvin to the park and let them run around for a bit."

Canis is Jack's dog. He's a Lab/pointer cross. *Canis* is also the Latin name for dog.

I know, I know. I'm dating a nerd.

"Canis is needing some exercise and attention." Jack is still talking. "I've been working too late."

"Well, I second that motion," I say.

"I didn't make a motion."

"Oh. Well, you should have."

I see a blond coming out of the auditorium finally, and I wave. "Mrs. Mitchell! Over here!"

She sees us and makes her way across the crowded hallway. "Good grief." She's grumbling by the time she gets to us. "This place has no sense of traffic flow," she says. "Whoever was the architect for this building did a very poor job."

"Well, it used to be a YMCA," I say. "We're just happy to have a building." For a while, the church was meeting in a movie theater at the Hudson Mall. We never knew what theater they would put us in, so some weeks we were told to continue to our left to theater two. Other weeks we were told they were all full, so church was canceled.

Everyone hated it.

I began attending Grace Bible Church right before we started renting the YMCA. It was closing down, and it was a good opportunity for us. Later, we bought it.

We've painted and redone floors, but a building like this will always feel like a gym.

Mrs. Mitchell is looking around, lips pursed. "If you took out that wall right there, then you would not have this funnel effect going on. The foyer needs to be a welcoming area for new-comers. You could even . . ." Her voice trails off, and she taps lightly on the wall we are leaning against. "What's behind this?"

"A closet, I think," I say.

"If it is not a necessity, take it out. You could put in an espresso bar there instead. It would also give it a more open feeling."

I glance at Jack while Mrs. Mitchell is talking. He's just staring at her, eyes wide, mouth open.

She catches his look and frowns slightly. "I was an architect major."

"Wow," I say. "I didn't know that."

"Well, it was a long time ago. And I have not done architecture in years. After my ex-husband excelled in real estate, there was not a need for me to work."

I suddenly have this flash of brilliancy. Probably due to the words *espresso bar*. I point to Mrs. Mitchell. "Wait here!"

I'm running to find our senior pastor, Pastor Steve. He's always wandering the hallway, visiting with people after the service. I finally find him talking to a blond couple, their three towheaded kids running around them.

I wait as patiently as I can, and finally Pastor Steve stops talking. "Hi, Maya, how are you?" he asks, all pastoral-like.

"I'm fine. Listen, I have a great idea," I say, grinning. "What if I found an architect who desperately needed something to do but not necessarily to be paid? Would you guys redo the foyer area?"

Pastor Steve rubs his cheek. "We've actually been talking over this exact thing in our elder meetings. That foyer is a little small." He looks at me. "You know an architect?"

"She hasn't done any work in years, but you need to hear her ideas." I nod toward where she and Jack are standing. "Want to meet her?"

"Sure," Pastor Steve says. He walks over. Jack's talking to Mrs. Mitchell about the zoo.

"So, anyway, we're looking at there potentially being a polar-bear cub sometime in this upcoming year," he says.

"Pastor Steve, this is Jen's mom, Candace Mitchell."

A knowing look briefly crosses Pastor Steve's face as he holds out his hand. "Nice to meet you, Candace. I'm so glad you could join us this morning."

She shakes his hand, though a little hesitantly. "Thank you."

"I heard you have some ideas about remodeling? Mind if I grab our head elder and let him listen in?"

She pauses. "Sure."

Steve leads her over to our head elder, Mike Benson. Jack and I take this as our cue to leave. We start walking back toward our Sunday school class, and I find Jen in the hallway.

She's waving at Andrew and Liz, who are leaving together.

"Guess who has a lunch date?" she sing-songs to us, then looks behind us and back at us, frowning. "Where's Mom?"

"She's telling Pastor Steve and Mike Benson how they could redo the foyer so it's more open," I say.

Jen sighs. "Oh, no."

"No, no!" I say. "It's a good thing! Your mom needs a job besides breaking up you and Travis, and Pastor Steve needs the foyer redone."

"And your mom is an architect," Jack says.

"True," Jen says. She purses her lips back and forth across her face and finally shrugs. "I guess if she wants to do it."

I nod. "Let her do it. What are you doing today?"

"Travis told me we have to take a break from wedding plan-ning, and we can't even mention the word *wedding* the whole day," she says.

"A rule that you just broke twice," Jack tells her.

She rolls her eyes at him. "Anyway, so we're going to have a picnic for lunch, and then he's coming over to the apartment. I'm hoping to talk Mom into watching a movie with us."

I smile at her. She's trying. Surely her mom will see this.

A few hours later, I'm exhausted from chasing Canis and Calvin at the park, and my face, shoulders, and thighs are sunburned pretty good. Jack is driving us to San Diego, and at the slow, easy pace he's driving, we'll make it there by Thanksgiving.

"Seriously?" I say, leaning over to look at the speedometer. "It's a highway, Jack. Open her up!"

"I'm only going five under."

"And the wind effect from these other cars speeding past us is only going to catapult us back in time," I say.

He makes one of those little annoyed noises from the back of his throat but pushes the pedal down a touch more. "Fine, Rudolph."

"Not funny." I touch my sunburned nose tenderly. I slathered about a gallon of that after-sun aloe stuff all over my face, shoulders, and thighs, but all it's done is make me sticky.

I might have issues getting off this seat. I think my legs are glued to it.

Calvin is napping on the backseat; we dropped Canis off at Jack's apartment before we started toward Mom and Dad's. I told Jack we could bring him too, but Jack said no.

"He doesn't do too well in new places. And he jumps. I don't want him jumping on Kate right now."

He's probably right. An eighty-pound dog jumping on you cannot be a good thing when you are pregnant.

He pulls up to the house at five on the nose. I peel my legs off the seat, poke Calvin, and close the door after he jumps out. Jack's suddenly standing in front of me.

"Hey," he says. "I'm sorry about your sunburn."

I look up at him. "I'm sorry about ragging on you for being a slowpoke."

"I had fun with you today."

erynn mangum

"Me too."

He leans down and kisses my cheek, then holds my hand as we go up the front walk.

Mom's waiting by the door, as usual. "Hi, honey!" she says, opening the door. Calvin wriggles in, all happy and excited to be among people who spoil him rotten. I give my mom a hug.

"Hi, Mom."

"Oh, no," she says, holding my chin. "That is a horrible sunburn!"

"You're telling me." I grimace. She hugs me more lightly.

"I'm sorry, honey. Nice to see you again, Jack," she says in the middle of giving me my hug. She looks all cute, in a stylish-mom kind of way. She's wearing black knee-length, form-fitting shorts and a longer, more drapey short-sleeved lacy top.

I love my mom.

My dad comes in the room then, and Calvin goes berserk. Dad laughs, pats Calvin's head, and hands him a huge bone.

"And we wonder why he likes coming over here," I say. I give Dad a hug.

"Well." Dad grins. "So, how was the drive? I noticed you didn't bring your car. Is everything okay with it? I might need to change the oil soon."

This is how my dad takes care of me. He fixes stuff for me. I give him a tighter hug. "I'll bring it next week."

Zach opens the door right then and shakes Jack's hand before giving me a hug. "Hey, sis. Thought of you this week. A patient of mine was in love with Nick Lachey."

I frown at him. "So you thought of me?" I was never in love with Nick Lachey.

"Yeah. Isn't he the guy from 'N Sync you liked so much?"

Proof yet again that my brother spent his entire teenage

years with his nose crammed in a book. His classmates voted him "Most Likely Not to Remember the '90s."

I have to agree.

"No, he wasn't from 'N Sync," I say.

Mom's hugging Kate, who starts laughing. "Tell him, Maya. I tried to, but he doesn't listen to me." She's clutching a box of Oreos. "Sorry, Mary," she says to my mom. "Again, it's all I can keep down."

Kate's got a cute little belly now, and it's very obvious she's pregnant. I think the worst part of being pregnant would be those first few weeks when you just look like you have been visiting the doughnut store a little too often.

Mom waves off her concern. "Don't worry about it. You eat what you need to."

Kate gives me one of those awkward pregnant-woman hugs and then gives Jack one. We all start moving toward the kitchen, which smells amazing. Mom's barbecue ribs are legendary in this house. Dad always says that's the reason he married her.

There are bowls of coleslaw, potato salad, and macaroni 'n' cheese on the island. Dad peeks at the ribs.

"Gosh, I wish I could eat this!" Kate says, sighing. "This looks amazing!"

"Just try some, honey," Zach says.

Kate starts shaking her head vehemently. "No. Last time I tried something, I was sick the rest of the day. I want to enjoy tonight."

Jack, meanwhile, is salivating by the island. "Wow. Thank you so much for having me, Mrs. Davis."

"Jack, please stop calling me that," Mom says. "It's Mary. Mrs. Davis is my husband's mother."

"Well, thanks for having me then, Mary." He grins. "It looks awesome."

"I think these are done," Dad says to Mom. She looks at the ribs and nods. Dad pulls them out of the oven and sets them on the island. Zach, Jack, and I just stand there, dabbing away the drool from our chins.

"Stop it," Mom says, backhanding me and Zach. "You're breathing on the food. You're a doctor, for goodness' sake, Zachary. You should know better."

Ooh. She used my brother's full name.

Zach rolls his eyes at me. "Half of the reason kids get sick with the flu and stuff these days is because they overwash their hands, Mom. They have no immune system to back them up."

Mom ignores him.

Dad takes Mom's hand. "Let's pray."

Jack puts an arm around my shoulders as we bow our heads. "God, thank You for this meal and for my family. Please keep them safe as they drive home. And bless my wife, who created this amazing dinner. Amen," Dad says. He pats Mom lightly on the rump. "Start us off, Mary."

Maybe it grosses out other kids to see their parents being all affectionate with each other, but it has always made me feel very safe. I grin.

Dad comes over to me and plops an apron over my head. "Here you go, Maya."

I sigh, but concede and tie it behind my back.

We gobble up dinner so quickly that there's barely any conversation until all the ribs and most of the mac 'n' cheese is gone. By the time I stand to wash off my hands, face, and arms, hardly any food is left.

The guys are all still chowing down on the ribs, and Kate is happily crunching on her Oreos. I scrub at my hands and then sit back down to finish off my mac 'n' cheese.

"So, who is up for Scattergories tonight?" Dad asks, winking at me.

"I'm sorry. Did you mean who wants to lose at Scattergories tonight?" I correct him, grinning back.

"That's it. You two cannot be on the same team tonight," Mom says. "You are obnoxious."

"Hey!" I protest. "We are not obnoxious!"

"Enthusiastic," Dad says. "Unlike some people, we enjoy family togetherness while playing games."

Kate elbows Jack. "Bet you didn't know she was this competitive, did you?"

Jack just sighs. "Oh. I knew."

He gets a glare from me for that response, but I don't let it dampen my excitement about Scattergories.

Dad and I rock at that game.

"I'll play as long as you two are on separate teams," Mom says, waving her hand at me and Dad. "If you guys are on the same team, I don't want to play. So, it's different teams or a different game." She looks at Jack. "She comes by the competitive stuff naturally."

"I think they're scared," Dad says to me. "We intimidate them."

"Well, they should be scared! No losses yet, my friend!" I hold up my hand for a high five.

Dad checks to make sure all the rib sauce is gone before he slaps my hand. "And I'm your father, not your friend."

"No losses yet, my father!"

Mom decides that the best way for us to pick teams is to draw numbers, so after dinner is cleaned up and we've moved to the living room, she passes around a little bowl with pieces of paper in it.

I draw number two. I glance over at Dad as he draws.

"Okay," Mom says once she gets her number. "We've got three teams. One and two, three and four, five and six." She holds up her paper. "I'm number five."

Kate waves hers. "I'm six. We're on the same team, Mary." She's still crunching on Oreos, but now she's sipping a Sprite and patting her protruding belly. She looks over at me. "Night sickness."

"Sorry," I say.

"Me too. I hope this doesn't mean that the little guy is nocturnal."

I grin. "It's a boy?"

Kate shakes her head at me. "You'll find out soon enough, Maya."

Jack opens his piece of paper. "I'm number four."

"I've got five," Zach says.

They all look at me and Dad. I grin wider.

"I'm two."

"I'm one," Dad says, laughing.

"You're kidding," Mom says, mouth wide. "You're still on the same team? Did you guys cheat?"

"How do you cheat at drawing numbers? The papers were folded!" I say.

"I think we're just supposed to be on the same team," Dad says.

Dad and I end up winning by a long shot.

Kate's booing at the end of the game. "Cheaters never prosper," she says, pushing herself to a standing position.

She's gained a lot of weight. I don't think I'd realized how much until just now. "How far along are you now, Kate?" I ask.

She makes a soft groaning sound as she straightens. "Um. I am nineteen weeks. Nearly halfway there."

"Just be prepared for longer than forty weeks," Mom pipes up. "I went forty-three with Zach and forty-five with Maya."

Kate puts her hands over her ears. "Don't tell me this stuff, Mary! It's depressing enough to look down and just see chub."

"It's for a good reason, right, babe?" Zach says, hugging his wife. He looks down at her. "Ready to go?"

"Yeah. I'm about dead on my feet."

Jack glances at the clock above the fireplace and nods to me. "Sorry, honey, but we should go, too," he says. "I need to get up early tomorrow morning."

He may have said it innocently, but my entire family perks up at the word *honey*. I can see Mom almost physically holding herself back from saying anything.

Zach isn't so tactful. "Honey," he says. He looks at Kate. "Honey."

She swats at him as Jack grins. "Hush," Kate says. "Let them be romantic."

"It's my little sister. Honey," he says again. He shakes his head and then moves toward the door.

The rest of us get off the floor, and I gather my sleeping beagle and my purse. "Come on, tired pup," I say, poking Calvin with my foot. "Let's go home."

He sighs and stretches, then pushes himself off the floor and wags over to Mom and Dad for his good-byes.

"Bye, Mom. Amazing dinner, thank you." I give her a hug. "Bye, Dad. We're still on top." I make an invisible check in the air and give him a hug.

He laughs. "Bye, Maya."

Jack and I follow Zach and Kate out the door. "Bye, guys," Mom calls from the doorway. "Drive carefully."

"We will," Jack says to her.

"Maybe," Zach calls back.

"Zachary," Mom says, in her "this is a warning" voice.

He grins. "I will, I will."

"Good. My daughter-in-law and grandbaby are in that car," Mom says.

"And your son. Don't forget about your son," Zach calls back. He waves. "Thanks for dinner, Mom!"

"Love you guys." Mom waves at all of us.

Jack lifts Calvin into the backseat, and he immediately conks out. Then he opens the passenger door for me.

I settle in and watch him walk around the car. He climbs into the driver's seat.

"Fun night," he says, turning the ignition.

"Very fun night. Sorry about the ragging Zach gave you."

Jack grins. "I like your brother." He pulls away from the curb and reaches for my hand. "It's good that he's protective of you."

I smile over at Jack. "So, what time are you supposed to be at work tomorrow?" I ask, changing the subject.

"Six." He says it with a groan, and I wince.

"Yuck."

"Yeah. Feeding time, though. And some of those animals should not go hungry." He gets a serious expression on his face. "That's when zoo accidents happen."

"I thought you told me it was when people didn't respect the wild in the animals that zoo accidents happened," I say.

"Well. Both, then."

I laugh.

I crawl onto the sofa bed at eleven thirty and pull my Bible onto my lap. Jen is sound asleep in my room. She didn't even bat an eye when Calvin slunk into his bed. Mrs. Mitchell is asleep in Jen's room.

I stare off at the refrigerator. It's going to kick on at any minute.

Jack called me *honey* in front of my family. He's told me he loves me, so I knew it was moving in this direction, but this is *serious*.

Zach didn't call Kate *honey* in front of everyone until the week before they got engaged. By that point, all of us and every person around knew they were headed for the altar.

Vvvrrrrrr! There's the refrigerator. I look back down at my Bible.

Is it weird that it doesn't weird me out to think about me and Jack together? Like in one of those "together forever, amen" *Princess Bride* kind of ways?

Considering how weirded out I was about us dating, I think it's very strange that I'm not freaking out more. Maybe it's because of the wedding fever going on in this apartment. Or maybe it's because Jack is my best friend in the whole world.

I look down at where I opened my Bible — Psalm 40 — and start reading a little bit.

"I waited patiently for the LORD; and He inclined to me and heard my cry. He brought me up out of the pit of destruction, out of the miry clay, and He set my feet upon a rock making my footsteps firm. He put a new song in my mouth, a song of praise to our God; many will see and fear and will trust in the LORD. How blessed is the man who has made the LORD his trust" (verses 1-4).

Wait patiently. Trust the Lord.

This is what I'm reading here. "God, help me to patiently trust You," I whisper quietly. I push the Bible onto the coffee table and grab a sticky note.

Reasons I Need to Trust God:
1. Future or non-future with Jack.
2. Mrs. Mitchell will not leave.
3. That leftover mac 'n' cheese I had for lunch
looked fairly questionable,
now that I think about it.
4. The future. Period.

CHAPTER SIXTEEN

It's Monday morning. I'm busy whipping up a mocha MixUp for a girl who is so skinny that she looks like she needs all the calories she can get.

Ethan's ringing up another customer as I hand the MixUp to the girl. "Two medium caramel macchiatos to go," he says, handing me two paper cups and moving to the next people in line.

It's a crazy morning. We get one of these on average about once a month. I guess today is the day.

I start frothing the milk and mashing every button on the espresso machine.

It's been two weeks since Jack called me *honey* in front of the family. Mrs. Mitchell has been gone from the apartment every day working with our church's head elder, Mike Benson, to draw up plans to redo the foyer. She's not charging them anything for her work.

That whole thing totally has God's handprints all over it. We couldn't get Mrs. Mitchell to church in the whole six years Jen and I have been living together, and now she's been there almost every day for the last fourteen days.

See what I mean? God definitely orchestrated something.

Jen and Travis have a caterer and an itch to just get married and be done with it. They have over a month and a half to go, and I think they've reached the point where there isn't much left to do.

I knew they should have picked an earlier date.

"And a large cappuccino, iced," Ethan says. He fills the cup with ice, and I pass the macchiatos across the counter and start making the cappuccino.

"I just saw Alisha drive up, too," Ethan says, between customers.

She'll want her americano, so I start that as well. I have so many things going I can hardly focus.

It's just as well. These last few weeks have flown by so quickly that I haven't really focused on anything. I didn't know that when I asked God for patience, He would make the days fly like they were connected to Peter Pan's shadow.

I blow out my breath, trying to concentrate. Ethan gives me a sympathetic look as he passes yet another paper cup over to me. "Medium mocha."

These are the days when I wish we had three baristas working and at least two espresso machines. The line is still all the way down toward the fireplace.

Alisha walks in, and I see her eyebrows go up. In between shots of espresso, I wave. "Hey, Alisha."

"Today's the day, huh?" she says, smiling at all the customers.

I hand her the americano and then hand the customer a mocha. "Apparently," I say.

Ethan disappears for a second and returns with the grocery list for this week. "Here you go."

"Thanks, Ethan." She watches me make another cappuccino and nods. "Looks like you kids are doing well. I won't keep you.

See you guys soon!"

She leaves.

The rush finally ends at eleven. Ethan and I both fall back against the counters, exhausted.

"I definitely need a new mattress if we're going to have more days like this," I say, rubbing my eyes.

"You still haven't bought a new mattress? Maya, seriously!"

"I know, I know," I say. It's not a huge deal. I've kind of gotten used to the creaks and groans and the spring that pokes right in the middle of my spine.

The timer on the oven goes off, and Ethan brings a new batch of cinnamon rolls out from the back. I have the frosting all ready to go, and I start lathering it on there.

The cream-cheese sweetness melts into all the cracks and crevices in the hot rolls, and the whole place smells like sugary cinnamon. A few customers sitting at some of the tables lift their heads to follow the smell.

It's amazing. My mouth is watering as I ice the cinnamon rolls.

Ethan is watching me. "Don't drool on the food."

"I can't help it. We're out of cereal." Which means I had a handful of M&M's for breakfast. And not only are those not filling at all, but they definitely melted in my hand on the way over here.

I should ask for a refund.

"Healthy," Ethan says, rolling his eyes. I finish icing the rolls, and he starts separating them for the display case. He puts one on a plate and slides it over to me. "Eat. It's on me."

I look up at him, surprised. "Really?" Alisha lets us have as many free drinks as we want, but food we have to pay for. She made that rule after Lisa and I had been working two weeks. Alisha said that between the two of us, we ate sixteen cinnamon rolls.

I counted higher.

"Really. You look pathetic." He slides the tray into the display case and sighs at me. "You can thank me when you're dying of a heart attack. It might be healthier to eat a spoonful of sugar."

"I'll run later," I say, grabbing a fork. I pull off a piece of the still-steaming roll, and it almost melts in my mouth. I close my eyes to enjoy it.

Our chef is a culinary genius.

Ethan is shaking his head at me when I open my eyes back up. "You're ridiculous," he says.

"Thanks." I finish off the cinnamon roll, wash my hands, and start cleaning off the area in front of the espresso machine. I tied back my hair this morning in a loose curly ponytail, but it's not staying back too well.

I'm wishing for the short haircut I had before Jack and I start dating. It was a pain in the neck sometimes, yes, but at least it was short enough that I didn't have to worry about pulling it up at work. Alisha's rule is that if it's longer than shoulder length, it needs to be in a ponytail.

Mine used to sit about an inch off my shoulders.

"So, how's religion class going?" I ask while I'm wiping the counters and swiping at my hair.

"It's going. The final is next week." Ethan is watching two little kids play on the sofa while their moms sit at a table talking. "I haven't really learned that much, but I took it for extra credit, so learning really wasn't a priority."

"Did you guys study Christianity?" I ask in a nonthreatening way.

Ethan nods. "Briefly. We mostly spent time on Buddhism, Islam, and Hinduism." He rolls his shoulders. "Weird stuff, religions."

I nod, because I agree. Religions are weird. "So, you consider yourself nonreligious?"

He gives me a look. "Look, Maya, I've seen your cross necklace, and I know there's a fish sticker on your car. Plus we've talked about it a little bit, so I get that you're a Christian. I just don't need a crutch."

"Too bad," I say, finishing with the counters. "Most people with a broken leg like their crutch."

He gives me a weird look. "What?"

"It's just . . . I recognize that I need a Savior. If you want to compare sin to a broken leg and Christ to a crutch, then, yes, by all means, I need a crutch."

Ethan just sighs. "Let's not talk about this anymore," he says.

I let him off the hook for now. I don't want to be one of those people who bang others over the head with a Bible. And there are customers coming.

But this conversation isn't over.

On Wednesday night, I'm running down the stairs to the parking lot after Jen. Bible study starts in twenty minutes, and I guess she needs to get there early to talk to Andrew about something to do with her and Travis's vows.

So, I came home from Cool Beans, changed from my work clothes, put on a pair of jeans and a blue T-shirt, and scarfed down dinner while watching *What Not to Wear*.

Mrs. Mitchell was reading a *Good Housekeeping* magazine. She watched me eat, frowning. "You will destroy your metabolism eating like that. And goodness knows you need that metabolism."

Even though we've seen a few changes, not everything has changed.

Jen starts the car, and I slam the passenger door. "Sorry for rushing you, Maya," Jen says.

"Not a big deal. I could have taken my car if it bothered me that much." I balance my Bible on my lap and click my seat belt.

"It just, well, there are less than six weeks left, and I don't know what else to do."

Jen is cute. I smile over at her. She's wearing her long blond hair straight today, and her blue eyes are spotlighted against a black lacy, short-sleeved shirt.

"What?" she asks, glancing over at me and seeing my smile.

"Nothing. You're getting married." Sometimes, I think I need to remind her of this fact.

She grins. "Yeah."

"Does it weird you out?" I ask.

"Does what weird me out?"

"That you're getting married. You have to live with Travis for the rest of forever. You won't ever be just Jen again — you'll always be 'Jen and Travis.'"

She laughs. "Yeah. Sometimes it does. I'm going to be Jen Clayton." She quirks her head. "Doesn't that sound like a news anchor or something?"

"Kind of, yeah."

She makes a right turn, lips pursed. "Want to know what really makes me nervous?"

I'm not sure how to answer this. On the one hand, sure, I'd

love to be her listening post. On the other hand, she's getting married, and I don't really want to hear about the scary thoughts the intimate details of marriage are giving her. We're closer than sisters, sure, but there are still some things that you shouldn't discuss with sisters.

I squeeze my eyes shut for a quick second and then let my breath out, prepared for the worst. "Uh. Sure."

She licks her lips and then settles her top teeth on her bottom lip, chewing on it for a second. "Okay," she says finally. "I'm a little worried . . . I'm kind of scared that maybe Travis and I will end up like my mom and dad." She finishes the sentence so quietly that I can barely make out the last part over the whirring of the car's air conditioner.

I just gape at her. "Seriously? That's your big concern?"

"Well, it's a valid one!" Jen protests. "I've been living on my own for six years. I've gotten used to making my own decisions, doing my own thing. And now, I'll have to consult with Travis before I do anything. No more just throwing a Lean Cuisine in the microwave for dinner; I have to cook something. I won't be able to just blow $200 on new clothes without consulting with him first. And want to know the real reason my mom and dad got divorced?"

"Your mom bought new clothes?" I ask.

She sighs. "No, they never communicated! I don't have one memory of them ever talking before they got divorced. They did afterward, but it was just screaming on the phone the whole time over who was going to take me for Christmas so the other one could go spend Christmas somewhere like Ireland."

Jen's fists are closed so tightly over the steering wheel that her knuckles are turning a light purple color.

I can feel myself tearing up for the little girl who had to deal with all of this. "I'm so sorry, Jenny," I say, reaching over for her shoulder.

"It's just . . . I don't want to be like that. You know?"

"You won't be like that, Jenny. You guys are more than just in love — you and Travis have Christ at the center." I rub her shoulder. "Your parents didn't have that."

She sighs. "True."

"And what is this about never consulting anyone?" I ask, lightly flicking her with my fingers. "You ask me how much money I think you should spend on clothes, and it doesn't affect me at all!"

She smiles lightly. "I guess you're right."

"Of course I'm right."

Jen pulls into the parking lot at Cool Beans. I look through the windshield and frown.

"I feel like I was just here."

She grins. "Well, two hours ago, you were."

"I don't like this work shift."

She grabs her Bible, and we climb out of the car. "So you'd rather work sporadic hours and miss the weekends with Jack?" she asks.

"True," I concede. "Hey, before we get off the wedding conversational train, I really need that list of people you want to invite to the shower."

She nods. "I have the list at the apartment; remind me to give it to you."

As maid of honor, it is my duty to throw two showers: The Wedding Shower and The Bachelorette Party/Lingerie Shower. The first one is intimidating because it's probably going to be about sixty people from church. The second one is frightening because, like I said earlier, there is some stuff I just don't want to know.

It's six weeks to the wedding, so we're right on time for the showers. I'm throwing the first one in two weeks. We're going to do it at the park by our apartment because there is no way sixty people will fit in our tiny living room.

The sofa bed barely fits in the living room.

And the park has a place for tables and chairs, and there are lots of shady trees. Andrew told me I could borrow a bunch of tables from the church.

So, I'm hoping it will be nice. Mom is coming to help me decorate.

We walk inside Cool Beans, and there are only a few people here. Andrew is alternating between moving chairs around and talking with the beautiful redheaded Liz.

Lisa is working tonight, and she waves at me from behind the counter. "Hi, Maya!"

"Hey, Lisa," I say, walking over while Jen goes to talk to Andrew. "How's the evening shift so far?"

She shrugs and grins. "Easy. We had, like, six or so people since you got off." She nods to the area Andrew is setting up for the Bible study. "It'll pick up. Wednesday nights are good for business." She winks at me. "And tips."

I laugh. Lisa is adorable, and she earns the most tips at Cool Beans by far. She's this short little sprite, full of energy, and she's always laughing.

I can see Peter in the back room spreading frosting on a new batch of cinnamon rolls, and he waves the spatula at me. "Hey, Maya! How's Jack doing at the zoo?"

"Good," I call back to him.

Lisa looks at me. "So, you've been seeing him more, I hope?"

"Yeah." I nod. "The training part is over." I saw him three times in the past five days.

It's like old times. It's nice.

"Good!" She grins. "So when are we going to be planning a big shower for you, Miss Maya?"

I blush and open my mouth.

She cuts me off. "Oh darn, there's a customer. See you later!" She's grinning like crazy, and I just shake my head.

"We'll talk later," I say.

She waves her hand at me and turns to focus on Matt, who is also blushing, but probably because Lisa is giving him her full attention.

"Uh. Yeah. Hi," he stumbles, "I'd, uh, like a coffee."

I sigh. I almost want to butt in and just tell him how to flirt, but I figure that's poor form.

I'm staring at the menu, trying to figure out what I want. I realize someone is awfully close to me before I hear them speak.

"Haven't you memorized this by now, babe?" Jack says in my ear before kissing my cheek from behind.

He ends up getting a mouthful of curls, because I turned to look at him right as he spoke.

"Pleugh." He spits my hair out.

"Ew. Gross," I say.

"Sorry." He grins. "Hi, Nutkin."

"Hey, Jack." I go in for the hug and then look back up at the menu. "I think I want a decaf caramel macchiato."

Jack frowns at me. "Decaf? Are you feeling okay?"

"I'm still on the sofa bed. I want to sleep tonight," I tell him. It's no fun trying to fall asleep there. It works best if I'm dead tired before I even try to go to bed.

Jack just smiles and hugs me tighter.

"Okay, people, get your coffee and grab a seat," Andrew yells out. I turn around and notice that there are almost thirty people here already. There's a line forming in front of the register, and Jack and I stand behind a girl named Rebecca.

Lisa and Peter are moving like Hammy from *Over the Hedge* on caffeine. They are one constant blur as they ring people up, make their lattes, and slide hot cinnamon rolls on plates.

I look behind me, and there are still fifteen people in line. Andrew is getting antsy. Travis and Jen are here, about three people back.

Right then, Peter trips and spills a whole latte all over the floor.

"Oh my gosh!" Lisa exclaims.

Peter says a word that shouldn't be said at Bible study.

I look at Jack, shake my head slightly, and then go behind the counter, washing my hands and pulling on my apron.

"What are you doing?" Peter asks, swabbing off the floor with paper towels while Lisa tries to make a mocha MixUp around him.

"Helping." I look at the next person in line: Connor, a nice-looking guy who was in my social studies class sophomore year.

"Hey, Connor. What can I get you?"

He looks at the menu. "How about a medium cappuccino?"

"I can maybe do that." I ring him up and give him the change. Lisa starts frothing the cappuccino, Peter finishes on the floor, washes up, and then starts whipping up the next person's caramel MixUp.

The three of us get the rest of the people their coffee in about ten minutes. Not too bad. Andrew nods his appreciation as I set a huge cinnamon latte in front of him and then sighs in frustration when he looks up from his notes and sees the pink-and-red mug with hearts on it.

"I thought I was done with the girly mugs when you stopped

working this shift," Andrew says.

"But this one just had your name on it," I say, patting his shoulder.

He picks up the mug. "I do not see Andrew written any-where on here."

"It's on the bottom."

He pulls the little sticky note with his name on it off the bottom of the mug and just shakes his head. "Oh, wow." Then he clears his throat. "All right, we need to start," he announces. The room gradually quiets.

I go behind the counter to the back and pull off my apron.

"Thanks so much, Maya," Lisa says, mopping where the latte spilled so it's not all sticky.

"No problem." I look over, and there are two empty seats beside Jack. He's waving — half sign language, half some weird arm motions — and I think he wants me to ask Lisa to come sit with us.

Either that or he wants a cinnamon roll.

"Want to sit with us?" I ask Lisa quietly, since Andrew is already rolling off the announcements.

"Um . . ." she says, face twisting. "I don't know. It doesn't seem fair to Peter."

"I'm studying," Peter calls softly from the back. "Go sit with them."

"Why not, then?" She shrugs, sticks the mop back in the bucket, and follows me to the chairs. I sit next to Jack, and she settles in the chair beside me.

Jack leans over. "I thought you were going to get me a cin-namon roll."

I grin.

"Jen?" Andrew calls, looking around before he finally finds

Jen sitting right in front of him. "Oh, hi. You usually sit in the back. Need anything for the wedding?"

"Actually, if we could get some of you guys to help move tables the morning of the wedding, that would be great," she says.

"Five and a half weeks," Andrew says. "Stick it in the back of your brains. And while you're sticking it there, flip to Proverbs."

I do as he says and then hand Lisa my Bible. I'll share with Jack. She smiles gratefully.

Andrew starts reading from chapter 15: "All the days of the afflicted are bad, but a cheerful heart has a continual feast. Better is a little with the fear of the LORD than great treasure and turmoil with it. Better is a dish of vegetables where love is than a fattened ox served with hatred" (verses 15-17).

He looks up and glances around the room, all pastoral-style. His eyes are serious, and everyone is paying attention in a somber, reflective way.

Then Andrew takes a sip from his "hearts" mug and ruins the moment.

Liz snorts but tries to mask it as a sneeze. A couple of guys in the back start whispering something about Andrew's touchy-feely side.

Andrew glares at me. I grin back at him.

"We're talking about opposites, people," he says. "Notice: Affliction is bad; cheerful heart has a feast. Little with God; a lot with turmoil. Veggies with love; meat with hatred. And lastly, me with a pink mug."

Everyone laughs.

He talks for about an hour and then wraps it up. "I'm not advocating vegetarianism; just be thankful for what you have. Whether it's an apartment, a bed, a family, whatever. Be thankful."

He has one of the guys pray, and then the normal stretching and chatter that happen after a Bible study begin.

I turn to talk to Lisa.

"Seriously, Maya. Pink?" Andrew says, standing right in front of me.

"Hey! I gave you a sermon illustration that earned major points," I say. "You should be thanking me."

"I think your lesson was about being thankful for things you normally wouldn't be thankful for," Lisa reminds him, grinning.

Andrew just stands there glowering at the both of us, and then leaves.

I laugh. "Totally put him in his place. I thank you, Lisa."

She grins, squeezes my shoulders in a hug, and goes to the back to start the cleanup process. I don't envy her.

Jack stands and stretches. "Bedtime for me." He leans down and kisses my cheek. "But I'll see you this weekend, right?"

I nod. "You'd better."

He grins. "Night, Nutkin." He slips out before he gets delayed talking to people. His six o'clock alarm tomorrow is going to come early.

I look around, and everyone is talking. There's a group of girls around Jen again, oohing over the ring and asking wedding details. She's smiling, but I can tell she feels a little cornered.

I mash my wayward curls behind my ears and stand. I might as well help Andrew get a head start on putting all the chairs and tables back in their places.

It hits me as I'm putting two chairs back next to their table that Jen is moving out.

She's not going to live with me anymore.

I stare at the chair and try to blink back the sudden tears that fill my eyes. We've lived in that apartment together for six years. We've done it all together. Movie marathons. Laughing so hard we can't stand up straight. Fighting over whose turn it is to empty the dishwasher. She's spent Christmas with my family every one of those six years.

She's like the sister I never had, and the thought of not coming home to see her gets me somewhere in my gut.

I sniff the tears away until a later time and finish with the chairs. By the time I put the last chair in its place, it's only me, Andrew, and a scrubbing Peter and Lisa. Jen gave me her car keys about ten minutes ago, saying that Travis wanted to take her home.

Andrew lifts the couch back over in front of the fireplace and looks at me. "What happened?"

"Jen's moving out," I say.

Andrew frowns at me. "You thought they were going to live together in your apartment?"

I shake my head. "No." I knew she was leaving and our little traditions were going to change. But there's the whole logistical side of her moving out that I haven't even thought about.

There is no way I can make rent and still afford food if it's just me living there.

Which means I need to look for a new roommate.

Here come the tears again.

Andrew is watching me, and he sighs. He glances over at Peter and Lisa, who are nowhere close to being ready to leave, and points to the sofa he just moved. "Sit," he commands me.

I sit.

He sits next to me and angles slightly away so he can stare at my face and make me feel awkward.

"You guys will still be friends," he starts.

Oh, boy. The "Living with Change" sermon. A favorite of his. I hold up a hand, because once you've heard it four times, you don't need to hear it again. "Andrew."

"But things are going to change."

"Andrew."

"She'll need to spend a lot of time alone with Travis in the beginning because those first few weeks of marriage are key."

I'm only half-listening to him. I'm using the other half of my brain to wonder why pastors think they know everything there is to know about life issues. Take Andrew, for example. He's never been married. He's never been engaged. I mean, he doesn't even have the guts to properly ask Liz out!

So, I'm not sure why he thinks he knows about the beginning of marriage being a key thing.

Unless he meant that literally, because there probably will be key exchanges involved.

I realize I don't even know where Jen is moving to. Are they going to live in Travis's apartment? Get a new apartment? Buy a house?

All these questions are more easily answered in *The Game of Life* rather than life itself.

"So," Andrew finishes up, "just try to be understanding. Jen is going to need a lot of emotional support from you right now."

I nod. "I know." I think I've been pretty good at not breaking down around Jen. Not yet, anyway.

"Good."

Peter and Lisa are done cleaning and are giving me dirty looks because the worst thing about the Wednesday-night shift at Cool Beans is the people sitting around talking when you want to leave.

I take the subtle hint. "We should go," I say.

"Yep."

We both leave, and I wave to Andrew as I get in Jen's car. I close the door, put the key in the ignition, and just sit there for a long minute.

Jack isn't working at Cool Beans anymore. Jen is getting married. Zach and Kate are having a baby.

Everything and everyone around me is changing.

I don't like change.

Jen's lounging on our sofa bed, flipping through the TV channels, and crunching on a bowl of her fat-free popcorn when I get home at eleven.

"Where were you?" she asks. "I was starting to get worried."

"Andrew was talking to me."

"Oh." This is explanation enough. She pats the bed, and I drop my purse, kick off my flip-flops, and climb up next to her.

"What's on?" I ask.

"Not much. Stacy and Clinton are attacking some girl who has hair the color of our kitchen cabinets, including the streaks; one of the *Rocky* movies is on; and I'm just getting to the Food Network." She flips there, and it's Bobby Flay. "Nice," she says.

Bobby's talking about some fantastic new way to grill flank steaks, and I'm lounging back on the cushions, thinking.

Jen moves out in five and a half weeks. Which means I have that long to find a new roommate or a one-bedroom apartment.

I really don't want to live by myself, but I also really don't want to live with someone besides Jen. The only other roommate I've ever had was horrible. Jen has spoiled me.

"What are you thinking about?" she asks, elbowing me in the ribs.

I sigh. "You're moving."

She immediately clicks the mute button. "I was wondering how long it would take for that to come up."

"I don't even know where you're moving to," I say.

"Travis and I are getting an apartment close to the church," Jen says quietly.

"How come you didn't tell me?"

Now it's her turn to sigh. "I know there's a lot that has been changing, and I just didn't want to add that little fact to the rest of it." She gives me an affectionate look. "You don't handle change well, Maya."

"Well, thanks."

"You're welcome." She grins. "But, yeah. I'll pay rent here until the end of next month."

"Why? You're leaving in the middle of the month. That's silly."

She shakes her head. "No, it's not. It's not fair to make you suffer for the extra two weeks' rent when it's me causing the problem. Plus, our lease is up at the end of next month anyway, so it works out well. You can either renew it without my name on the lease or get a place of your own."

We both are quiet for a long minute, watching Bobby grill some yellow and orange peppers next to the steaks.

"This is weird," I say finally.

"Yeah. Really weird." She nods.

"Are you sure you have to move in with him? I mean, you guys could get married, and he could just visit," I joke.

She giggles. "I don't think he would go for that."

"No, probably not."

We're both quiet again, and I wrap my arm around her shoulders. "I'm going to miss you, Jenny."

She hugs me tightly, and we don't say anything else until she flicks off the silent TV and we go to bed.

"Good night, Maya."

"Night, Jen."

By Monday, I'm convinced that Jen's shower is going to be the worst day of her life and that I'll be living on the streets in less than five weeks.

"You aren't going to be living on the streets," Mom tells me. I'm talking to her as I drive to Cool Beans. It's eight forty-five in the morning.

"So you think the shower is going to be horrible, too?" I ask.

"What? No! I was just addressing the situation I thought was most troubling to you," she says. She makes her voice all soothing. "The shower is going to be beautiful."

"And literal, if today is any indication," I say, peering out my windshield at the straggly raindrops scattering down from the sky. It's almost like the faucet in heaven has a leak.

I don't like lazy rain. If it's going to rain, I want it to fall from the sky, screaming in terror as it bounces off the earth.

Which sounds more morbid than it is.

Mom's still in soothing mode. "I'm sure it won't rain. Just try not to worry about everything. Now, about the apartment. When is your lease up?"

It's actually up the day after the wedding. Jen and I had our dates wrong. I could have sworn it was two weeks later.

This is not good. Now we're both going to be moving right before the biggest day of her life.

"The day after the wedding," I tell Mom.

"Oh my. Okay. Well, I'll be over in Hudson on Saturday. We'll give the shower and then go look at apartments. Does that sound good?"

I pull into the parking lot at Cool Beans. I'm a few minutes early, so I unbuckle my seat belt and keep talking. "Yeah. Thanks, Mom."

"And don't worry about the shower. You mailed the invitations?" she asks for the fifth time.

"Two weeks ago."

"Good girl. I have the decorations, and I'm picking up the cake on Saturday morning before I drive up."

"I have the tables and chairs and the rest of the food." Which isn't much. Since the shower is at two on Saturday, Mom and I decided that not too many people would be eating. So, we are serving light hors d'oeuvres and cake.

"Very good," Mom says. "See? It'll be fine, honey."

"Mom?"

"Yes?"

"I love you."

I can hear the smile in her voice. "I love you too, honey. Go have a good day at work."

The phone clicks, and I put my cell in my purse and climb out of the car. It's not even drizzling as much as it's just like 98 percent humidity.

My hair is going to be something today.

I get a text as I'm unlocking the door to Cool Beans. I pull my phone out and go inside, flicking on the lights.

It's Jack.

Nutkin. I realized that I need to eat dinner and you need to eat dinner. Let's eat together.

You know how in romance books the guy always gives the girl a week's notice on dates? So she has time to buy a new outfit, get her hair cut, and paint her toenails?

Yeah. Jack doesn't believe in advance notice. I barely have time for a shower after work before a date, and it's been five months since I got a haircut.

I guess some guys are good with the advance stuff, and some guys aren't.

I text him back as I go behind the counter. *Sure! Sounds good!*

Ethan walks in as I'm pulling on my cherry red apron. "So I'm not sure if it's raining or if people in planes are spitting," he says.

"Yuck. And good morning."

"Morning." He joins me behind the counter, blocking a yawn with his fist. "Find an apartment yet?"

I had told him about the hunt on Friday. I sigh.

"I'll take that as a no."

"Everything is so expensive," I complain. "I'd have to earn triple the tips and get a raise in order to afford some of these places on my own. And they aren't even the nice places." I look at him. "Where do you live?"

"Hunter's Run Apartments," he says. "Over by Cal-Hudson. They aren't too bad. They aren't good, but they aren't horrible either." He starts grinding the decaf blend, a spicy Colombian. "Where all did you look?"

I looked at four different complexes on Saturday. The nice thing about having a college in town is there are lots of apartments. The not-nice thing is they all had a waiting list because it's officially summer but people will be moving back for the fall semester.

I tell him the names of the complexes. "They each had a

waiting list. Except for the one I didn't like." Its ceilings were less than six feet high. If I ever wanted to have Jack over, he wouldn't be able to stand up straight.

It's not worth the chiropractor bills.

"Why don't you just move in with Jack, then?" Ethan asks.

I've always read the word and never understood the sound it made, but right here, right now, I honestly do it. I guffaw.

Ethan frowns at the sound that just protruded from my throat. "What was that?"

"A guffaw, I think."

"I don't think that noise exists."

"Well, I just made it."

"Whatever." He finishes the decaf and pours the grounds into the coffeemaker. I start on the light roast. I'm blending a light Breakfast Blend with a sweet almond-chocolate-flavored coffee.

"So, how come you guffawed?" Ethan asks a minute later.

"What?" I ask over the grinder.

"How come you did that 'ha' thing? Does Jack have a tiny apartment?"

Well, yes, he does, but that is not the point. "Ethan, I can't move in with Jack," I say, shutting off the grinder and pouring the grounds in the coffeemaker.

"Why not?"

"We're not married."

Foreign concept, I guess. "Wait, so you mean you guys have never . . . ?" he says, eyebrows as far up as his forehead will allow.

I shake my head and pull out the beans for the dark roast.

"Wow," Ethan says. "Is this the Christianity stuff again?"

"Well, that and common sense." Okay, so nothing is off-limits in this conversation. I look over at him. "It's a command, yeah, but I also don't have to worry about getting pregnant or getting some kind of weird disease. More than that, though, my life is way less complicated." And should we get married, our wedding night is going to be amazing. Seems like God knew what He was talking about.

Ethan doesn't respond, which is just as well, because our first customer walks in right then.

It's five o'clock, and Lisa's car is pulling into a parking space before he mentions it again.

"So, even though I could never do that, I'm impressed you guys can," he says, pulling off his apron.

I'm in the midst of counting the tips, so I miss the nonexistent segue back into this conversation.

"What?" I say.

"The no-sex thing. I'm impressed."

"Oh." Awkward. "Thanks." I hand him his tips. "And you could do it."

"Yeah, right."

I pocket my tips and pull off my apron. "You could. When it's not even an option, it becomes easier."

He shakes his head. "I don't think so. Christianity just isn't for me. I'm not about rules."

Lisa walks in then, whistling. "And how was your day on this wonderful drizzly day?" she asks, all chipper and excited.

Lisa is the only person I know who is still happy on rainy days. Every person who came in here today grumbled about having to work on a perfectly good sleeping-in day.

"I'd kill for a snow day," one lady told me menacingly.

I am glad I'm not in control of the weather. Sounds like a dangerous job.

My alarm wakes me up at nine on Saturday morning. I roll over and moan.

"Time to get up, Maya."

I crack an eyelid open, and Mrs. Mitchell is standing next to the sofa bed, showered, dressed, and coiffed.

"Ugh," I moan again.

"It is Saturday," she says to me.

I close my eyes and burrow my head in my pillow. Exactly. I should not be getting up on Saturday.

I ended up reading Proverbs 31 last night, and that part about the woman of excellent character staying up late really spoke to me. So I stayed up until past two watching *Iron Man* with Jack, Travis, and Jen.

The part about the Proverbs 31 lady rising early didn't speak to me as much.

Obviously.

"Maya, it is the day of Jennifer's shower," Mrs. Mitchell says, poking me in the foot. "You really need to get up. We have a lot to do."

I yawn, my eyes watering.

Jack hugged me for a really long time last night before finally letting go. "I love you," he said for the sixth time before he left.

I almost got scared that he was like Sandra Bullock in *Premonition* and knew something bad was going to happen on his way home. So I made him text me when he arrived safely at his apartment.

He finally texted me at 2:23. *I'm home. I love you.*

Make that seven times last night.

Which meant I wasn't asleep until after two thirty.

I flip to my back and blink up at Mrs. Mitchell. She's wearing a knee-length black skirt by a designer whose name I can't pronounce and a red cashmere, lightweight, three-quarter-length sweater set. Her blond hair curls under all around her face, and her makeup is flawless.

She looks beautiful.

I know Mrs. Mitchell has had lots of plastic surgery, but judging by Jen, she didn't need it. She might have looked better without it. I think about my mom with her laugh wrinkles, and I guess that Mrs. Mitchell would look a lot softer without the Botox.

"You look pretty," I say, stretching.

A surprised look crosses her face, and I suddenly realize I've never complimented Mrs. Mitchell before. On anything.

"Thank you," she says softly. "This is appropriate as mother of the bride, right?"

She's never asked for my approval either, so I imagine we now share the surprised look. I nod. "Looks perfect."

I push myself up to a sitting position and yawn again.

"How late were you all up last night?" Mrs. Mitchell asks, going into the kitchen.

"Late."

"I am glad I went to bed when I did." She's pulling a box of fiber-packed, fat-free, tasteless granola from the cabinet and her fat-free milk from the fridge.

What a way to wake up.

"What time is your mother getting here?" she asks.

Mom had texted me yesterday. *Wll B thr @ 10. <3 U*

"Ten," I say. The shower is at two. We figured we should

start setting up around eleven, since we have to move all the tables and chairs to the park. Jack and Travis are helping, so at least we have some muscle.

"You need to take a shower," Mrs. Mitchell says. There is no room for argument in her tone, and I realize whatever moment we shared earlier is gone.

I sigh and climb out of bed.

Thirty minutes later, I'm showered, and my hair has been blow-dried and curled. I'm wearing a blue sundress.

Mom knocks on the door as I finish the last bite of my cereal.

"Morning, honey," she says, handing me three huge bags of decorations. "I left the cake in the car for now, but I wanted you to see what I got." She smiles at my dress. "You look very nice, sweetheart."

Jen comes out of my room, yawning but dressed and showered. "Good morning, Mary," she says, giving my mom a big hug.

"Good morning, beautiful bride-to-be," Mom says, hugging her tightly. "Are you excited for today?"

Jen grins.

Mrs. Mitchell is standing back, looking unsure of herself.

"You've met my mom, right?" Jen asks Mom.

Mom is gracious. "Yes, how are you? Your skirt is just adorable."

I love my mom. With the two mothers in the same room, the differences between them are even more apparent. I suddenly realize that I'm proud to be Mary Davis's daughter. Mom may not be the most stylish mom, but she's dressed age-appropriate and everyone around her can see Jesus in her.

"Thank you," Mrs. Mitchell says, still looking a little off-kilter.

I start to open the bag, and Mom freaks out. "Wait! Jen can't see!"

I jump and hand the bag back to Mom. "I'll see everything at the park."

"Fine."

"Let me get my stuff." I grab my phone and text Jack as I go find my shoes and purse. *We're getting ready to leave.*

He texts back right away. *On my way, love.*

I can't help but smile.

By ten minutes until two, the whole park looks like a white wonderland. Mom has white tablecloths with cranberry doilies and white candles on all of the tables. There is tons of food: cookies, tiny finger sandwiches, and a beautiful cake that says *Congrats, Soon-To-Be Mrs. Clayton!*

Jack gives me a kiss on the cheek as he leaves. He and Travis are making their escape before the women show up. "See you tonight, Nutkin." He waves at my mom. "Bye, Mrs. Davis!"

"Mary. For goodness' sake, Jack. It's Mary."

"Bye, Mary." He grins.

Travis kisses his fiancée, and the boys leave. I look at Jen, who is just radiant today.

"Here," I say, handing her a bag with a good number of bows for her rehearsal bouquet. "Open it before everyone else shows up."

She grins at me. "What did you do, Maya? I told you not to get me any presents." She gasps as she pulls the piece of paper from the bag. "Maya!"

It's a certificate for a manicure, pedicure, and massage before the wedding. I give her a hug. "You need some relaxing."

"Thank you so much!" She hugs me tightly and leaves to go put the gift on the table.

"Maya?"

I recognize the voice, even though it's been almost six years. I straighten and turn. "Hi, Mrs. Clayton," I say, repeating to myself that it's only awkward if I make it awkward.

She doesn't know whether to give me a hug or a wave. She settles for a leaning wave.

Yeah, just pretending it's not awkward doesn't help.

"How have you been?" I ask.

"Good. And yourself?"

"I'm fine."

"Good."

We stand there.

"Well," I say brightly, "enjoy yourself!"

"Thanks."

Awkward, awkward, awkward.

The rest of the shower is a hit—all of the women seem to have a good time. And Jen makes off with some amazing gifts.

I stand near the back just watching. Jen looks so happy. She's practically glowing. She's so beautiful, and I wonder if Travis realizes how lucky he is.

Mom closes the trunk of her car once it's over and gives Jen another hug. "Congratulations, honey." She looks at me. "Apartment-hunting time?"

"Why not?" I mutter. As much fun as the shower was—despite the awkward talk with Mrs. Clayton—it was a shower for Jen. Which means that she's moving out and getting married in exactly four weeks.

Four weeks is not very long.

I guess Mom notices the mood swing because she puts an arm around my shoulders. "Let's go. Maybe we'll find the prettiest apartment ever and cheer you up."

"Maybe," I say, to make her feel better. But I doubt it. I don't want to move.

Why can't everything just stay the same?

Four apartments later, I'm even more depressed. I climb back in the car and growl.

Mom's not happy either. "That was disgusting," she says, making a face. "Did you see the caulking on the bathtub? It looked like toothpaste. There was so much mold in there."

My stomach twists. Now I'll be grossed out brushing my teeth. "Eiegh."

"One more. Then we're calling it a day and going for a dinner-ruining ice cream," Mom says. She pulls out of the complex.

I smile at her. "Really? Ice cream?"

She laughs. "You are a daughter after my own heart," she says, patting my leg. "You can always move back home."

"Yeah, but the commute is not good," I say.

She smiles over at me. "I meant move from Hudson. You could find a job as a barista in San Diego. Or maybe teach English."

I majored in English education. Which was stupid, because now I can't find a job since I hate teaching.

Something twists in my stomach at the mention of moving from Hudson, and I don't think it's a late reaction to the toothpaste caulk.

"Probably not, Mom," I say after a minute.

"Sure? It would save you a lot of money. You wouldn't have to pay for rent or food," she says, and I hear a little of the wistful empty nester in her voice.

"Yeah . . ." I'm clenching my hands together.

Moving from Hudson means I don't get to see Jack as often. Or Jen. And as meaningless as my job may seem, I love it, and to me, it has meaning.

"You don't want to move that far away, do you?" Mom says.

"No."

"Any reason why?"

Aha. Suddenly the guilt trip makes sense. I narrow my eyes. "Mother."

"Daughter."

"You just wanted me to talk about Jack."

She grins. "And here's the last apartment."

She's sneaky, but she's not getting away with it. We climb out of the car, and I'm immediately feeling brighter.

There are three buildings, and they are adorable. Red brick with white accents around the doors and windows and blue shutters.

We follow the sign leading to the office and knock.

A cute pregnant lady comes waddling over. "Can I help you?"

"Do you have any apartments available?" I ask. "And what's the rent?"

She nods and tells me the rent. "I have one opening up next month. Would you like to see the model?"

Both Mom and I nod.

"Okay, follow me," she says. She leads us to the building in the middle. Slowly we walk up one flight of stairs. "Sorry," she huffs. "One month to go." She pats her extended tummy.

I smile.

There are two doors leading off from the stairs, and she opens the door on the right. I walk in and immediately know.

"This is it," I say to Mom. The living room is bright and cheerful. There's a fireplace and a decent-size kitchen. One bedroom, but that's all Calvin and I need.

"Do you accept dogs?" I ask the lady.

She nods. "Under sixty pounds."

Calvin is definitely under sixty pounds. And unless he breaks into the food again, he'll stay there.

I look around the apartment and grin. Mom is busy asking the lady about deposits and credit checks and all the paperwork stuff.

"Welcome home," I say to myself quietly.

CHAPTER SEVENTEEN

Almost a week to the wedding.

I can't believe it got here so fast. The past three weeks — filled with counting RSVPs, throwing a very awkward lingerie shower, and helping Jen double-check on all the details — have flown by. In addition, both of us have been splitting belongings and packing like no other.

Our apartment looks like a war zone.

Mrs. Mitchell is still here, but I haven't seen her much. Construction started on the church at the beginning of the month, and she's been over there making sure it's done right and finished before the wedding.

Jen and I are in the middle of going through the kitchen stuff. "Is this your omelet pan?" she asks me, holding up a blue nonstick skillet I've never seen before.

I give her a look. "Do I look like I know how to make omelets?"

"Must be mine." She puts it in a box. "This is your sauce-pan though." She hands it to me.

Ah, the pan I use to make Bertolli instant dinners. I hold the pot close. I have fond memories with this saucepan.

Jen rolls her eyes. "It's a pot, Maya. Put it in the box and move on."

"Hey," I protest. "I've made amazing things in this saucepan."

"All of which came from a box." Jen grins. "Very amazing."

"Origin is not as important as taste," I say.

She looks at me and sighs. "You're never going to switch to organic foods, are you?"

I laugh.

Jen finishes putting her pans in a box and scoots down to the cookie sheets. We're both sitting on the floor; I'm crunching on a bag of buttered popcorn.

Jen looks up at the clock on the microwave. "It's almost seven. They're really still working at the church?"

"Maybe," I say. "It's construction."

Jen looks at me.

I listen to what I just said. "True. They were done for the day three hours ago, huh?"

"Where is she? Mom's never this late."

Just the fact that we're worried about her is proof how things have changed here. Not so much with Mrs. Mitchell, but Jen and I are different.

More tolerable, I suppose.

"What?" Jen asks, noticing my expression.

"I love Mr. Darcy."

"You're weird."

"Well . . ."

"Well. Let's finish with the kitchen."

"Yes, ma'am."

Later that night, Travis and Jack are both over. Mrs. Mitchell got home at nine, mentioned something about a late working night, and went straight to bed.

Travis is throwing stray Styrofoam peanuts at Jen. "Please tell me you didn't pack all of your stuff with these."

"I packed all of my stuff with those," she says.

"So these are going to be all over our apartment now, too?" he moans.

I slap his arm as I walk past. "Yup! Aren't you excited?"

"I couldn't be more," he says, rolling his eyes.

I settle next to Jack on the couch, and he wraps an arm around me. I watch Travis and Jen and just smile.

They are cute together.

"So, honeymoon in Hawaii," Jack says.

Travis nods. "Oh yeah."

"I bet Jenny's been packed for a week already," Jack grins.

Jen sticks out her tongue. "Have not."

"Five days is basically a week," I say.

"So? I don't want to forget anything. Hawaii is a long way to fly back for something," she says, flipping her hair and managing to hit Travis in the face.

"Honey, I think that if we leave something, we can just get it when we get back," Travis says, rubbing his eyes where Jen's hair got him.

Jack laughs.

Travis ducks out early, claiming he's tired from packing up his apartment. Jack takes his time leaving. I finally walk him out at nearly eleven.

"So, how are you doing with all of this?" he asks me, holding one of my hands. We're on the porch, and the dimly lit porch light is the only bright thing around.

"Okay," I say. I had one minor meltdown this morning, but nothing worth mentioning.

"Good." He smiles at me. "So, I was thinking maybe on Wednesday I would kidnap you and give you a break from all of this. What do you think?"

"Are you supposed to warn the person of kidnapping? Doesn't that ruin the effect?" I ask.

"True," Jack concedes. "So never mind. Forget I said anything."

"What were we talking about?" I say, grinning.

"Very good." He's lingering, and it's obvious he doesn't want to go. "So, you signed the lease for the new apartment?"

"Signed it. I'm officially living there for the next six months."

"It's a nice place," he says. I drove him past there last week because he kept bugging me with questions about how safe the neighborhood was.

"That it is."

He glances at the clock on his phone and sighs. "I guess I should let us both go to bed. Good night, Nutkin."

"Night, Jack."

I close the door after him and turn to find Jen grinning in the living room. "What?" I protest.

"He loves you," she smiles.

"Yeah . . ."

"And you love him."

"Yeah . . ."

She grins wider. "I think it's only a matter of time." She makes a face. "Of course, I've thought that for the past six years, so you guys get the award for the slowest moving couple ever."

"Well, thank you, Jen. That means a lot."

"Seriously, though," she says, helping me pull out the sofa

bed. "Has he kissed you yet?"

I shake my head. "Not really." Jack sticks with my cheeks. I've never really wondered about it until now.

Jen shrugs. "Maybe he's waiting for some sort of sign from you."

"Like what?"

"Well, have you told him you love him?"

I nod. "Yeah."

She frowns. "I don't know, then. Maybe he's nervous. You guys were best friends for years. Maybe he's scared it will ruin everything."

I straighten the sheets on the bed and then pull the quilt out of the hall closet. My nightly routine. "I think by this point, we've already ruined everything. If we don't continue down this path, we couldn't be friends anymore."

"True," she says. "I don't know. I do know that tomorrow is my last day of work before the wedding, so I'm going to go to bed and actually enjoy getting up tomorrow." She gives me a hug. "Night, Maya."

"Night, Jen."

I change into my PJs and climb into bed, pulling over my Bible.

Some sort of sign?

I bite my lip. While the thought of Jack kissing me doesn't freak me out anymore, it still makes little squiggle lines run through my rib cage. I haven't kissed anyone since Travis, and that was almost six years ago and better left forgotten.

I open my Bible and pause.

"Do not arouse or awaken love until it so desires" (Song of Solomon 2:7, NIV).

I check the reference. I'm in Song of Solomon. Who would

have thought that the most sensuous book of the Bible would have the best warning against it?

I grab a sticky note.

Stuff I Need to Remember:
1. Pick up dresses from the alterations lady Wed. morning with Jen.
2. Finish packing.
3. Pick up Jen's dad at airport Thursday.
4. Do not awaken anything — is awaken a word?

Wednesday at noon, I take my lunch break. Ethan is half-watching the register and half-reading a book called *Religion in the New Millennium.*

I wish he weren't so closed off to Christianity.

God, open his heart someday, please.

I pull out my peanut-butter sandwich. No jelly. Just peanut butter. Jen and I are down to the last few ingredients in our home, but neither of us wants to buy more food because that just means moving one more thing. And Mrs. Mitchell isn't buying anything because she bought a plane ticket home for the day after the wedding.

Finally.

"Maya, customer for you," Ethan calls from the front.

I smile. It has to be Jen coming for a lunch-break tea. I try to swallow the bite of peanut-butter sandwich I just took, but it's stuck to the roof of my mouth.

"'Oming!" I yell as best I can.

I scrape the roof of my mouth with a napkin and wash my hands, drying them on a paper towel before I walk to the front.

It's Jack. Or most of him anyway. His entire chest area is

covered with a gargantuan bouquet of lilies and roses and daisies.

I stop dead in my tracks and stare at him. "Jack?"

He grins. "It's Wednesday. I'm kidnapping you."

I'm shocked, to say the least. "I'm working," I mumble. "And shouldn't you be working?"

Jack shrugs. "Vacation kicked in this week. I took a day off." Lisa walks in the door right then and waves to all of us. Jack smiles at me. "And so did you."

Lisa, who is usually all smiles and sunshine anyway, is even more so. "Hello, everyone!" She pretty much bounces over. "Nice to see you, Ethan. Good-bye, Maya."

On the one hand, I'm super excited to have a half day off and to spend it with Jack. On the other hand, my hair is in a messy bun; I spilled the vanilla flavoring all over my shoes this morning so I smell like a Glade PlugIn; I'm wearing my work attire: black shirt and jeans; and the most makeup I put on this morning was mascara.

I don't feel very pretty. I like to look nice when I'm around Jack.

Everyone is just looking at me, so I force a smile. "Okay. See you guys later," I say, waving to Ethan and Lisa. I grab my purse from the back and leave my apron behind.

Then I follow Jack out to our cars. "These are for you," he says, handing the bouquet to me.

"They're beautiful," I say. The bouquet is enormous. The sweet and spicy scent of the flowers is overwhelming.

Jack smiles at me. "Now. Go home and shower, and I'll be there in thirty minutes."

A rush of relief takes over. "Thanks, Jack! I'll be ready soon." I jump in my car and drive as fast as I can to my apartment. Boxes are everywhere, crowding the walkways and completely taking over the kitchen. I run for the shower.

Thirty minutes later, I no longer smell like an air freshener exploded, and I have on cute black Bermuda shorts and a loose teal top. My hair is still air-drying, but it's curling well. If I don't touch it, it should look fine.

The doorbell rings right then.

Jack is standing there wearing jeans and a polo shirt. "Hello, beautiful," he says, all cheesy.

I grin.

"Hungry?" he asks.

I'm starving. Like I said, we don't have much food left here, and so far, lunch has consisted of one bite of a sandwich. I nod. "Yes."

We walk down the stairs to his car and he pulls out of the parking lot. "Surprised?"

"Um, yeah. I thought by Wednesday you meant tonight," I say. "Considering, you know, that we both have work." I annunciate *work*.

He rolls his shoulders. "Work, schmerk. It'll be there tomorrow. Today, though, you're mine." He reaches for my hand.

He's driving away from Hudson toward I-8, and I start to wonder if he remembers that he promised me lunch. Like I said, I'm starving.

"Are we getting lunch?" I ask.

He nods. "Patience, Nutkin. Patience."

"Well, I'm kind of hungry," I say, trying to be nice about it but really meaning, *feed me.*

"A few more minutes," he says.

He pulls off onto the road leading to the little picnic area where he first told me he loved me. It doesn't look nearly as creepy during the day as it did that night.

He stops the car right in front of the picnic table and nods. "We're here!" Then he grabs a cooler from the backseat and shakes it in my face. "See? I promised we would eat."

"Thanks. I really am starving."

"I kind of figured that out by this point," Jack says. We climb out of the car and walk over to the table.

Jack has a picnic blanket that we spread over the sticky wood, and he points to my side of the table. "Sit."

I sit, now having some understanding of how Calvin feels.

Jack puts a bottle of water in front of me. "Here you go."

"Very funny, but not very filling," I say.

"Hush, Pattertwig." He pulls a bowl of grapes and strawberries from the cooler, a package of crackers, a plate with swiss, Havarti, and cheddar cheese and sliced deli meats, and a plastic bag filled with chocolate-chip cookies.

I peer at the cookies. Jack doesn't cook. So either those are Chips Ahoy, they're from the batch I gave him six weeks ago, or someone else is baking him cookies.

I eat quickly, and everything is delicious. Jack is watching me eat, a grin on his face.

"What?" I say once I've polished off six meat-and-cheese-filled crackers.

"Nothing. I'm glad you like it."

I grin at him. "Thanks for kidnapping me, Jack. And for feeding me."

"You're welcome."

Soon, there is nothing left but cracker crumbs and the untouched cookies. I open the bag slowly, sniffing.

"These are homemade," I say.

"Oh?" Jack says, pretending not to be interested. "So?"

"So. Did you make these?"

He doesn't answer. Smart man. I take one out of the bag and nibble on it. I frown. I know these cookies.

"Jen made these!"

Jack smiles. "So, I recruited Jen. Are you still mad?"

"When did she make these? And why didn't I smell them in the apartment?"

"She made them at my apartment." Jack shrugs. "You're like the Cookie Monster. I didn't want the surprise ruined."

I grin and pop the rest of the cookie in my mouth. "Well, thank you very much."

"You are very welcome," he says again.

We finish off the cookies, and then I look around. The picnic area is totally surrounded by trees. Even though it's a warm day, it's not that warm right here. There are birds singing in the trees, and everything feels completely quiet and calm.

It's perfect.

I smile over at Jack, who's looking at me from across the table. "Thank you for today."

He nods and comes over to my side of the picnic table, scooting next to me on the bench. "Can I join you?" he asks.

I grin. "Maybe."

He smiles. "I love you."

He's been saying this a lot lately. I squeeze his hand. "I love you back." I pick up the empty plates and the dirty napkins to start cleaning up.

"Those can wait, Maya."

Uh-oh. Real name. I squint at him. He never calls me by my real name.

"I love you," he says again.

Maybe he's dying. Maybe he caught some awful disease from the giraffes or something. Is zookeeping a dangerous job?

"Are you okay?" I ask.

"Actually, there's something I need to ask you." He slides off the bench and drops to one knee. My jaw drops. "Maya Davis, will you marry me?"

I think he pulls out a ring, but I don't even see it. Both hands are covering my mouth. "Oh my gosh," I mumble through my hands.

He grins. "Is that a yes?"

I can't even say it, but I nod. "Oh my gosh," I say again. He starts laughing and stands, pulling me up with him.

"So, yes?" he asks quietly. "Maya, I've wanted to marry you since the day I saw you again in class five years ago. Marry me?"

I look at him. "Yes." I can't tell if he's getting teary or I am.

He tucks one hand under my hair and wraps his other arm around my waist as he pulls me close. My heart is pounding so loudly that I can't even hear the birds anymore. He gently leans down and touches his lips to mine.

A real kiss.

When he pulls away a few minutes later, I'm smiling. "Some sort of sign," I say, grinning.

"What?"

I shake my head. "Nothing."

He holds out the ring again, and this time I see it. It's simple, white gold, one solitaire, and it's beautiful. It's sending glitters of white light all around the picnic table.

I take in a deep breath. "Wow!"

He grins. "You like it?"

"I love it." I reach up for another kiss. "And you." I smile at the picnic. "This was perfect!"

He pulls me back in close, and we stay like that for a long time.

Friday night. One o'clock in the morning.

The only light in our apartment is the moonlight filtering in through the blinds. Jen and I are both in our PJs on the couch, staring off into space.

Both of us should have been in bed hours ago. We're supposed to be at the community center by eight tomorrow morning.

I'm finding it really hard to move from the couch though.

Apparently, so is Jen.

She sighs. "I'm so excited he finally asked you," she says again. She reaches for my left hand, where the sparkling diamond glitters in the moonlight.

I smile contentedly. The last two days have been filled with laughing, crying, and lots and lots of real kisses.

Jen's all packed up. All of her boxes are already at the new apartment, as is the other couch. I get to keep the couch with the sofa bed.

Mrs. Mitchell is staying in a hotel tonight since Jack and Travis moved Jen's bed over to the new place earlier this evening.

Mrs. Mitchell almost seemed emotional when she left. She reached out and squeezed Jen's shoulder before she walked out the door. I've never seen Mrs. Mitchell give any kind of physical affection.

Maybe something is starting to change.

All of my boxes are stacked in the empty dining room. Jack and my dad are going to move my bed, the couch, and the boxes to my new apartment on Sunday.

"I don't want a long engagement," Jack told me yesterday.

"Okay. How long?"

He shrugged. "Maybe four months? Like Jen and Travis?"

Works for me. All except for that lease I just signed. Jack only shrugged again. "Mine is up in four. We'll move into your new apartment. I like it better than mine anyway."

It's a tiny place for me, him, and two dogs, but I guess we'll be okay.

Jen's dad is at the same hotel as her mom. I picked him up from the airport on Thursday, and the whole time we were together, he was on the phone with his work. He never said hi, never asked who I was, nothing.

He's personable. Not.

"The wedding is going to be beautiful," I say quietly. The rehearsal went like clockwork, and the decorators are arriving in the morning. Jen's dress is hanging in her empty bedroom, along with my maid-of-honor dress. "Really beautiful," I add.

"Yeah," she says.

More silence. Almost six years are culminating tonight, and I really don't want the night to end. Once it ends, everything is changing.

Jen looks over at me. "Remember when you first brought Calvin home?"

I grin. It was four years ago. Jen about had a heart attack.

"Is that a *puppy*?" she gasped. "Are we even allowed to have dogs? What if we get kicked out? Is this a joke?"

Jen laughs now. "He was so cute and so sad looking!"

"That's because he couldn't walk without stepping on his ears," I say. Beagle puppies have to be the cutest puppies ever.

"So cute," Jen says again. She stretches and looks at the clock. I'm half afraid she's going to go to bed, but she doesn't move from the couch.

"Remember when Andrew and Jack and those guys from church copied the key to our apartment?" I ask. That was five years ago, and we'd only been going to the church for six months.

Jen growls. "Yes."

I grin. They poured seven huge trash bags of Styrofoam pea-nuts all over the floors. Once again, Jen about had a heart attack.

"That is not a happy memory," she says. "It took us a week to get all of those picked up."

"It's funny now."

"Not really," she says, but she's smiling. "I remember when you and Jack met up again. You brought him home for dinner that night."

I smile, remembering. "Yeah. He was dorky then."

"He has gained some much-needed weight," she says, nod-ding. "He was all cute and shy." She looks over at me. "I wonder if he's loved you from the very beginning?"

"Probably not in second grade," I say, twisting my ring around on my hand. Amazing how quickly I picked up the engaged-girl habit. "Remember when you first called me to tell me about Travis?"

She was giddy. Jen never used to be giddy.

She grins. "Yeah." She doesn't remark on the next few months where I tried to hide the fact that Travis and I had dated before.

It's quiet again. It's past one-thirty, and my eyes are starting to close without my permission. I snuggle into the couch.

"It's late," Jen whispers.

"No, it's still early," I protest, despite my drooping eyes. "We've stayed up later than this before."

"True," Jen concedes. She's also burrowing into the couch. "Maya?"

"Yeah?"

"I just wanted you to know that you've been the best room-mate and best friend I could ever ask for," she says quietly into the darkness.

I can feel the corners of my eyes getting wet. "You're

basically my sister," I stutter. "I can't imagine a better one."

She leans over on the couch and rests her head on my shoulder. "Oh," she says suddenly. She pulls a crumpled piece of paper from her pocket. "Look what I found earlier."

It's an old sticky note of mine. I peer at it in the moonlight.

> *Reasons It's Okay to Like Change:*
> *1. God is in control.*
> *2. God is in control.*
> *3. God is in control.*
> *4. Without change, we would not have*
> *any ice-cream flavors except vanilla.*

I start laughing. "Where was this?"

"Buried in the junk drawer in the kitchen." She lays her head on my shoulder again. "We should probably go to bed."

Time to face the inevitable. I nod. "Yeah."

She pushes herself off the couch, and I do the same. She gives me a long, long hug. "Good night, Maya."

I watch her stumble to my room, and I look at the note in the moonlight again.

God is in control.

"Night, Jen."

I settle on the sofa bed, and I've just pulled the covers up to my chin when I hear footsteps in the hallway.

"Maybe one last girls' movie night?" Jen asks.

I jump from bed and run for the ice cream I stashed in the freezer earlier today. "Chocolate or rocky road?"

ABOUT THE AUTHOR

ERYNN MANGUM plans her life around caffeine, but when she's not tipping the coffee mug, she's spending time with her husband, Jon O'Brien, or hanging out with family and friends. She's the author of *Miss Match, Rematch, Match Point,* and *Cool Beans*. Learn more at www.erynnmangum.com.